Love at
First Like

ALSO BY HANNAH ORENSTEIN

Playing with Matches

Love at First Like

HANNAH ORENSTEIN

ATRIA PAPERBACK

New York London Toronto Sydney New Delhi

An Imprint of Simon & Schuster, Inc.
1230 Avenue of the Americas
New York, NY 10020

First Atria Paperback edition August 2019

ATRIA PAPERBACK and colophon are trademarks of Simon & Schuster, Inc.

For information about special discounts for bulk purchases, please contact
Simon & Schuster Special Sales at 1-866-506-1949 or
business@simonandschuster.com.

The Simon & Schuster Speakers Bureau can bring authors to your live event.
For more information or to book an event, contact the
Simon & Schuster Speakers Bureau at 1-866-248-3049 or visit
our website at www.simonspeakers.com.

Interior design by Joy O'Meara

Manufactured in the United States of America

1   3   5   7   9   10   8   6   4   2

Library of Congress Cataloging-in-Publication Data

Names: Orenstein, Hannah, author.
Title: Love at first like / Hannah Orenstein.
Description: First Atria Paperback edition. | New York : Atria Books, 2019. |
"Atria fiction original trade"—Title page verso. | Includes bibliographical
references and index.
Identifiers: LCCN 2019005677 (print) | LCCN 2019008102 (ebook) | ISBN
9781982121464 (ebook) | ISBN 9781982117795 (pbk. : alk. paper)
Subjects: | GSAFD: Love stories.
Classification: LCC PS3615.R4645 (ebook) | LCC PS3615.R4645 L68 2019
(print) | DDC 813/.6—dc23
LC record available at https://lccn.loc.gov/2019005677

ISBN 978-1-9821-1779-5
ISBN 978-1-9821-2146-4 (ebook)

For my family, Audrey, Jack, and Julia Orenstein

· Part 1 ·

April & May

· Chapter 1 ·

Tonight's date was the kind of disaster that makes people give up on finding love forever. For starters, I had eyeballed his height from his Tinder photos; I had guessed he was about six feet, maybe four inches taller than me. Instead, I arrived at the bar, Golden Years, to discover that he was approximately five-foot-four. When I ordered a whiskey, he made fun of me for being the kind of girl who orders whiskey to impress a man. (It stung because he's half right; that's why I first started drinking it, before I developed a taste for it on my own.) He spent the first round of drinks quizzing me: had I been to this restaurant, or that museum, or that new club that had just opened up downtown? My plans to excuse myself were dashed when he insisted the bartender bring us a second round. It turned out his alcohol tolerance is much lower than mine, and by the time our glasses were empty again, he slid off his bar stool and tottered toward the door. "Eliza, you got the bill, right?" he called over his shoulder. "That's what the feminists always say they want!"

Now, alone at the bar, I wince at the check: sixty dollars plus tip for my hot date. I lock eyes with the bartender, a guy with a mop of dark hair wearing a gray hoodie with the sleeves scrunched up. I lean over the bar.

"Can you believe that guy?" I mutter, shaking my head. I toss him a flirty smile and cross my arms under my chest to give him a better view of my cleavage. "Hi, I'm Eliza, by the way."

The bartender glances up from polishing a glass.

"Raj. Hi. Sorry about your date," he says. For a split second, his dark eyes flash sympathetically. But then he shrugs. "Better luck next time," he says, returning to his task.

So I'm stuck with the bill. I slide my credit card across the bar. While I wait for the bartender to run it, I pull my phone from my purse and begin deleting the neat row of dating apps from my home screen. Enough is enough. Muscle memory triggers a spree through my phone: I toggle through my work email, personal email, and Instagram. I'm scrolling through my feed when my heart drops.

Holden is engaged. Holden, engaged? Holden, my on-again, off-again ex whose birth name is Hayden but who goes by a J. D. Salinger reference because he thinks it makes him sound smarter. Holden, the one who used to say that monogamy isn't natural and that he would always want the freedom to pick up and move to Borneo or Mexico City or wherever else pops into his head. Holden, the guy with a Bernie Sanders tattoo who forgot to register to vote. I repeat, *Holden* is engaged.

Right there, at the very top of my feed, a photo of him kneeling in front of his girlfriend, Faye, who appears as if she's based her entire personality off a Free People catalog. A fringed, floor-length robe slides artfully off one shoulder as she claps a hand over her mouth in surprise.

"Two souls became one today," Holden solemnly captioned the photo.

I navigate to Faye's profile, where she's posted not only that photo, but also a close-up of the diamond ring on her hand against a backdrop of lush green trees. Her caption: "I went hiking with the love of my life today . . . and I said YES!!!" She geotagged a misspelled version of the Appalachian Trail.

I sign the check and get the fuck out of the bar. My apartment is just across the street. It should be an easy walk—except, of course, it's suddenly pouring. Water squelches into my shoes as I break into a sprint. My purse slaps against my side.

Holden and I were caught in flash floods like this once. We were on vacation in Nashville for our one-year anniversary (if you didn't count the three-month break we took halfway through), and the sky just opened up. We huddled under a tiny awning while he scrolled through Yelp reviews of nearby restaurants. I had begged him to just pick a restaurant, any restaurant.

"Eliza," he said slowly, clearly annoyed. "I can't eat just *anywhere*. I'm a *chef*, all right?"

He was not a chef. He was a cook at a second-rate grill on Long Island during the summers and was looking for a full-time job at a restaurant in Brooklyn. My shoes were waterlogged for the rest of our trip.

Fucking Holden. Engaged. I'm not like some of my friends who, at twenty-seven, are still deeply shocked whenever people our age announce they're getting married. I acknowledge that twenty-seven is a perfectly reasonable age for Holden to propose to Faye. And fine, whatever, maybe he's changed. It's not exactly like we've been in touch often during the past four years since our final, brutal breakup. And more than anyone else I know, engagements are my bread and butter. Ever since my sister Sophie and I opened up Brooklyn Jewels last year, diamonds have become my world. I guess I just always assumed that between me and Holden, I would pair off for good first. I'm not good at losing; I'm not used to it. And his engagement means that I've officially lost the breakup.

I reach the door of my building and I'm home. I live in a second-floor walk-up on top of the shop. I dig my keys out of my purse and jam the right one into the lock. I know before I'm even inside my apartment that I won't want to stay. From the sound of it, you'd think my neighbor was personally hosting New York's most crowded EDM festival. I can feel the bass of his soundtrack vibrating in my chest. My walls are so thin that I need noise-canceling headphones just to sit in my own home.

I drop my rain-soaked purse on the floor of my bedroom, strip out of my damp clothes, and pull on my oldest sweats. Then I grab my phone, swing by the galley kitchen to pick up my bottle of Jack Daniel's and the cleanest glass from the cupboard, and head downstairs to the quiet shop.

Holden and Faye may have a diamond ring, but I have an entire store full of them. It's not a huge space, but we have a storefront in one of the most coveted parts of the city with a stable of chic customers to match. And it's *ours*. Sophie and I opened it last year after years of planning; I handle the business side while Sophie masterminds our jewelry design. Running our own business felt like a natural choice after growing up underfoot in Mom and Dad's store, the largest boating shop in Portland, Maine. When we were young, we loved to hang out after school at the jewelry boutique next to Mom and Dad's place. Helen, the owner, was like the eccentric, indulgent aunt I always wanted. She'd let me try on every sparkly thing in the store and tell me stories about her two failed marriages and her romantic dalliances in far-flung destinations. As I got older, I started asking more serious questions about the jewelry: the story behind why she acquired each piece, how she works with customers to create bespoke works of art, and what makes each item so valuable. She taught me that jewelry isn't just a product; in order for a customer to make a purchase, they have to develop a sentimental attachment to it that goes far beyond the price tag.

Helen retired and shut down her boutique during my senior year of high school. She said she was too old to run the business anymore, and I knew she was right, but I was upset. I missed spending time in the shop with her. It was a pivotal year for me; I was applying to colleges and browsing course catalogs, dreaming up a future for myself. That's when the first seeds of my idea to open my own jewelry shop began to sprout. Eight years later, Brooklyn Jewels was born.

Grandma and Grandpa each left money for me and Sophie in their wills when they passed. We pooled it to open this store. The first year for any small business is notoriously make-it-or-break-it. We just hoped to stay afloat. We never expected to land the occasional celebrity client or build such a massive following on Instagram (100,000 strong and counting). I use @brooklynjewels as both my professional and personal account—it's 90 percent jewelry shots with a few personal photos thrown in. Sophie never wanted to be the face of the brand, so I've gladly stepped in. We're even doing well enough that we could afford to hire Jess, our resident sales specialist/office manager/all-around wizard. She's Helen's grandniece. When she got laid off from her position assisting a fashion stylist, we stepped in to hire her as a favor to Helen.

The store's back room is a combination of an office for me and a small production studio for Sophie. My favorite item in the room is

Helen's old leather armchair, and I slump into it. I use a heavy hand to pour myself a drink, and then I pull up Faye's ring shot again. It looks like an old European-cut diamond on a gold band—small, but surprisingly expensive, since that cut is no longer made. The only available stones in that style are antiques. I try to zoom in to get a better look at the diamond's quality, but my finger slips and I accidentally graze the "heart" button. *Fuck*. I liked it. I liked Faye's engagement announcement.

In desperate times like these, I have a game I like to play. I unlock one of the TL-30 safes in the back. (You can't get insurance for a fine jewelry business without them. The safe's door is six inches thick and can survive a continuous half hour of destruction by every imaginable thief's tool before it'll break—and the minute it senses damage, it triggers a call to the police.) I select a three-carat, round-cut ring with side stones. It's not what I'd ever choose for myself, were I really to get engaged (too glitzy, too heavy, too trendy), but I slide it onto my left ring finger anyway.

Here's my dirty secret: when the irony of being a single girl who sells engagement rings for a living becomes too much, I blow off a little steam by making fake engagement announcements. I stage ring shots and pair them with overwrought captions like, "I can't wait to marry my best friend!" or "'You don't know how long I've waited for you.' —Stephenie Meyer, *Twilight*" and pile on hashtags like #engaged, #isaidyes, #waitingforthewedding. Of course, I never actually post any of them; I save them as drafts. It's like writing a nasty letter to an ex to unload all your feelings, then ripping it into pieces.

But now I need a backdrop—the shop feels too stale. I fling open the front door, stepping out into the twinkling darkness. I splay my left hand out in front of me and use my right hand to snap a picture. The rain has stopped by now, leaving a glinting sheen to the street. Behind my hand, pretty string lights pop. The streetlights cast an angelic glow. Perfect.

I shut the door and return to the cozy armchair. Even after all this time, it still smells faintly of Helen's perfume. I take a hearty swig of my drink and pull up the photo on Instagram. I up the contrast and saturation and take a second to dream up a schmaltzy caption: "They say when you know, you know . . . and I know I want to spend the rest of my life with you." I add a red heart emoji for good measure and jab my finger at the screen to triumphantly save the post to my drafts.

It's silly, but the pressure that's been building up behind my eyes ever since I left the bar seems to ease up a tiny bit. It's not fair—I spent the first three years of my twenties in a joke of a relationship, and the next four completely single. It's not that I'm a leper. But running a business doesn't exactly leave me with tons of free time or energy to bother much with dating apps. When I *do* go out on dates, they either fall flat or they just don't blossom into real relationships.

I have a Word document on my laptop that I've been keeping since college, titled "LIL BLACK BOOK <3." The name seemed cute at eighteen. It's organized by year, a chronological list of every single guy I've gone on a date with. A name gets italicized if we sleep together and bold-faced if I actually like him. Only one name is highlighted in pink: Holden. It means he was actually my boyfriend. The list is too depressing to look at for long, but I like to keep it up to date so I can scroll through it when I'm old and married and nostalgic for the adventures of my youth.

There haven't been any pink or bold names in ages. Instead, recent dates included Todd, the startup engineer who drinks Soylent instead of having real meals because he claims eating food tanks his efficiency; Marcus, the guy who rambled for four hours straight and then texted that he didn't feel chemistry because I was "too quiet" for him; and Zachary, who mentioned after we ordered forty dollars' worth of oysters that he's saving himself for marriage.

And meanwhile, Holden has apparently found the person he wants to spend the rest of his life with. I was in love with him, once upon a time. It's not so easy to remember now; so many years have passed that it feels like recalling the hazy details of a movie I fell asleep halfway through watching. I believe that what I had with Holden was real at the time. But that doesn't mean it was good, or right, or the kind of love that should last forever.

The music is no longer blasting from upstairs. I lock the ring back in the safe, trudge up to my apartment, and flop down on my own bed. The whiskey lulls me to sleep.

Morning hits like a truck. I'm jolted awake, not by the harsh light streaming through the narrow window and not by the hot, sticky sensation of my tongue glued to the roof of my mouth, but by my phone vibrating at full blast. Sophie is calling—and I can't remember the last time she actually used her phone to make a call. My thoughts in order: Who died? Was it Mom, Dad, or Waffles the cat? Is it dumb that I'd be almost as sad about the cat as I would about a real human being?

"Sophie? Is everything okay?" I ask. My voice is groggy with sleep.

"What the hell did you post on Instagram last night?" she snaps.

I rack my brain. "I didn't post anything on Instagram last—" Wait. Shit. "Can you hold on for a sec?"

I can't see her, but I know the exact haughty way in which she probably just rolled her eyes. Liv is probably patting her knee, as if that could help calm her down.

I open Instagram and am horrified to find an avalanche of notifications. Fourteen thousand people have liked my ring photo, which apparently did *not* save as a draft, but instead, must have been posted to my feed. This is terrible. I scroll through five hundred comments. Sasha, an old friend from college who I haven't seen in months, wrote, "Omg WHAT?!" Rachel, a girl I met while drunk in line at a bar bathroom three years ago and haven't seen since, wrote, "I'm crying!! This is beautiful!!!!!" Kate, a cousin I see a couple times a year, wrote, "I didn't know you were dating anyone???" Holden commented, "This is simply wonderful news." And the rest are variations on "Congrats!" or "So happy for you!" Some are from followers whose names I recognize, but most are from total strangers. As if that's not freaky enough, it looks like the account gained more than a thousand new followers overnight. My phone is warm to the touch, as if all the activity is overheating the delicate device.

I sit up in bed, steadying myself against a mountain of pillows. My heart thumps against my rib cage.

"Okay, Sophie, I know what happened. . . ." I tell her everything about the date, Holden's engagement, and my bad habit of letting off steam on Instagram. I leave out the part about the whiskey.

"Mom and Dad are gonna flip," she says. "Kate's probably already sent a screenshot to Aunt Linda, who probably called Mom."

I check my phone's notifications, which are overflowing. Sure enough, buried among emoji-laden texts, an avalanche of Instagram likes, and an email from Helen, are three missed calls from our parents. It's not even 8 a.m.

"You're taking the photo down, right?" Sophie asks.

It's clear she doesn't really mean it as a question. Because Sophie is five years older than me, she's convinced that she's right about everything.

"I'll call you back," I say, hanging up before she can protest.

I stare at my phone, scrolling through the endless stream of praise. I'm amazed at how many people think I'm actually engaged, but even more so, I'm surprised by how positive the reactions are. People are happy that I appear happy. Nobody knows how crushed and alone I felt last night. America is a sick place in which girls still grow up thinking that getting someone to fall in love with them is some kind of achievement. I know it's not, because I see that anyone can fall in love at any time; it's not like Holden *deserves* to be in love, and yet, he is. It's unfair that we give relationships such importance; I can't even begin to count how many Thanksgiving dinners I sat through during which Aunt Linda asked about my love life instead of, oh, I don't know, the business I was building. I recognize that I'm not totally innocent here—selling engagement rings as a dream luxury item means that I'm part of the problem. If only people saw what I see now: I might look "engaged," but instead of feeling happy, I feel hungover, defensive, and panicked.

My phone buzzes with an incoming email. It's a Google Alert for the shop. We're mentioned in a story on a wedding blog that trumpets the news: cofounder Eliza Roth—yours truly—is engaged. *"While nothing is known about the mystery man quite yet, one thing is clear: he knows how to pick out a rock,"* it says. Within minutes, there's a rush of new followers on Instagram. Judging from their profile pictures—mostly engagement photos with their significant others—they must have seen the story. I want to be happy about the good publicity; any press is cause for celebration, and this site is massively popular. But instead, I only feel panic creeping up my chest and closing in around my throat.

An automated email from the e-commerce platform we use comes in, alerting us that we made a sale. It's unusual for us to sell a product without some kind of catalyst; typically, our customers prefer to buy pieces in person from the shop, so online purchases mostly happen when we send an email blast about a flash sale or a celebrity wears one of our pieces. (Not to brag, but Blake Lively purchased a five-carat, emerald-cut, platinum-band vow renewal ring from us last month, and both Ariana Grande and Cardi B like to wear our stackable rings.) Sales online tend to be smaller than ones in-person. It makes sense—before you drop an entire paycheck on a piece of jewelry, you probably want to see it up close. So, I didn't have any expectations of greatness when I read the e-commerce email.

A new customer bought a $10,000 diamond necklace. Engagement rings aside, it's the most expensive piece we carry. And now, it's sold.

If it looks good for me to be engaged to a mystery man, and that translates directly into sales, then damn it, I'll be engaged to a mystery man. What's the harm? I call my sister back.

"You saw the sale?" I ask.

"Yeah, I did." She sounds awestruck.

"That photo is working to our advantage," I say, summoning my firmest voice. "I'm not taking it down."

· Chapter 2 ·

I shower. I put on an underwire bra and pants with a real waist-band. I make myself look like I have my shit together, which for me, means piling on jewelry like armor: my signature stack of thin silver Brooklyn Jewels bangles, each embedded with a different family member's birthstone; the chunky amethyst pendant Helen gave me as a bat mitzvah gift that ignited a lifelong love affair with jew-elry; the round-cut diamond studs Sophie made for me to honor the shop's launch, topped by a delicate pair of mismatched studs in my second holes—a star and a crescent moon—from an indie designer whose work I admire. Some people think jewelry is an overpriced fashion statement, but it's so much more than that. When chosen with care, each piece tells a story of who you are and what matters to you. I don't feel like myself without all of this.

I pick up a large coffee from the café next door and make it to Brooklyn Jewels by 8:30 a.m. I always like to get here early. Jess will be in by 9, and Sophie typically makes it in twenty minutes later. That's half because she's a slowpoke in the mornings and half because she's coming from Park Slope, the neighborhood she and Liv moved to in anticipation of the babies that are taking longer to come than either of them expected. I don't think it's healthy for her to be in Brooklyn's greatest per capita concentration of strollers after two rounds of IVF. I keep telling her to move to Williamsburg, or at least closer to the shop, but she claims that living within ten blocks of the bar Union Pool again would give her hives. As a person who's had more than her fair share of hookups in the Union Pool bathroom, her point resonates on a cellular level.

Everything looks different in the daylight, and the shop is no exception. I flick on the lights, flip the white-lacquered sign in the window to OPEN, and unlock the safe so I can set out jewels in the window boxes and the glass display case. The routine calms me, and I take extra care with it today, adjusting the placement of each piece until it's flawless.

I should set what is now, I guess, "my" ring into the case, too. We keep engagement rings and bridal jewelry on one side of the store and other fine jewelry pieces on the other. There's a spot just waiting for it. But instead, I slide it onto my finger and flex my hand under its weight. Sunlight streams through the shop's window and hits the bulky center stone at a fiery angle, radiating sharp bursts of light from my hand. The bauble is monstrous. I always pictured myself with a pair of our vintage-inspired ballerina bands stacked around a classic solitaire, or maybe a pear-shaped diamond for a more modern look. (It's impossible to choose just one dream ring when you sell them for a living.)

I'm Windexing the glass counters when Sophie pushes through the door. It's 8:58 a.m. She's early and her eyes are wild. She wears a tomato red caftan that makes her copper red bun look even brighter, and her oldest clogs. Sophie always looks more polished than this;

it's like my news has sapped the energy she'd need to iron a silk Everlane button-down or to swipe on some mascara.

"I can't believe you're actually doing this," she says in lieu of a greeting.

"You saw that ten-thousand-dollar sale," I point out. "You can't think that's a coincidence."

"It's clearly *not,* but also, you must be deranged if you think you can pull this off." She crosses her arms over her chest and leans a hip against the counter. Sophie's always been more tightly wound and risk-averse than I am. Design is her release; she relaxes when she sketches out a new piece. I can see her gearing up to slip into big sister mode. "Have you called Mom and Dad? Have you thought ahead to what's going to happen when you don't actually wind up getting married to anyone? Are you just going to string people along forever? And how, exactly, are you planning to take that ring from the shop without paying for it? Because if you borrow it indefinitely, we're losing out on money there."

I put up my hands in defense. "I'll figure it out. I'll call Mom and Dad back. It'll work out somehow."

She slumps over the counter, rubbing a hand over her face. Her own (real) engagement ring, an Art Deco, emerald-and-diamond piece she sourced at an estate sale, glints back at me. She and Liv got married three years ago on the coast of Maine.

"I'm worried this could backfire on us," she says. "You know, hurt the business."

That's a more legitimate concern. But there are certain entrepreneurs—Whitney Wolfe Herd of Bumble, Emily Weiss of Into the Gloss and Glossier, and Leandra Medine Cohen of Man Repeller—whose businesses are bolstered *because* the founders have enviable lives. Maybe I can be one of those. Maybe that's the reason today is already one of the most successful days in our company's short history.

"I'm going to make this work," I say. "I promise."

Sure enough, it's a shockingly good day at the shop. Three more online orders roll in; though none are as big as the first, combined, they pay a month's worth of rent for my apartment. Sophie busies herself by packaging them up and shipping them out. Two more blogs pick up my "news" and write fawning stories about me and the company. The @brooklynjewels account blows up with new followers. The energy in the shop is frantic but hopeful.

At noon, a girl about my age wanders in. Jess is supposed to take the lead with customers, but Sophie and I are equipped to handle sales in a pinch. That's the reality of running a small business like this one—everyone has to wear a million hats. Jess greets the customer first, but the customer gives me a shy look and approaches my side of the counter.

"I'm on my lunch break, and I just wanted to pop in and check out your pieces," the customer says. "You came up on my Instagram Explore page and I just love your work."

"Well, thank you!" I say. She peers into the cases, and I use that opportunity to throw a pointed smile Sophie's way as if to say, "See?"

"My boyfriend and I are just starting to talk about getting engaged, and while nothing is definite yet . . ." The customer trails off, kneeling down to examine a round-cut diamond with side stones, the smaller (and more affordable) version of the piece I'm wearing. She smiles and straightens up. "I'd just love to try that one on. You know, get a sense of what I like before I start dropping hints to him."

I unlock the case and remove the ring for her to try. She squeals a little when she slides it on. Her eyes dart from her hand to mine.

"I saw yours this morning and was totally obsessed," she explains.

She tries on two more pieces but keeps coming back to that first ring. She tries it on once more and looks at it longingly before twisting it off her finger.

"I'll be back—next time, with my boyfriend," she promises.

After years of watching Helen work with customers, and more than a year of handling customers here, I can spot when a potential buyer bullshits me. She isn't. I know she'll be back.

When I walk to the nearby vegan restaurant, By Chloe, to pick up my favorite avocado pesto pasta on my lunch break, I call Mom and Dad.

Mom picks up. "So are you going to tell us what's going on?" she demands.

"So what happened is—" I start.

She cuts me off, calling for my dad. "Paul? Paul! Come here. She finally called us back." Then to me, "Honey, I'm putting you on speakerphone. You have a lot of explaining to do."

That would be fair for any parent to say under the circumstances, but she has even more of a right to be clued in. When Sophie and I first told our parents about our idea for Brooklyn Jewels, they helped us out and invested; they have a 10 percent stake. Any decision I make with the business doesn't just affect me—it affects them, too. And since another boating shop opened up a few blocks from theirs last year, they're worried that their own business might suffer. I spent the morning thinking about how to explain the photo to them, and I think I've got it. When Dad says "hi," I take a deep breath.

"It's a *marketing stunt*," I say, as if it's the most obvious explanation in the world. "It drums up interest in the business. If I'm the face of the company, then it's good for people to be intrigued by my life. Basically, all our Instagram followers are single girls who are dying to get engaged—so this panders to them. It's aspirational content."

"I don't know about that, honey," Mom says, sounding concerned.

"It seems a little far-fetched," Dad adds.

"It's going to be fine," I recite for what feels like the millionth time today. "You don't grow unless you take risks! You taught me that."

"Right, but this seems . . ." Dad struggles to find the right word.

"Creative!" I shout.

"Ill-advised." He settles on a word of his own at the exact same time.

There's a long moment of silence. "Please trust me on this one," I say.

I can hear him sigh. Mom speaks first. "We want to," she says.

"Wow, look at that, already at my lunch place. Gotta go," I say. I hang up before they can protest.

By Chloe is a hotbed of the kinds of customers who go for our pieces: well-off, well-versed in indie brands they learned about on Refinery29, and artsy (or they want their Instagram followers to think they are). I recognize pretty much all of the employees, since I eat here at least twice a week. I order my regular dish, and when I hand over my credit card to the cashier, her gaze follows my ring. She looks up at me appreciatively.

"That's pretty," she says, nodding at my hand.

It's the first time we've ever had a personal conversation. "Thank you," I say.

If I'm going to do this, I'm going to do it for real. I linger by the napkin dispenser as I wait for my pasta to be ready and pull out my phone. I upload the ring photo from last night to both Facebook and Twitter. I refresh each platform once, and watch dozens of likes and comments spill in. People are so quick to be happy for me. It stings a little bit. Not even my post announcing the launch of our shop got so much positive feedback in such little time. An engagement marks a new phase in your life, sure, but it's not an achievement.

Next, I open Gmail. I do some work as our company's de facto publicist, and so I already have the email addresses for various editors at jewelry blogs, wedding sites, and women's magazines saved in my contacts. I draft an email to all of them pitching a big story with the announcement that I'm engaged. I ask if they'd like to cover it.

It's a risk, for sure. But so is doing nothing. Nobody's exposed me as a fraud just yet, and our company's bank account is flush. I call that a small victory. And today, that's all I need.

· *Chapter 3* ·

Carmen and I have had a standing happy hour date every Thursday since we got fake IDs our freshman year at NYU nearly a decade ago. At first, we went to Sigma Burger Pie, the frat-themed dive bar behind the library that miraculously let you pay for PBRs using Campus Cash. When the police shut it down after less than a semester, we migrated to Crocodile Lounge, where beers cost $4 and every round got you a free personal-sized pizza. After graduation, we traded up; these days, we mostly hang out at wine bars and don't flinch at the cost of the cheese plates. So it doesn't matter that today has been a beast of a day—today is Thursday. It's time for happy hour. It's tradition.

It's her turn to choose the spot, so I trek up to the Upper East Side to meet her at AOC East, the French wine bar. We've never been here before, but that's typical. Carmen doesn't have regular spots; she gets bored too quickly. It's out of the way for both of us, but she swears the wine list is worth it.

When I arrive at AOC East, I feel transported to Paris. The

walls are musty brick and cranberry paint, stacked with book-shelves filled with classic editions and landscape paintings in gilded frames. A French flag hangs proudly on one wall and the ceilings drip with dainty string lights. The low chatter from other tables is all in French. It's not hard to spot Carmen at a table by the window. She's resplendent in a pink jumpsuit, white sneakers, and gold hoop earrings. Last year, she made the switch from doing marketing at old-school giant L'Oréal to the relatively newer Tinder, and she's been reveling in the lax dress code ever since. She wears magenta lipstick and sips a glass of what must be French rosé (the only kind she has determined worthy of drinking) carefully. Her eyebrows shoot up when she sees me.

"Hi! Okay, gimme all the deets," she commands.

We'd been texting about everything that happened since this morning, but it's different in person. Here, she can fake gagging noises when I tell her about Holden commenting on my Instagram, and she can slip the ring off my finger to try it on herself. The waiter comes by to drop off a glass of French rosé that matches hers; it's part of our tradition to order for each other if we're running late so we never miss the happy hour special.

"So, if you're faking an engagement, don't you need . . . a fiancé?" she asks.

"I have a plan!" I explain. "What if I pretend that I'm madly in love but he has a super-private job and can't appear on any social media?"

"Like that consultant you dated once," she recalls.

"I think that was a line he gave girls so he never had to be Instagram-official with any of them, but yes," I say. "Like he works for a really private hedge fund, or the FBI, or he's a billionaire who thinks he's above it all."

"Right, because there are so many of those floating around," she says, deadpan.

"What if he was a victim of a house fire and is recovering from debilitating injuries and isn't ready to show his face yet?" I ask. "Or maybe that's a little dark. What if he's one of those off-the-grid types?"

Carmen rolls her eyes.

"Okay, okay, but seriously, what if I just find some aspiring actor to pose as my fake fiancé?" I ask. "I can throw a stick on Broadway and hit a dozen potential candidates."

"Eh," Carmen says, squinting. "Actors are flaky. And besides, do you really want to pay some rando off the street?"

I shrug. "Do you have a better plan?" I ask.

"I do," she says. Her eyes sparkle dangerously. "I thought of it at work today, inspired by *The Bachelorette*."

"Excuse me?"

"We get a dozen, two dozen, whatever, eligible dudes in one place, and you get to choose from all of them."

"That sounds unreal. How are you expecting to pull that off?"

She grins. "It's more real than paying someone off."

The plan, I gather, goes like this: Carmen grabs my phone, pulls up Tinder, and tweaks my profile so I look like bait for future Stepford husbands, catnip to guys whose grandparents' names adorn hospitals and who refer to the Hamptons vaguely as "out east." I'm glad she explains this as she goes, or else I would've been offended when she deletes nearly every single photo from my existing profile. When she swipes, she's like a NASCAR driver—making life-changing decisions at lightning speed as she careens around bachelors. She's judicious, not generous. I trust she knows what she's doing. She must know tricks I don't, because by the time we order and finish a cheese plate, she's amassed a pool of suitors who I'm sure consider themselves worthy of making the *Forbes* 30 Under 30 and *Town & Country*'s Top 50 Bachelors lists. I'm not so convinced. She launches into high flirt. She hides the phone from me, but I can see her type fiendishly fast, then press the phone to her chest to throw back her head and cackle. She signals for the check.

"Where are we going?" I ask.

"Dorrian's. Two blocks from here."

I can't help but make a face.

"That's why I didn't tell you!" she says. She's already fishing twenties out of her purse and gathering up her things. "We have two guys confirmed already to meet us there, and if they suck, I bet we can snag a bunch more once we're on their home turf."

"And they're . . . hot? Eligible? Gullible?" I ask.

She makes a face. "Well, we'll see. 'Hot' can be a flexible term."

I take off my engagement ring and tuck it into the zippered compartment of my wallet.

I have to hand it to Carmen, Dorrian's is a smart choice, albeit not one I would've ever made myself. The bar is an old Upper East Side watering hole that briefly shot to national fame in 1986 when it was splashed across tabloids in conjunction with the "Preppy Killer"—a prep school kid got drinks with his date here, then dragged her into Central Park to rape and murder her. While the bar *is* stuck in the past, there's nothing openly morbid about it today: tables are topped with cheery red-and-white gingham cloth, framed black-and-white photos depict Kennedy lookalikes sailing or playing polo, and felt Ivy League pennants hang from the walls. It's essentially the townie bar for people who grew up in this money-soaked neighborhood and never left.

My first instinct is to sidle up to the bar for a drink, but Carmen stops me.

"Someone will buy you one," she says confidently.

I don't really get nervous on first dates anymore; the first fifty or so sort of beat that out of me. But there's something spine-tingling about knowing I could potentially cross paths with my future fake fiancé tonight. Carmen was right—*I feel like the Bachelorette.* There could be a simple way out of this mess.

Carmen's first match appears in the well-worn wooden doorway. He looks like a walking human khaki and introduces himself as Keith. He runs a hand through his dark blond hair.

"I hear you need a plus-one for your cousin's wedding this weekend?" he asks.

"She *does*," Carmen purrs. "Why don't you tell her a little about yourself?"

He pivots toward me as Carmen whispers in my ear, "I'm going to go round up more troops," and slips past me.

"Well, uh, I'm getting my MBA right now," he offers up.

"Cool," I say, nodding. I do not think this is cool. I studied marketing and entrepreneurship at NYU's undergrad business school, and the students fell into two clear categories: the first, like Keith, wanted to get MBAs, launch management careers, and speak in corporate buzzwords for the rest of their lives; the second, like me, wanted to gain just enough business sense to launch a company, then get the eff out.

"Yeah, it's good," he says.

"Yeah."

"You ever think about getting your MBA?"

I am just about to flee back to Carmen when she returns, this time flanked by two guys in Nantucket red shorts. They introduce themselves as Jordan and Kyle. Soon, I'm fielding three offers to buy me drinks, and trying desperately to remember which nearly identical jawline matches up with which guy's name. It's not the worst way I've ever spent a Thursday night.

"You're beautiful," Jordan says, leaning in two inches closer than a stranger ever should. "You know, I know a thing or two about beauty. My grandfather was a pretty serious art collector back in the day."

Kyle wilts ever so slightly by his side, as if he's heard this line before. He dips his head and fiddles with the straw in his gin and tonic.

"Like, he was really tight with Jackson Pollock before anyone looked at his stuff," Jordan continues, not waiting for me to respond or nod or react in any way. "I could take you over to the Met sometime, show you some of my family's contributions."

"Mmm," I say noncommittally.

There's something very sad about a dude who believes his best chance to land a date is to brag about his grandfather's accomplishments more than a half century earlier.

Kyle works up the courage to jump in. "When did you say this wedding was?"

"Uh . . . Saturday? Saturday night," I say.

"In the city?" he asks.

"Greenpoint," I say, just to test how they'd respond to the suggestion of visiting Brooklyn.

To get there from here, you'd have to transfer from the 6 train to the L to the G—it's basically impossible.

Jordan wrinkles his nose. "Far."

"We'll be out east by Saturday," Kyle adds.

"We could always double back in your uncle's jet," Jordan counters.

"Not if it's raining," Kyle says.

At this, Jordan and Kyle both nod their heads heavily and sip their gin and tonics in silence.

"If you'll excuse me, I have to . . ." I trail off. They don't seem to notice that I don't complete the sentence. Carmen is talking to two guys by the door, and I pull her away from them.

"Excuse us for one sec, gentlemen," she says.

"Okay, Chris Harrison, let's talk. These dudes are duds, and you know it."

"They're all *suuuuper* eligible bachelors who would look amazing on Instagram and are dumb enough to not question whatever scheme you're cooking up," she counters. "Isn't that what you're looking for?"

"They're just so . . . boring," I whine. "Keith, Jordan, and Kyle do not get roses."

"Right, because your whole 'tortured artist who hasn't showered in three days' thing has been working out really well for you." She raises one smug eyebrow.

I mentally review my last few dates. There was the guy who left me with the bill the other night. There was the guitarist who ghosted me after I downed espresso shots at 10 p.m. to stay awake for his midnight gig in Bushwick. There was the cute, floppy-haired movie critic who took me to the dive bar on his block for dollar-beers night, then asked me to cover the $4 check. I still have the crick in my neck from hooking up with the photographer who slept on a twin-sized mattress in a crawl space lofted above his microscopic studio.

"Look, you are a successful, badass entrepreneur. You can do way better than the unwashed schmucks you dig up from god knows where." She holds up my phone hopefully. "The best ones are still on their way, I promise. Give me twenty more minutes and then we can head out if it's a disaster. Deal?"

I tilt my neck to the right and revel in the satisfying crack. "Deal."

I make a promise to give Carmen's plan a chance, and soon, the night gets better. I wouldn't necessarily call it *great*, but at least I'm *entertained*. I meet a producer who has a podcast about podcasts; a redhead who only identifies himself as an equestrian; a model who appears to be under the impression that this is a casting call; and an anesthesiologist who immediately places his hand on the small of my back and explains, "This is where I'd put the epidural when you go into labor with our children."

I head to the quiet end of the bar to collect my thoughts. I wouldn't date *any* of these guys on my own terms. But for the sake of my current situation, I could see myself not totally hating the podcast producer, Isaac, or the equestrian, Finn. They're the most interesting, least creepy of the bunch, and they certainly have the right amount of square-jawed magic to reel in likes on Instagram, should our relationship ultimately progress to that level.

"Can I ask you a question?"

To my left, there's a man leaning against the bar, holding a gin and tonic. He's dressed sharply in a navy suit and lilac shirt, open at the collar. His cheekbones jut out at swoony angles and his wavy dark hair makes his brown eyes pop. He looks like a Disney prince who got lost at Ralph Lauren.

"Is this some kind of casting call?" he asks.

"Something like that," I say.

I don't recognize him; he's not one of Carmen's recruits.

"What are they auditioning for?" he asks, gesturing to the crowd of men sprawled across the middle of the bar.

I hesitate. "To be my boyfriend."

He laughs out loud, then stops. "Oh, you're serious, aren't you?"

He falters and stares down at his shoes to hide his grin. In any other circumstances, my cheeks would've flushed. But today has been intense—I feel beyond embarrassment at this point. He composes himself and extends his hand.

"I'm Blake," he says. "Pleasure to meet you."

"Eliza." I give him my sturdiest handshake, the one I give to my wholesale suppliers who try to jack up their prices.

"So, Eliza, tell me about yourself. I might want to be in the running."

I straighten up and flip my hair over my shoulder. "I run a jewelry business with my sister. We have a store in Williamsburg."

"Jewelry? Me, too," he says.

"No way, what do you do?" I ask. The industry is on the smaller side; I'd expect to run into people I know in the Diamond District on 47th Street, but not necessarily uptown at this preppy dive bar.

"I founded Bond and Time," he says simply, like that's not a big deal or anything. "It's like—"

"Rent the Runway for high-end watches," I finish, cheeks flushing.

"So you've heard of me," he says, cocking an eyebrow.

I make a sound that's probably not so ladylike out of the corner of my mouth. "I mean, I've heard of your company. Probably at an industry thing. Or maybe I follow your company on Instagram, I can't remember."

I definitely follow them on Instagram.

He shrugs. "I don't have anything to do with that. Social media isn't my thing. I don't even have my own account. I outsourced that to a PR agency. Do you think they're doing a good job?"

"You could increase your followers and engagement," I say.

Once, a few years back, when Mercury must have gone retrograde and life got topsy-turvy, I briefly dated a string of guys like Blake—the kind who wear dry-clean-only suits regularly and have a signature cologne. I learned that they secretly enjoy being called out on their shit. So I hold my gaze and wait for his response.

He nods deeply. "Noted. So, why exactly are you holding a casting call to find a boyfriend?"

I consider telling him the truth. Blake doesn't seem like one of the dopey men in khakis across the bar. Plus, as a fellow entrepreneur, I'm sure he'd go to any length possible to ensure his business will succeed. I'm on the verge of explaining the scheme Carmen and I cooked up, but then I lose my nerve. He's too cute to mess things up with.

"I need a date to bring as a plus-one to a friend's wedding this weekend," I offer.

"It's a shame, then. I'm out of town this weekend," he says. He takes a sip of his drink, and when the glass leaves his lips, I see a grin lingering there. "I'm around other weekends, though. I hope that doesn't take me out of the running."

My stomach flip-flops. "Not necessarily."

He pulls his phone out of his pocket; it's buzzing. He gives it an annoyed glance and sends the call to voicemail.

"Unfortunately, I have to head out," he says. "But I'd love to be considered for, you know, the position. Could I take you out sometime?"

His smile is just as genuine as one could hope for in this ridiculous scenario. I get that sensation that every girl who's ever felt beautiful and valuable and important has ever felt: like you're zooming over the top of a roller coaster, untouchable, winning, perfect.

I grab his phone and enter in my number. I don't leave a last name—too traceable. For now, I'm just Eliza. I return his phone when he closes his hand around it, the gleaming face of his watch winking back at me.

"It's been a pleasure, Eliza," he says.

For a split second, I wonder if he's moving toward me for a hug or a kiss, but then he slips past me into the crowd. If I need a fake fiancé who won't ever question why I look engaged on Instagram, Blake might be my jackpot. All I need to do now is convince him.

· Chapter 4 ·

Click. A flashbulb pops. *Click*. Another one. *Click*.

I clench my left butt cheek to give myself a better grip on the metal stool I'm leaning against, precariously balancing in silver stiletto booties. Unbelievably, those emails I sent actually panned out. My story was picked up by jewelry blogs and wedding websites right away, and then I caught a big fish: a women's magazine. It was an easier reel than I ever could have dreamed. *Elle's* digital director apparently follows Brooklyn Jewels on Instagram and was eager to assign a piece about my business and, yes, my engagement. Now, less than a week later, it's happening.

It's my first time ever doing a magazine photo shoot, and to be honest, it's not what I imagined. I know that magazines aren't exactly thriving at the moment—I didn't expect to share a private plane to a secluded beach in the Maldives with Pat McGrath as she did my makeup—but I expected a tiny bit more than this. The photographer, reporter, and I are stuffed into what probably used to be a storage room. There are scuff marks on the walls and a mishmash of camera equipment and clothes strewn about. My hair and makeup were done by a woman summoned from the beauty editor's phone via Glamsquad. My outfit is sweet, though—the fashion editor was waiting with a rack of clothes for me when I arrived, and I got to choose. I asked why everything was white, gray, and silver, and she shrugged like it was obvious: "To play up your engagement ring, you know?" I slipped into charcoal gray leather leggings, a whisper-thin white camisole, and a white jacket dripping in silver zippers. This morning, I had spent a half hour debating which accessories to bring. Ultimately, I went with my signature bangles, hammered silver hoops, and a simple diamond pendant on a silver chain, all from Brooklyn Jewels: they create a pretty effect without stealing focus from my ring.

The photographer, a petite woman with an intricate floral tattoo snaking up one arm, looks up from her camera. "Can you adjust your hand? Move it onto your thigh again?"

Oh. Right. She had suggested that I casually rest my left hand on my thigh so that my engagement ring is visible in photos. I move my hand. The photographer smiles. *Click.*

I am not a model; I never dreamed of being a model; I never even fantasized for a moment during a particularly juicy rerun of *America's Next Top Model*, I swear. And yet, something about this whole ordeal—the photo shoot, the interview, the office outside full of editors who can create a trend or launch a brand's success with a single story—feels inevitable.

People always ask how a girl like me who grew up around boats in the most picturesque seaside city wound up moving to New York City. The subtext: *Who would give that up?* Back in middle school and high school, Mom, Dad, and Sophie would go out on our boat on the weekends when the weather allowed for it. It was their passion. But the thing is, I get seasick. Not just a little bit queasy, but debilitatingly nauseous. So, while the rest of my family was gone, I hung around Helen's boutique with a stack of glossy magazines, poring over each page carefully. I liked the fashion spreads and the celebrity interviews, but that's not what drew me in. No, I couldn't get enough of the profiles of women to watch—chic women with booming careers in cities like New York and Los Angeles. It's like Diane von Furstenberg said after marrying a prince and building a multimillion-dollar company well before turning thirty: "I didn't really know what I wanted to do, but I knew the woman I wanted to become."

I knew the woman I wanted to become. I knew I wanted to do something *big*, something that would land me on this stool, in front of a photographer, waiting to be interviewed for one of the publications that I read as a seasick teen back in Portland.

As I get more comfortable, the photographer comes closer, moving from full-body shots to close-ups. I take a deep breath, flip my hair, and flash my biggest smile. *Click, click, click, click, click.* I offer what I hope is a glamorously coy, close-lipped gaze. *Click.* I rest my bejeweled hand on my chin and look flirtatiously off to the side. *Click.* The woman I wanted to become. *Click.* The woman I'm becoming. *Click.*

Once the shoot wraps up, I slip into a stall in the bathroom to change out of the fashion editor's clothes into the ones I arrived in: a short black skirt and the most *Elle* garment I own, a delicately embroidered white blouse with a high collar. I knew they'd give me clothes to wear for the shoot, but I wanted to arrive in style, like I belonged here. Standing barefoot on the cold tile floor, I miss my glittering skyscraper booties from the shoot. I wish my regular black ankle boots gave me a little bit more lift. But when I see my reflection in the mirror, I regain my confidence: I look like I've been FaceTuned. Somehow the makeup artist carved out cheekbones and made my eyes sparkle. My hair bounces.

Taylor, the reporter, is waiting for me in the hall. She's wearing a chic outfit—vintage Levi's, leopard-print pumps—and box braids that cascade halfway down her back. I check her hand when she holds the door to the elevator bank open for me: no ring. That's a good sign. It means that, hopefully, she won't ask gushing questions about my fiancé. Maybe it'll be strictly focused on the company.

She takes me downstairs to grab coffee. I follow Taylor through the cream-colored granite cafeteria with soaring, double-height ceilings, we each pour ourselves a cup, and we take a seat at a round table.

When we sit, she asks for permission to record our conversation. I feel a rush of nerves. For the first time, it's possible that the story about my "engagement" will be in someone else's hands. I can only control what I say—I'll have to choose my words carefully.

"Of course, you can record," I tell her.

To my delight, Taylor runs through the questions I've always imagined a reporter would ask. I tell her that Sophie and I grew up underfoot at my parents' store, watching them run a business. I tell her about everything Helen gave us: inspiration, an education, a vision for my career. I explain that after Nana and Pops passed away, we were left with a sizable chunk of money that we'd each gain access to upon turning twenty-five. So we hatched a plan—we'd go into business together.

That fall, I enrolled at NYU to study entrepreneurship and marketing. When I graduated, I landed a well-paying but criminally boring sales job. I could leave the office at five on the dot to read books on startups, attend lectures by entrepreneurs, and study the hell out of the jewelry industry. I wrote a business plan and submitted it to competitions that offered seed funding for startups. Meanwhile, Sophie had been working as a graphic designer in Portland and living at home to save money. She moved to New York to study diamonds and jewelry design at GIA (the Gemological Institute of America). By the time we were twenty-five and thirty, respectively, we were ready: Sophie knew how to create beautiful pieces, we had two years' worth of funding locked in, and we signed a lease on a storefront in Brooklyn.

Taylor asks thoughtful questions—about the challenges of launching a business, about Sophie's design process, about how we grew such a loyal fan base in Hollywood and on Instagram so quickly. I tell her my favorite story, about how Meghan Markle happened to wear one of our necklaces a month after we launched. Like many politicians and royal figures, she uses fashion as a tool for diplomacy; whenever she and Prince Harry travel, she wears designers local to that country. A Brooklyn Jewels necklace sat atop a Calvin Klein dress and a Michael Kors coat. The minute our brand was identified and named by fashion reporters around the globe, our business skyrocketed to success. Life hasn't been the same since.

"So, your fiancé. What's his name?" Taylor asks.

She drops the question so smoothly into the conversation that I would've blurted out a name if there was one.

"Oh, he . . . I . . ." I falter. I give her a tight-lipped smile. "He's a very private person. I'd prefer to keep his name out of this."

"That's interesting. You don't seem like a private person," she observes, checking her notes, ". . . sharing your life with one hundred thousand followers on Instagram."

"I love connecting with Brooklyn Jewels's customers and fans there, and sure, part of that means sharing pieces of my life," I say as calmly as I can. "I share as much as I'm comfortable with."

"But why not share your fiancé's name?" Taylor presses.

I sip my coffee to stall. "He has his reasons to stay out of the spotlight. He may make a more public debut when he feels comfortable, in his own time." My next move is important. I have to steer the conversation in the right way. "What matters is that I've met a wonderful guy, we're very happy, and seriously, would you look at this *ring*? I mean, he did well. I'd love to tell you more about it. . . ."

Taylor listens as I explain that I'm wearing a Brooklyn Jewels original that was handcrafted by Sophie using stones from an Israeli diamond dealer who comes to New York once a season with gems hidden in every pocket and strapped up both legs. I note that the ring exemplifies two of our customers' favorite styles, the three-stone setting and the classic round-cut diamond. I add that we also stock less expensive versions of this ring for the bride on a budget. I pivot Taylor toward what I want her to write about: my work, not my life.

When the interview is over, Taylor walks me to the lobby. I have one last card to play to ensure she writes the story I hope she'll write. I pull a small black velvet pouch from my purse.

"I brought a little something for you," I say, handing it to her.

She pulls the black cord drawstring and tips the contents into her palm. I've given her a dainty, gold chain bracelet with a tiny chip of opal on it.

"Your birthstone, right?" I ask. I did my research.

She's touched. "Yes, this is gorgeous. Thank you so much," she gushes.

I help her clasp it on and we hug goodbye. From the photo shoot to the interview to the gift, I feel as if I've nailed today. For the first time in two hours, I exhale. I push through the revolving door of the grand lobby and exit onto bustling Eighth Avenue. I can see the expanse of Central Park two blocks to my left; the trees are newly green again. To my right, there's a crowd of tourists streaming my way. I lean flat against the side of the building to catch up on my phone's notifications: a busy mix of emails, Instagram likes, and texts—two from Carmen and one from Blake.

"Hey there, stranger. Found a plus-one for your friend's wedding?"

I can't help it—my lips curl into a pleased grin. Once upon a time, my impulse might have been to write back, "I did! How was your weekend? Didn't you go on a trip? How was it? :)" But nearly a decade of dating in the city has taught me how to stretch out my interest like taffy: the less eager I appear up front, the longer I can capture a guy's attention. I scale back my response.

"I did."

"So the casting call worked?"

"Ha. I guess so."

"Bummer—does that mean I can't ask you out?"

I love my life.

"I never said that," I type back.

It's the first day of spring that hints at the summer to come. Sun beats down in steady golden rays on my bare legs. I hit Send on my message. And I watch his response bubble up.

· *Chapter 5* ·

I can't wait for my date with Blake this Saturday afternoon, and yet, I'm yawning. Like, massively. I've been up since 6 a.m., sliding jewelry on and off my fingers and wrists and ears, modeling it all for our Instagram. I shoot most of the photos and videos myself on my iPhone. I take excellent care of my hands—weekly manicures, no picking at my cuticles, no matter how stressed I get—specifically so we don't have to hire a hand model for these shots. Through a combination of trial and error and research on our competitors, I've nailed what our followers want to see. So I stack three of the same ring in different carat sizes on my hand for potential customers to compare, enormous rocks for users to *ooh* and *ahh* over, and show off our signature setting, the three-stone, round-cut ring I wore in the engagement announcement. This morning, I took hundreds of photos, narrowed them down to the best couple dozen, and started the tedious process of editing each image. Over the next few weeks, I'll add captions and hashtags and roll them out one at a time.

I don't usually work this early on Saturdays, but I'm feeling frantic. I got a letter from my landlord yesterday with bad news. When Brooklyn Jewels's two-year lease expires in mid-November, our rent will go up by 20 percent. And since my apartment is in the same building, the rent on my studio will jump by 20 percent a month, too. We have until late October to decide whether or not to renew the leases. I always knew that we could've locked in our original rate—which is already exorbitant—for longer, but I hesitated to sign beyond a couple years. Thirty percent of small businesses fail in their first two years. I worried that if we committed ourselves to a brick-and-mortar storefront for longer than that, we'd inevitably fail.

So that explains why Blake catches me in full yawn, mouth wide open, eyes scrunched up at the East Seventy-Ninth Street entrance of Central Park. I'm lucky I had the good sense to clap a hand over my mouth so that his first glimpse of me is not a front-row view of my molars. I've remembered to take off the engagement ring.

"Sorry, am I boring you already?" he jokes.

God, he is cute. He's dressed more casually today, in olive green chinos and a lightweight navy knit with the sleeves pushed up just so.

I punch him playfully on the arm. "No, I got up early. I've been working."

"I feel that," he says, nodding. "I remember those days."

"You don't need to work weekends anymore?"

He shrugs diplomatically. "Things are more or less stable these days, though, of course, it's never easy. But I can usually clear a Saturday afternoon if I have a good enough reason."

He's flirting in a way that makes me smile. Blake invited me to join him at the park for a picnic, and I said yes despite the trek. He said he'd bring a blanket, a baguette, and some cold cuts. I instantly volunteered to bring the cheese and the wine. If we're going to spend any amount of time together, Blake is going to learn one thing: I love my cheese.

I lift up the Bedford Cheese Shop bag dangling from my wrist. "This is a good enough reason for you?"

He peers into the bag to investigate.

"There's gouda, goat cheese, and truffled brie," I explain.

"Excellent," he says.

We traipse off into the park, following the winding pathways under shady trees.

"So, you were out of town last weekend?" I ask.

"Visiting my brother in Boston," he supplies. "He and his wife had a baby in February. I went up when she was born and wanted to go back for another visit."

"That's sweet," I say. I can't help but think of Sophie. I know her heart hurts when she hears about babies—I have something resembling sympathy pains.

"She's so tiny. So cute. Belle, that's her name."

"Baby Belle, Babybel. Like the cheese," I say automatically.

The moment the words are out of my mouth, I want to die of embarrassment.

He stops in his tracks and laughs.

"Did you just compare my niece to a *cheese*?" he asks incredulously.

"One-track mind," I say, lifting the Bedford Cheese Shop bag again.

We amble onto the Great Lawn, my favorite part of the park. It's a lush oval of grass, smooth and sunny in the middle with baseball fields around the perimeter. Every few feet, there's a cluster of people: women testing the newly warm weather in cutoffs and sandals, stretched out on towels with books; couples lounging with heads in laps; groups spread out with dogs, babies, Frisbees; a shirtless guy doing yoga under the shade of a tree; two Little League teams facing off in bright uniforms. Blake points to an open spot.

"There?" he asks.

"Sure."

He pulls a big gingham picnic blanket out of his navy canvas backpack. We settle in: I arrange the cheese, discreetly unscrew the rosé to pour into plastic cups, and stash it back into my tote bag before the police at the edge of the park can see; he sets up a mini speaker to play a Spotify mix, tosses the packets of turkey and salami on the blanket, and starts to slice the baguette. And then . . . silence. I smile at him. He smiles at me. I hate those first dates that alternate between spurts of biographical information—where you grew up, how many siblings you have—and awkward silent lulls. I don't want that to happen.

He picks up the goat cheese I brought and studies the wrapper longer than he needs to. "It's a good thing this isn't Camembert," he says.

I latch on to what he said too quickly, eager for the awkward moment to pass. "What do you have against Camembert?"

"When I studied abroad in Paris, my friend and I rented this little flat in the Sixteenth," he says. "We bought Camembert our first day there, and before we knew it, the entire place reeked of stinky cheese. We spent the first week in our apartment with all the windows open to air it out. It was January."

"Ha."

"Where did you study abroad?" he asks.

"I didn't."

"Oh. Sorry."

Another lull.

"I wanted to. Study abroad, that is. But the classes I wanted didn't line up with the cities I was interested in, and so I figured it wasn't worth it."

"Yeah, that makes sense."

Another lull. We both fidget with our food and sip our rosé.

"You brought Solo cups, huh?" he says, lifting an eyebrow.

I look down at my plastic cup. "Yeah?"

"I can't remember the last time I drank out of one of these. Spring fling, senior year, maybe?" The memory of it makes him grin.

"Oh, come on, what else are you supposed to drink out of in the park?"

"Clear plastic cups," he says simply, as if it's that obvious. "Plastic wineglasses. Not . . . *Solo* cups."

Another lull. A familiar wave of disappointment washes over me. I've been here before: cute guy, good on paper, flirty texts, zero chemistry in real life. I see the afternoon spinning out before me as a dull stretch of small talk ruining what should be the most glorious first weekend of spring. Without meaning to, I let out an audible sigh.

"I'm sorry, this shouldn't be one of those dates," he says, wincing. His brown eyes crinkle.

I'm embarrassed that he senses my disinterest.

"What do you mean?" I say, faking bewilderment.

"I mean, we don't need to talk about dumb college stuff like semesters abroad and Solo cups. Tell me something that matters. Tell me more about what you do."

I admire his confidence to call out our stilted mood. The vibe lightens up. He leans back on his elbows and I relax onto my side. I tell him about how Sophie and I launched our business, and he chimes in with his own startup horror stories. He grins and compliments my ambition; he says it's impressive. We bond over what characters the old-school Diamond District dealers are, and he makes me laugh with a surprisingly accurate, gruff impression of a guy whose family has been operating their tiny storefront on Forty-Seventh Street since they escaped Nazi Germany. He nails the hoarse accent in a way that proves he's spent his fair share of hours negotiating with them, like I have. From there, the conversation slides smoothly out of work territory, ping-ponging from my grisly love of true crime documentaries to the elderly resident who walks a pet turtle on a leash outside his building every Friday night.

"I don't believe you," I protest.

"Then maybe we'll have to go stake out the building together next Friday night," he says, his hand grazing my knee.

My heart does an anxious flip. I'm not ready to banter back and forth about a second date. I like Blake. He's a perfectly nice guy, though I don't feel that intangible, electric spark between us, either. But right now, I don't need the love of my life—although I want that someday. I need a fake fiancé. Someone who looks good on paper, and maybe with a filter, too. It would be so convenient and easy if Blake could be that guy for me, though I'm not sure I feel the chemistry.

Blake leans across the gingham picnic blanket to kiss me. I turn my head ever so slightly to offer him my cheek instead. If he's disappointed, he doesn't make a show of it; he pulls back and offers me a small smile.

"Should we head out?" he asks. "It's getting a little chilly."

I'm grateful for the out.

💍

I bring the leftover cheese to Sophie and Liv's apartment that night. It's a little melted from sitting in the sun all day, but it'll do. If I need to have a tough conversation with Sophie about money, I'd rather do it with three wedges of cheese between us. I savor the walk down their tree-lined block full of brownstones. Their neighborhood looks like Nora Ephron's version of New York: classic, gorgeous, expensive. Sophie couldn't afford Park Slope on her own, but Liv's lawyer salary helps. When I reach their building, I take a deep breath to collect myself before I hit the buzzer.

My sister and I have always been close. That's not to say we don't get bogged down in the same occasional, passive-aggressive ruts that other pairs of siblings do—we do. But we both want to see this joint dream through so badly, we're able to let those minor dramas slide. From the start, we've had a clear plan in place: we'd play to our strengths. I might weigh in on a piece of jewelry and she might offer an opinion on how we spend our budget, but she has the final say on the creative side and I have the final say on the business side. That makes what I'm about to discuss with her even worse. She's savvy enough to weigh in on our finances, but the ultimate decision will be mine. And I need her input.

The buzzer blares. I push open the front door and walk up a flight of stairs to their apartment on the second floor. Liv is waiting for me by the door, and I can smell Sophie's cooking wafting into the hall—something spicy, though I can't identify what. I hug Liv. She's in an old, oversized T-shirt from her college marching band and clutching a plastic-covered library book (Sophie's type: nerds).

To borrow a phrase from every New York real estate listing ever, the apartment is "cozy." But they've managed to make it homey, too. The living room walls are painted like pale sunshine and covered in custom art, mostly from their friends. An afghan made by

Liv's mom is thrown over their tweed couch, and a pair of shelves are overflowing with stacks of books organized by the colors of the rainbow.

"I can't remember the last time you voluntarily gave up your Saturday night to hang out at home with us," Sophie calls from the kitchen. She's in an apron stirring something in a wok on the stove.

"Yeah, about that . . ." I slide onto one of the bar stools at the island that separates the cramped kitchen from the living room and plunk down the blocks of cheese. "I'm not exactly here for a fun Saturday night."

"Well, jeez, *thanks*," Liv says, pushing up her glasses.

"No, no, I mean, I got some not-so-fun news from Roy." Our landlord.

"Oh." Sophie stops stirring. She turns away from the stove to lean her elbows on the kitchen island.

"It's our rent," I say, letting the explanation tumble out in a rush: the rent hike, the October deadline to make a decision.

My words hang in the air.

Liv is the first to speak. I've come to love her over the years, but I despise when she interjects herself into our work. It's not like I run over to her law firm and negotiate divorce settlements for her. (Of course, she's a divorce attorney. Sophie says opposites attract.)

"That neighborhood is absurd," she says. "You're paying top dollar for the privilege of living in an Urban Outfitters commercial. Can't you ditch the hipster nonsense and move the shop somewhere else?"

"The neighborhood is part of the appeal," I insist. "Our customers are there. We get amazing foot traffic."

"But we're already stretched so thin." Sophie groans and pushes her hair back. "We're just barely making rent every month as it is."

"Our sales are on the upswing lately," I point out.

"Sure. This month. What about next month?"

The answer rolls around my mouth and I'm not sure I should say it out loud.

"What, you think your little marketing stunt is going to boost our sales permanently?" Sophie asks.

Liv pads into the kitchen and plants herself by Sophie's side. She purses her lips at that thought.

"Look, maybe it's nuts, but it's working. Don't tell me you haven't noticed the wave of new followers and sales to new customers. And it's only going to get better in time."

"Eliza . . ." Sophie looks at me with big, pleading eyes.

"What?"

She sighs. "I really doubt that we can afford to renew the lease at the higher rate. It's a lot of money. It might be too much. Think practically."

I picture us shutting down the shop, losing the business, me living on that tweed couch. The mere thought of it makes my head feel fizzy with pressure. I pinch the bridge of my nose, waiting for the right words to come.

"We can make it work. We'll cut our salaries!"

Sophie and Liv exchange heavy glances.

"No," Liv says simply.

"We can't do that," Sophie says after a beat. Her face falls. "We really need the money."

"You're doing another round of IVF," I guess.

Liv snakes her arm around Sophie's waist. "We want to," she explains. "But our insurance won't cover another round. It'll be fifteen thousand dollars this time, entirely out of pocket."

"That's why we're at home making our own stir-fry instead of going out," Sophie says. Her eyes go wide. "Shit! The stir-fry." She whirls around, turns off the burner, and uses pot holders to move the wok to the other side of the stove.

"What about laying off Jess?" Liv suggests.

Sophie and I both make faces.

"She's Helen's family, we can't do that," I remind her.

Sophie hesitates. "Yeah, but . . ."

"Ditching Helen's family is off-limits. Neither of us would be here without Helen's influence in the first place."

"But you have your own family to think about, too," Liv points out.

"I know that! I *know* that," I say. "Come on, though. Jess was already laid off once. I can't do that to her again. That would be so depressing and sad."

"Yeah, but it's nothing personal," Sophie argues. "It's business. Jess would understand that—and if she doesn't, that's not your problem."

"We don't even pay her *that* much," I protest.

"Well, come on, Eliza," Sophie says. "She makes twenty-two dollars an hour. That's not nothing."

I wince. She's right. But Jess is great at what she does, and it wouldn't be fair to cut her job just yet. There are a lot of corners I'd be willing to cut to save money: moving in with a roommate; boosting our prices; eating and drinking at home more often instead of going out. But leaving Jess behind isn't one of them.

"Look," I say. I flatten my palm against the island and speak as calmly as I can to Sophie's back. "We have six whole months to decide. Give me six months. I can make this work."

She turns around to face me. Her jaw is set. "It has to."

· Chapter 6 ·

We have the happiest, smuggest, most self-satisfied customer in our store, and Jess is about to burst his bubble. I'm perched at the counter answering questions and engaging with comments from users on Instagram, which can take upward of an hour every day. But I can't help but watch Jess handle him. This guy, a wiry, bearded dude in a plaid flannel, thinks he's brilliant because he snuck one of his girlfriend's rings out of her jewelry box and insists that he needs a ring the same size.

"Which finger does she wear that on?" she asks patiently.

He balks. "It's a ring. It's her ring size."

"Every finger is a slightly different size," she explains. "Unless she wears this on her left ring finger, you can't guarantee that an engagement ring sized off this one is going to fit."

This is actually a pretty common mistake. When we first opened the shop, I was surprised by how many guys—smart guys, guys with complicated jobs, *doctors* even—did not realize that fingers vary in size. It'd be hilarious if it wasn't so frustrating.

While Jess walks the guy through his various options (figure out which finger she wears this on; bring home a ring sizer and measure the right finger; buy any ring and have it sized properly after the proposal—at great expense), my phone vibrates with alert after alert. There's a flood of Instagram notifications, and I scroll to figure out where they came from. A sudden spike like this is never random. Sure enough, I figure out that it's from the *Elle* piece published online ten minutes ago.

I skim it breathlessly, not daring to relax until I've finished, just in case I said anything terribly dumb or Taylor picked up on the fact that I'm kind of a fraud. But it's *good*. I'm relieved. Taylor notes that I'm newly engaged but won't name my fiancé, although she praises that as a feminist move designed to keep the spotlight on my professional accomplishments. The piece's primary focus is on my journey to entrepreneurship, and frankly, Taylor makes me sound like a rock star. I certainly look like a rock star in those silver stiletto booties. It's better than I could have dreamed. I share the piece on Facebook, Twitter, and Instagram.

When I've come back to earth, it appears that the guy has given up.

"I don't know," he says morosely. "I just don't know which of her fingers this fits on."

"You could always ask her," Jess suggests.

She's good with customers—better than either Sophie and I will ever be. She's endlessly patient, naturally friendly, and has a sixth sense that tells her when to push a sale and when to stand back.

He looks appalled. "But then it won't be a surprise!"

I know the stats. Among straight couples, nearly 90 percent of men propose with an engagement ring, and less than half of them consult their girlfriends about the decision. I'm not knocking my job, but it makes no sense to me to send a typically clueless man into a jewelry store to pick out the most expensive accessory a woman will ever own—one that she'll hopefully wear for the rest of her life. I don't think anything about an engagement ring should be a surprise. I certainly wouldn't want to be surprised. But then again, I'm the girl who picked out her own hulking diamond without a man in sight.

The guy mutters that he'll "figure it out on his own" and leaves.

"Ugh," Jess says, once the door has swung shut.

"You did the best you could," I point out. "He wasn't in a position to buy right now."

"True." She sighs. "His fiancé will surely have fun with a lifetime of him."

Jess never fails to make me laugh. I show her the elle.com story.

"God, I miss this," she says, scrolling to examine the photos.

In her past life, before she landed at Brooklyn Jewels, Jess styled the accessories on photo shoots exactly like this one. It was her job to select the jewelry and the shoes—well, to *assist* the woman who selected the jewelry and shoes. From what she's told me, the job mostly entailed packing and unpacking boxes of accessories sent in from publicists all over the city and praying that nothing got lost in the process. I think that's why she's so diligent and organized here.

"The booties are amazing." She sighs. "Gianvito Rossi?"

"I don't know," I admit.

She zooms in to read the credits. "Gianvito Rossi," she confirms.

Her eye is good. She's told me how thankful she is for this job, but I know her ultimate dream was always to work as a stylist for fashion magazines. With print publications like *Glamour* and *Sev-*

enteen gone, and the rest of the industry on red alert, that dream seems less and less likely.

"The interview is great," Jess says finally, once she's finished reading it. "It positions us at the next major, hot jewelry brand. So legit."

If only she knew how precarious our position is right now.

"Yeah, hmm," I say, taking my phone back and abruptly changing the subject.

Soon another customer comes in. She's probably in her early twenties, with teal eyeliner flicked out in a flawless cat eye and two neat French braids.

"Hi, how can I help you?" Jess asks as she looks up from the glass case, a smile frozen on her face.

"Hi," the girl says. "I was just looking. I'm single. I mean, seriously, *just looking*."

"Enjoy. Let me know if you have any questions."

The girl peers into every case, inching toward me across the shop.

"You're Eliza, right?" she asks.

"I am."

Her gaze darts to my hand. I'm not wearing the ring. I move my hand to my hip so she stops staring.

"Can I get a selfie?" she asks shyly. "I love your Instagram."

I feel like I'm watching myself from outside my own body as I make my way around the counter and stand a few inches from her. She wraps an arm around me, bounces up on her tiptoes and juts out her chin to look closer to my height, and extends her phone in front of us. *Click.* Nobody's ever asked me for a selfie before.

She spends nearly half an hour lingering by the case of our least expensive pieces. She goes live on Instagram while she selects her favorites and gingerly tries them on. Ultimately, she chooses a delicate rose gold bangle after triple-checking the price. As Jess wraps it up in white tissue paper, the customer tells me softly that it's her present to herself after her boyfriend broke up with her last month.

"Trust me, it's less complicated to have jewelry than to have men," I tell her.

Jess laughs. Last I heard, she's been regularly hooking up with the same guy for three months, afraid to tell him that she wants more.

My phone buzzes again. It's like a pot of gold today: when I check my notifications, I see a slew from the customer who just left, followed by plenty of praise for the elle.com story and a resulting flood of new followers, two sales from the e-commerce shop, and plenty of emails. There's one I have to read twice in order to fully comprehend it.

Nora Mizrahi, a publicist, explains that she represents a variety of luxury event spaces, including the Wythe Hotel, a bougie hotel in my neighborhood with a killer rooftop bar and uninterrupted views of the entire Manhattan skyline. I've been there for birthday parties and happy hours. The hotel apparently hosts weddings, too. And if I'm reading this email right—which I think I am—Nora says they've had an unexpected cancellation for a wedding this October and would be able to accommodate my wedding on the Wythe roof-top entirely free of charge. There's a minor catch, as there always is: I would have to promote the hotel heavily on social media and in interviews. I read the email a third time, just to be sure that I am not hallucinating, but Nora's words seem to gel together. She's offer-ing me a free wedding. I know that at 100,000 followers, I qualify as an influencer to a degree. If I wanted to, I could probably get free clothes, free makeup, free dinners. But a free *wedding*? I can't wrap my mind around it.

I have never been a careful person. I still have childhood scars on both knees from flinging myself down the hill outside our house on my first bicycle sans training wheels. In college, I was the first one in line for another round of tequila shots. Even now, I'm running a jewelry business when I know millennials are supposedly "killing" the diamond industry. It's not that I don't care about facing consequences. Trust me, I do. But the upside—the adrenaline rush that comes with taking a risk, the reward that stems from making a bold decision—will always win out in my mind. Your life doesn't move forward if you sit at home saying no.

So before I have a chance to fully consider the ramifications of Nora's offer, I say yes, thank you, and hit Send. She emails back instantly to ask if I'm free for a phone call now to work out the details. Within the hour, we've hammered out the arrangement on the phone, she's emailed over the contract, and I've returned it with my signature. It's good to move quickly; I'm afraid if I don't, I'll back out. I post a smiling selfie on Instagram and announce in the caption that I've just locked in my dream wedding venue for October nineteenth. Thirty seconds later, I refresh the photo, and there are a dozen commenters celebrating my news. My wedding is exactly six months from tomorrow. All I have to do now is find the groom.

"So I have really great news and, uh, less than ideal news," Carmen tells me an hour later. "Which do you want first?"

This week's happy hour is at Le Boudoir, the Marie Antoinette–themed bar in Brooklyn Heights. We enter through the secret bookshelf in the restaurant above, on street level, and descend into a lounge with red velvet couches and a bust of the queen herself that serves as a tap. We both order a drink called the Guillotine, made with mezcal and honey.

"Hit me with the good news," I say, taking a slurp of the cocktail.

She straightens up to reach the fullest extent of her five-foot, two-inch height and brushes her hair off her shoulders.

"It's a lot," she warns me.

"I can handle it," I say.

Her eyes are bright and her lips are pressed together, like she can barely contain a secret. She pauses, as if recognizing that by saying her news out loud, it'll suddenly become real.

"I think I want to launch my own company," she says.

I can't help it—my hands zoom across the table to clutch hers. I nearly knock over our drinks in the process.

"Tell me! What's your idea?"

She takes a deep breath. "I'm happy at my job, I really am. But I miss working in skincare," she explains. I can tell—Carmen can happily spend a hot Friday night testing out face masks and researching the active ingredients in her moisturizer. "And working at a relatively new company these past few months has taught me so much. It's energized me."

"So . . ." I prompt, waving my hands. "Your idea. Spill. I wanna hear."

She grins. "Okay, but you have to be honest about what you think. I trust you."

"Of course, of course."

"It's a skincare app. You upload a close-up selfie and it instantly analyzes your skin type. From there, it sends you a box of products every month that's tailored to your skin's needs. You refresh the photo every season as your skin changes."

There's a hint of fear in her eyes, and I want to envelop her in the biggest hug. Because I get it, how terrifying it is to put your idea out there into the world. It seems audacious to think that *you* could have a valid business plan when there are, what, thousands or millions of new companies popping up every year?

"Carmen. I love it. That's so incredibly cool. And skincare is hot right now!"

She nods. Her eyes glow. "You think I have a chance?"

"I know you do."

She sighs with relief and slumps back into her booth. When Sophie and I launched Brooklyn Jewels, she was supportive, but made it clear that starting her own business was not her jam; she said she'd rather do excellent work for a company and collect a steady paycheck. I never thought she'd strike out on her own.

"I have a lot of questions for you about this whole process," she warns. "You know, raising money, the logistics of it all, when to quit my day job. But . . . those will come in time. Maybe over email, when alcohol isn't so involved."

"You know I'm here for you," I say.

I raise my glass to hers and give her a toast. I'm so proud of her, my perfect, beautiful, brilliant friend.

"So, do you want the bad news?" she asks, wincing.

"Lay it on me."

"Just as a preface, I want to let you know that what I did is totally against Tinder's policies and I could probably get fired, so please never tell a soul."

I laugh. "My lips are sealed."

"That was really Mary-Kate and Ashley's best movie," she muses.

"Right?!"

She mimes crushing the soda can against her forehead, like they do in the movie, but I call her out.

"Hey. You're stalling. What's the news?"

"I hacked into Tinder's database to look up that guy you went out with, Blake," she says, wincing. "He's actively swiping and messaging like . . . a dozen girls a day. And setting up dates."

"So? We went on *one* date," I say.

"Yeah, but that was before you set a wedding date six months away," Carmen says.

I had texted her about the free wedding the moment it happened. Now, the intensity of her words makes me sigh with stress.

"All I'm saying," she continues, "is that if you want him for your ruse, or fake wedding, or whatever it is, you probably want to jump on that before he gets too involved with someone else."

I know I didn't feel the *most* chemistry when we went out in Central Park, but it still stings that he picked up on that and actively decided against pursuing anything with me. I hadn't fully considered the significance of it until just now—hello, I was just a little busy dealing with an impending rent hike and my sister—but it's true. Blake didn't text me after our picnic date.

It's not that I want Blake to be The One. I don't. It wasn't love at first sight—he's a perfectly nice guy whose handsome looks will serve me well on Instagram, though the spark isn't quite there. But now that I have the clock ticking on an October wedding, I don't have the luxury of being choosy. Chemistry can build over time, can't it? My dad first spotted my mom during a freshman seminar at the University of Maine; they didn't wind up on their first date until the end of their senior year, when Mom says Dad finally grew up.

Carmen's news makes an idea click: if I'm giving up any semblance of a normal personal life for the sake of my company, it has
to be for the right person. Blake makes sense. If we were together,
we'd be a power couple: me in fine jewelry, him in luxury watches. I
can practically see the *New York Times*'s Vows column in print now.
I need to find a way to catch Blake's interest—for good.

· Chapter 7 ·

I hop on the subway to Blake's neighborhood first and figure out what the hell I'm about to do second. Cocktails with Carmen jolted me into action. As the 4 train whizzes toward the Upper East Side, my frantic impulses cool into a semblance of a plan. I want to knock on Blake's door and ask him to be my fake Instagram fiancé, but even I realize that's fairly bonkers for a large variety of reasons—namely, we've only been out once, it's a preposterous request, and also, I don't know his address. Instead, I shoot him a text to ask if he's free.

"Hey, are you around tonight? I happen to be in the neighborhood," I write.

I waver between adding a smiling emoticon and not. I add it. It looks desperate. I delete it and press send.

A torturous thirteen minutes crawl by. I refresh my Instagram, ignore the urge to pick at my cuticles, loudly sigh at the manspreader sitting across from me. I start a sudoku game on my phone and abandon it halfway through. I check to see if my text actually went through—of course it did.

And then, miraculously, Blake texts back.

"Yeah, just got home. What's up?"

I try not to worry about where he just got home *from*. A date? I wait precisely three minutes before typing a response so I don't appear too eager. It's important that I play this right. I get one shot at Blake.

"Can I come over? There's something I need to say to you," I text.

He writes back faster this time. "Sure," he says. He gives me his address.

The rest of the subway ride is a blur: I pop an Altoid, check my reflection in my phone, use the tweezers in my purse to remove a stray eyebrow hair, take my birth control when my regular alarm goes off at 9 p.m. I try not to dwell on the nerves sprawling across my gut.

When the train stops at Eighty-Sixth Street, I exit the station. I have to map Blake's cross streets on my phone; I'm not used to the Upper East Side, this neighborhood full of stately cream-colored granite buildings and designer flagship stores and foreign embassies proudly draped with colorful flags. When I see a liquor store, I dart in to pick up a bottle of wine; I figure it's the least I can offer Blake. Because the thing is, my plan isn't much of an actual *plan* at this point. I can seduce him over wine first and figure out what to say next.

Blake's building has a uniformed doorman to preside over the gleaming lobby. He asks for my name and calls Blake for approval before he waves me toward the elevator. The phone call embarrasses me, somehow, as if the doorman can see just how undignified I am by imposing on Blake like this. In the mirrored elevator, I press fourteen for his floor—not the penthouse, but certainly not cheap, either—and flip my head over to fluff up my hair at the roots. It's a trick that Mom taught me before my first boy/girl party in middle school; she says she learned it when she was my age, from Farrah Fawcett in a magazine. I catch my reflection: a little wild-eyed, a little frizzy, in black pants with a tote bag—not exactly Farrah Fawcett. The doors *ding* open. It's time to go.

I find Blake's door toward the end of the hall and knock. He opens it right away. I'm struck all over again by how handsome he is. He's in charcoal gray dress pants and his tie is loosened at the collar. At first glance, I'm utterly stunned that I rebuffed his kiss on Saturday. He hesitates ever so slightly before leaning across the threshold to give me a one-armed hug. And then, *there*, the awkwardness between us hits me. Something about our conversation, our connection, our chemistry is stilted.

I'm going to fix this.

"Hi!" I say in the warm voice oozing with charm I typically reserve for customers. "It's so good to see you. Thank you for, um, having me over."

He steps back, allowing me to enter the apartment. "Your text was mysterious. I'm curious."

I laugh to stall for time. His place is gorgeously masculine. Along one wall, there's a chestnut brown leather sectional with a green plaid blanket tossed over its arm. An angular brass lamp shines light on a meticulously organized bar cart and a sleek wooden coffee table. His suit jacket hangs over the back of a chair. This is a major upgrade from Holden's apartment, which basically just contained a mattress on the floor and a dead succulent on the windowsill. I set down the wine in its black liquor store bag and my tote, and turn to face him. I stuff my hands in my back pockets so I can't give away my nerves by fidgeting.

"I thought we could have some wine and I could apologize for not kissing you the other day in Central Park," I say.

A look of embarrassment flashes over his features before he settles into a bemused grin. He runs a hand over his chin.

"You did dodge me, didn't you?"

"I did, but only because I was a little nervous," I say. "Because I like you."

My stomach tightens when I hear my own impulsive words out loud. Maybe it was a ridiculous mistake to zip across the city and barge up here with sweet, canned lines like I'm every hero who's ever chased down a girl in a rom-com. Maybe Blake has moved on.

But instead, he takes three strides to close the gap between us and kisses me. He weaves his fingers through my hair and places a sturdy hand on the curve of my waist. The adrenaline that's been building ever since I first stepped onto the subway washes over me. *I did it.* I like that when we finally pull apart, I can see him smiling for real.

Like magic, the kiss cuts through the tension between us. I don't feel nervous as he opens the wine with a corkscrew from his bar cart and pours two generous glasses. We settle onto the couch, my legs curled up beneath me, his stretched out confidently. He compliments my bravado, showing up here; I volley back something about how good he looks in his work clothes; he brushes his hand across the pebbled leather of the couch to run a finger over my knee. It feels good to be bold. The chemistry begins to come alive.

I know this is only our second date, but I like how fresh this feels. We didn't wind up together because we both happened to swipe right in the middle of a loneliness-induced dating-app binge. We're not hunched over bar stools at some dive bar or cocktail spot that we've probably taken a dozen other dates to this year already.

We didn't spend a week texting back and forth about, oh, can you do Tuesday? No? Thursday? Six thirty p.m? Eight p.m.? This feels distinctly different than all of that—spontaneous and electric.

Conversation unfurls like a spool of ribbon. We debate if my Guillotine cocktail at the Marie Antoinette–themed bar is in poor taste (he says yes, I say it honors an icon), and he tells me about the weekend trip he took to Portland last summer. When his wineglass runs low, he doesn't refill it. Instead, he places it gently on the coffee table and leans across the couch to get closer to me.

He kisses me tenderly at first, with one hand cupping my cheek and the other lingering on my hip. I brace myself against his chest and trail my other hand across his firm bicep. I like how broad his shoulders are and how I can feel his muscles moving beneath his starched white shirt. He kisses me deeply—and then there's a crash.

He jolts upward. He must have knocked over the wineglass with his leg; there's a splash of dark red across the surface of his table and it spills on the carpet. He darts into the kitchen to grab a roll of paper towels and kneels down in front of the table to mop up the mess.

"Sorry," he mutters, grimacing.

"Real smooth," I tease, ruffling his hair.

"I guess it's time for a refill?" he jokes.

My glass was close to empty anyway. I pour us both more wine.

"Hold on, I'm going to grab some more cleaning supplies from the closet down the hall," he says.

An impulse washes over me. The wineglasses are tall with elegant stems, and they look chic against the backdrop of Blake's living room. Before I can think twice, I snap a photo of the scene. A picture like that—two wineglasses atop marble coasters, Pinterest-worthy decor—looks undeniably couple-y. I can post it later on Instagram. Blake's not on social media, so he'll never find out. I slip my phone back into my pocket just as he returns with a spray bottle and a wet sponge.

He gets down on his hands and knees to dab the stain from the rug, flipping his tie over his shoulder. There's something oddly domestic about the moment. I can't help but imagine what it might be like one day to live here with Blake and do mundane household tasks with him, like washing the dishes or making the bed. I snap back to reality when the stain is lifted and he sits back down on the couch with me. He sips his wine self-consciously.

However hot the chemistry was between us a minute ago, it's evaporated. It's clear neither of us knows how to kickstart it again. Thoughts of my engagement scheme and the shop's rising rent and his other dates lurk in the back of my mind and I push them away. I cast around for any subject that'll move us forward.

"So, you—" I say, just as he blurts out, "I just—"

"Go ahead," I say.

"No, you go ahead," he says.

I blush. I don't really want or need to ask him whatever bland question I had just brainstormed to get past this awkward moment. Instead, I scoot closer to him on the couch, swing one leg over his lap, and straddle him for a kiss. I slide my arms over his shoulders and pull him close to me. If he's surprised, he doesn't show it. He smoothly kisses me back as he stretches one arm out to put down his wineglass. He finishes loosening his tie and lets it slip from his collar. When I fumble with the top buttons of his shirt, he gently catches my lower lip between his teeth.

"I'm glad you're here," he says.

I sit back for a moment to catch his gaze. "Me, too," I say.

Blake runs his hands appreciatively from my hips to my waist to my chest. His hands are warm and he smells like a mix of leather and a heady cologne I can't quite place. The hem of my blouse has somehow shimmied up around my stomach. When he touches my torso, my skin tingles with anticipation. I can't remember the last time I felt this good.

I'm lost in his kiss when I feel his hands pull away from my waist. The sudden lack of contact jerks me out of the moment. I pull back.

"Is everything okay?" I ask.

There's a gleam in his eye. "Come to the bedroom with me," he says, running his hands along my thighs.

I try to slide off his lap as gracefully as possible without tipping backward off the couch. He extends a hand to me and weaves his fingers through mine. He stands and leads me down the dark hallway, opens the bedroom door, and shows me inside. Half of me feels glowing, seductive, lit up with desire, wanted. I want him. The other half of me feels victorious. My plan is working.

· *Chapter 8* ·

Blake has great sheets. Bright white, ultra-crisp, marshmallow soft like the touch of an angel. Blake also has a great body, as I learned last night, and a great, sunny view from his fourteenth-floor window that is currently pulling me out of a delicious slumber. I shift to stretch out the crick in my neck that formed overnight from lying in his arms, and he pulls the arm snaked around my waist even closer.

"Don't go," he mumbles, still half asleep.

I twist around in his arms to lay my head on the warm expanse of his chest. My insides feel like liquid gold. I've been single for four years now, and despite all the very real perks of a relationship—it's easier to meet the minimum delivery fee on takeout orders and sure, you can, like, share your entire life with someone—this is the one thing I miss the most. I savor the cozy sensation of snuggling up to Blake, from the lazy brush of his fingers against my bare hip to the way my cheek fits flush against his collarbone. He strokes my hair and tucks a loose piece behind my ear. My shoulder, crumpled under the full weight of my body, aches. But I don't dare move and break the spell until his phone's alarm trills a while later.

Blake groans, props himself up on his elbow, and hazily stabs a finger at his phone's screen to silence it. He drops back onto the bed and rolls over, leaving a good few inches of polite space between us.

"Morning," he says. His voice is all business again—no longer the sweetly sleepy voice that begged me not to leave a few minutes ago. He drops his gaze from mine. "Hope you slept okay?"

Yeah. The spell has been broken. Whatever last night was—fueled by an intoxicating combination of adrenaline and mezcal and Cabernet Sauvignon—is gone. In the light of day, there's a slight awkwardness between us. The easy comfort that bloomed last night has evaporated.

He offers me a white, fluffy bathrobe and averts his eyes when I slip it on. He makes me coffee, offers to make me eggs, and asks if he can call me an Uber back to my place. The question catches me off guard. My most recent hookup, a graphic designer training to be a tattoo artist, simply requested I leave so he could "chill."

I accept his offer of coffee, decline the eggs—that seems like too much—and escape to the bathroom for a moment alone with my thoughts. I slump against the sink. Blake is so kind, so attentive, so sweet. He's a nice guy, plain and simple. Is it wrong to be here, to pursue him like this, when my motives aren't strictly innocent? I try to flip the situation in my head to see if it feels sleazy when the gender roles are reversed. Men ruthlessly concoct all sorts of schemes to build a business or turn a profit, don't they? But as hard as I rack my brain, I can't fathom a situation where a guy like Blake would callously arrange a fake engagement with a girl like me.

My hair is mussed. Blake's robe slips off my shoulder. The contrast of my skin against the white terry cloth makes me look tan. I don't look quite like myself, especially not in this marble bathroom with vanity lights over the mirror. I still feel conflicted, but I also look like kind of a bombshell. I lean a hand on the counter with my wrist turned just so the reflection of my bare ring finger isn't visible. I pout into the mirror. *Click*. I take a selfie that I can post later online.

I slip out of the bathroom, collect my clothes from scattered corners on Blake's floor, and dress quickly. Blake raises an eyebrow when I emerge into the kitchen again.

"Leaving so soon?" he asks, cracking an egg into a glass bowl.

"I should head to work," I say, jerking my thumb toward his door.

He drops the eggshell into a garbage can, wipes his hands on a dish towel, and reaches for mine.

"Can't you head in whenever you'd like?" he asks. "Founder's perks?"

"I have a pile of work to do," I explain. I fidget with one foot to scratch the back of my other leg.

I tilt my head up and kiss him softly.

"I'll see you soon," I promise.

I collect my things, leave his apartment, and make a beeline to the elevator. My heart pounds the entire time. As I exit his building, make self-conscious eye contact with the doorman, and walk toward the subway, I try to process everything that's happened. My relationship with Blake—no, my *connection* with Blake; meeting in a bar and having two subsequent dates isn't nearly enough to merit the use of the word "relationship"—is just beginning to bud. I like him enough to see him again, sure. But do I like him enough to pin all my hopes on him and pray he'll somehow wind up as my actual fiancé or husband? And is this wedding ruse necessary enough to drag some innocent guy into my plans? I don't have any clear answers. I wish I did. All I know right now is that pursuing Blake is better than sitting idly by and waiting for this fake engagement to blow up in my face.

I'm late for work. I'm never late for work. Back in Williamsburg, I sprint up the stairs to my apartment, jump in the shower, and head down to the shop as soon as I can. Sophie's sitting on a high stool behind the counter and reading something on her laptop. She looks up at my wet hair and cocks her head.

"Where were you?" she asks.

Jess emerges from the back room holding a box.

Mornings are almost always dead in the shop. And sure, there are plenty of other things to do—polish pieces, pay bills, order inventory for next quarter—but for now, that can wait. It's time to sit down next to my sister and recount last night. I don't mind if Jess hears, too; we've become close since she took this job.

"I was late, true, but for good reason. . . ," I begin.

I explain who Blake is—she stops me, she knows all about Bond & Time—and why he could be the perfect person to get me out of this mess. I tell her about running over to his apartment last night.

It's not always easy to tell Sophie about my personal life. The five years between us sometimes felt like more. I was well into college by the time she got comfortable hearing about my dating life. I think part of her discomfort around the subject stems from the innate differences between us—she's cautious where I'm a risk-taker. She would never pull the kind of stunt I pulled with Blake last night. She doesn't need to have a black book saved on her laptop, since she could probably recite her entire list by heart in under ten seconds.

Sophie shakes her head at my story, but the expression on her face is clearly one of approval. She bites her lip and grins.

"You're nuts," she says. Her cheeks flush even just *hearing* about my hookup. "Just, you know, be safe, or whatever. Be smart."

That afternoon, I head outside to pick up lunch. I can't help but let my thoughts drift toward last night with Blake. My cheeks flush when the cashier interrupts my reverie to ask for my order. When I return to the shop, Jess is alone in the front room. Sophie's words from earlier echo in my head: *Be smart.* If I want to keep Blake as a viable option for me, I need a plan to explain away the engagement announcement on my Instagram feed.

"Hey, question for you," I ask, shifting my takeout under one arm and drumming my fingers on the glass counter in front of her.

"Yeah?" she asks.

I glance nervously toward the door. There aren't any customers about to walk in—we're alone.

"If anyone ever questions who runs our Instagram, do you mind saying it's you?" I ask.

"What do you mean?" she asks, her brow crinkling.

"Like, if *Blake* suddenly looks me up online and sees my quote-unquote 'engagement announcement.' I'll tell him the truth someday—but I just haven't gotten around to it yet. In the meantime, if he starts asking questions, can we say that photo came from you?"

It's embarrassing to ask so much from Jess. She looks confused, or maybe upset—it's hard to read the storminess behind her eyes.

"But I'm, like, *extremely* single," she points out.

"I know, I know. I'm asking if you would just pretend—only for Blake's sake, and only if he ever asks."

Maybe this was too much to ask. Maybe I crossed a line.

She sighs heavily. "Fine," she says. "As long as my name doesn't appear on those photos. I don't want my friends or family finding out."

"Trust me, *that* is something I understand perfectly well," I say, relieved. "Thank you so much, Jess."

I exhale as I move into the back of the shop to eat my lunch. I hunch over my phone to carefully edit the photos from last night. "When you borrow his robe . . ." I caption the selfie, posting it. I caption the picture of the two wineglasses with, "Date night in," plus the hashtag, and save it as a draft to post tomorrow.

I dig into my avocado pesto pasta and watch the likes and comments roll in. There's a flurry of praise ("werk it, girrrrrl," "#RelationshipGoals," "so happy for you, babe") and a smattering of emojis (pink hearts, kissy faces). And then the same sentiment pops up from a handful of users: "Who is he?"

My first impulse is to delete the comments so they don't attract attention. If I can get rid of the questions, I don't have to confront them. But my gut instinct tells me that's the wrong move. That would only make it seem like I had something to hide. So instead, I type out a carefully worded response: "We're so touched by the positive response to our engagement! Everyone's support means so much to us. But his privacy is important to him—and I want to respect that." I feel guiltier using this line now that I've had two more dates with Blake; it was easier during the elle.com interview, when I barely knew him.

A few minutes later, two users like my comment. A third replies solely with an emoji featuring a skeptical face—damn it. I need to convince my followers that this is real. But there's also a stream of people asking for details about the necklace I'm wearing in the bathrobe shot. I respond that it's available on our site. Ten minutes later, when I'm done with my pasta, I get a string of emails from our e-commerce platform. That necklace? The eight available ones in stock are sold out.

It's hard to celebrate a victory when it's tinged with fear. I make it through the rest of the day in a minor panic, wavering between triumphant moods—the necklace sold out! Blake seems to like me!—and utter misery—my scheme could be uncovered on a massive, publicly humiliating scale at any moment, and what if Blake and I don't wind up working out? Three times that afternoon, Sophie shoots dagger eyes at me because I'm drumming my fingers too loudly against the glass counter. I can't help it. Fidgeting gives me something to do.

I tell Sophie and Jess that I'll go ahead and close up on my own. Sophie's more than happy to skip out early—she says that she and Liv are looking forward to trying out a new zucchini noodle recipe. I need a moment to be truly alone, and I secretly enjoy the mindless, physical work of storing away jewels and wiping down the counter with Windex. I take my sweet time as I close up, playing electronic music as I work. I turn the locks on the front door with force, relishing the satisfying *clunk* as each one clicks into place.

I could go straight upstairs and go to bed, but I feel restless. I walk across the street to Golden Years, the bar where I discovered that Holden was engaged. (I cannot get over that.) There's nothing particularly special about Golden Years—it looks like any beloved local watering hole: glossy dark wood floors, lights strung up over the bar, well-worn booths with black-and-white posters hung above each one. But it's my go-to bar because it's nearby and reliably chill—I never have to shout over loud music or dodge heinous crowds. In this neighborhood, that's a feat. The cheap but perfect mozzarella sticks are simply an added bonus.

When I push open the door and feel the sweet rush of air-conditioning, I glance at the booths, but take a seat at the bar. I don't bother grabbing a drink menu—this isn't the place for a frou-frou cocktail or a glass of wine, unless you're okay with up-charged screw-top bottles of Chateau Diana. I have a usual beer order here. I scroll through Instagram on my phone until a bartender comes by.

"Hey, what can I get you?" he asks.

He looks vaguely familiar: a mop of dark hair; sweet, brown eyes; a hoodie with the sleeves pushed up. It takes me a moment to place him, but of course, I know him from here. He was the bartender who served me and that awful date. His name is Raj.

"Hi, one Brooklyn Bel Air Sour, please," I order.

He nods and goes to retrieve it. When he returns, he pours the bottle into a glass for me and keeps steady eye contact with the drink while he asks, "What, no whiskey this time?"

So I'm not the only one who remembers that night. Raj slides the bottle and the glass across the bar to me and finally looks up, giving me a small, tight smile.

"I think you were my bartender last time," I say.

"You were here with that short, drunk, angry dude who left you with the whole bill, right?" he asks, narrowing his eyes.

I take a heavy sip of my beer. The fruity, sour notes make today's stress fizz away. "That's me," I say.

He shakes his head slightly, like he's holding in a laugh. "How'd that go for you?"

"Oh, we're very much in love," I deadpan.

"So, what, you're meeting a date here tonight?" he asks.

I slurp down a healthy amount of beer so I don't snort. "Uh, no."

"Meeting a friend?"

"Nope. I just wanted to chill with a beer. And maybe talk to someone?"

"Chill as long as you'd like," he offers. "I like when customers hang out. Keeps things interesting."

Raj opens his mouth like he's about to say something more, but a burly dude in one of the booths on the other side of the bar summons him over with a graceless, "Hey!" Raj holds up a finger. "One sec, I'll be right back."

One second turns into one minute, which turns into a solid ten. I like watching him scuttle around the bar. It's like reality TV—as long as it lasts, you can tune out whatever's happening in your actual life. He takes a whole round of orders from the guy in the booth, pours each one, loads them up on a tray, and sets each drink down in front of the correct guy; he runs checks; he drops by what looks like an awkward first date at the bar to see if they need refills.

"Are you new here?" I ask when he swings back by my seat. "I mean, aside from recently, I haven't seen you around here."

"You're here often enough that you notice when the bar staff changes?" he says, smirking.

I can't help but laugh. "Yes."

He fidgets with the left sleeve of his hoodie. "Yeah, I, uh, I'm new. Got hired about a month ago."

"Congrats. Where were you bartending before?"

"Nowhere. I'm in between gigs right now," he explains. "I was the senior engineer at a tech startup. At first, I loved it. But I got burnt out after three years. It felt like I was tethered to writing code that didn't actually help anybody. And the meetings—" He groans and goes slack-jawed. "Pointless. The worst. So I left. I'm figuring out what my next move is. I thought I'd pull in some extra money here while I work that out."

"Wow. It's cool that you're making a change."

"Thanks. Just gotta figure out the next thing. I want to do something meaningful this time, you know?"

"Totally, yeah. It's best when you love what you do."

He leans his elbows on the bar and looks down, smoothing his hands over his head. When he looks back up, his cheeks are flushed.

"You're, like, the third person I've told, aside from my old co-workers."

"Seriously?"

"Easier to tell a stranger. You're not letting them down," he says, shrugging. He pauses, then adds, "Though, I guess if you're here as often as you say you are, you won't be a stranger for long."

I take a long sip of beer and weigh what I'm about to do. It's not a difficult choice—Raj's honesty stirs something in me. I want to be real with him.

"I have a secret, too," I offer.

He raises one thick eyebrow and drums his hands across the top of the bar. "Shoot."

"I accidentally led my Instagram followers to believe that I'm engaged," I say.

"But you're not. . . ." he says, looking confused.

"No," I say. "You know the jewelry store across the street? My sister and I own that."

"Whoa, really? You're pretty young to own your own business, aren't you?"

I shrug. "I'm old enough."

"Impressive," he says, whistling.

"I realized that if people think I'm engaged, my business does even better than it did before," I explain.

"So you're just not going to correct them," he finishes for me.

"Exactly."

He shakes his head and laughs, but then stops short when he figures out the problem. "Wait, but aren't people going to wonder *who* you're engaged to? And like, eventually, when you'll be getting married?"

I hadn't planned on revealing anything further, but it's not like Raj is going to blow up my secret. Even if he knows the truth, who is he going to tell? I hesitate, then dive into the story.

"Okay, so I'm fully aware this sounds preposterous, but I met this guy Blake at a bar the night after that whole Instagram thing went down. He's in the jewelry business like me," I explain, amping up my voice with bravado. I want to sound confident, even though I'm not. "We went out once and he was cool, but I don't know if the chemistry was fully there. But then a hotel offered me a free wedding six months from now. I said yes, and so I needed to rustle up a good fiancé, and Blake obviously made sense to step into that role."

"Obviously," Raj says. His eyes twinkle; he's humoring me.

"I haven't filled Blake in on my plan yet . . . and I'm not sure I will?" I feel guilty saying this out loud, so I skip quickly to my next thought. "A six-month timeline is fast, but it's not *unheard of*, right?"

"My parents got married two months after they met," Raj says.

"See!" I say, a little too excitedly.

"I mean, different circumstances," he counters. "It was an arranged marriage. They met just a handful of times before they decided to get married, and it wound up working for them. They've been together for thirty years."

"I love that it worked out."

"In a way, you know, you're kind of arranging your own marriage," he points out.

"I think of it more as a business arrangement that happens to involve a wedding?" I say, sounding as uncertain as a I feel about the entire scheme.

Raj throws his head back to laugh. I like it. Unlike Sophie or my parents, he doesn't have anything at stake, so his opinion is real. Unlike Carmen, he didn't forge an oath in tequila in an NYU freshman dorm room to be my best friend forever, so he won't sugarcoat anything to spare my feelings. He could reprimand me for my callous treatment of Blake. Whatever Raj's verdict is when I finish telling the story, I know it'll be honest and unbiased. That sounds even more refreshing than this cold beer.

"You're nuts," he says finally, pushing off the bar, stunned. "But I admire your balls."

"Really?" I ask. It's a hair too fast. I sound desperate.

He grips the bar and leans over it toward me. "Life's too short to play it safe. You want to win big, you gotta take risks." He grabs my empty bottle. "Tonight's drinks are on me."

· Chapter 9 ·

The weekend goes by in a crowded blur of customers. But on Monday, the shop is quieter than I'd like. Sitting in the back room, I can hear the blow of the air-conditioner—business is really that dead on a weekday morning. And that's when a plan strikes me. It's so beautifully simple, I don't know why I didn't think of it before. I pitch it to my sister, who's hunched over her desk, examining a new order of stones one by one with tweezers.

"What if we email Roy and ask for an additional six months at our current rent if we promise to renew the lease for at least the next year, and pay the new, raised rent once the deadline's up?" I propose. "This way, he gets the money he wants, and we get a few more months to raise it."

She looks up with a blank expression. I've pulled her out of her work.

"That'd give us nearly a year," she muses.

"Right—a whole year to apply for grants, court new investors, expand our e-commerce shop, grow our following."

"But what if doesn't go for it?"

I shrug. "Then he doesn't go for it. But at least we tried."

"He won't be mad at us for asking?" She picks at her nails at she talks, her telltale sign that she's stressed. She hates talking about money.

"He could be annoyed, maybe, sure. But I'd rather have him feel slightly bothered by us than kick us off the premises when we can't pay."

"You're so dramatic."

I hesitate before going in for the kill, because I know this will convince her for good. "Another year at this rent means another year before we have to even consider laying off Jess or cutting our salaries."

Sophie stops picking at her cuticles and we lock eyes. Before we formally made the decision to launch the shop, we sat down together, each with a sheet ripped from her designer's sketchpad and a marker. She said we should map out our ideal next ten years so we could both be on the same page about our goals and values, especially if we were tying our finances and livelihoods to each other for the foreseeable future. She completed a detailed outline in under two minutes: marrying Liv that next summer, one kid by their second wedding anniversary, and another within the next two years; she wanted a brownstone in Park Slope with a yard for a Labrador to run around in; she had even noted how much money she needed to set aside every month to maintain regular appointments with her colorist. I pointed out that the shop wasn't even mentioned in her outline.

"Well, *obviously*, it's a goal," she had said back then, rolling her eyes. She scrawled it in with her marker. "Such an obvious goal I didn't even need to write it down."

Here we are, three years later: she has one company, one wife, no kids, no dog, no yard. She has a half floor in a brownstone, but not even close to the whole thing. Her colorist still does a great job.

Sophie had leaned over my sheet to see what I had written and balked. I had written the name of our company ten times over in slightly different looping cursives, like an eighth-grade girl trying out her first name with her crush's last in the margins of her notebook. It's not that I never wanted anything besides this business. It's just that I wanted it so badly that the outer fringes of my life turned hazy. Maybe I wanted a relationship, but I couldn't tell you with whom, or what it'd look like. On Sunday mornings, would we run together in McCarren Park or would we call each other "babe" while passing pages of the *New York Times* back and forth? Would we move to an old walk-up with a leaky faucet but plenty of charm or one of those sterile high-rises going up on the waterfront with a lap pool and a sauna? Would we even want a baby?

Sophie's always wanted a baby. This company is mine. We've both known that for years.

"Email Roy," Sophie says finally. "It's worth a shot."

I type up the email and press send right in front of her, before she can change her mind.

I've kicked my outreach to editors, bloggers, and producers into high gear, pitching Brooklyn Jewels for every press opportunity I can dream up. I figure that our strategy should be full-speed-ahead right now. It seems worth the effort to pursue every idea that sounds even remotely within our reach, because that's just one more tool for attracting new customers.

So that's why I'm sitting next to Haley Cardozo, host of the radio show *Head Bitch in Charge*, a weekly feature on "powerful women who get shit done," as her slogan says. We're sitting in a glass-walled studio at the Sirius offices in a dizzyingly tall tower in Midtown. This is one of three press opps I've set up this week. An assistant instructs me to slip on enormous padded headphones and adjust the microphone so it's level with my face. She says I'll be on right after the show's first commercial break.

I thought I dressed boldly, but Haley's clad in a mint green pantsuit over a pale pink T-shirt printed with a portrait of Ruth Bader Ginsburg. Her canvas tote bag is from the *New Yorker*, and a gold nameplate necklace that spells out "HBIC" rests against her chest. The magenta highlights in her hair could probably be seen from Mars. By comparison, my purple slip dress, striped blazer, and stacks of Brooklyn Jewels wares—engagement ring included—are positively bland.

"You ready for this?" Haley asks. "It's live, you know."

"Let's do it," I say.

I try to push away my nerves. This only goes out to a million people or so. No sweat. Haley signals her assistant, who counts backward from three, then presses play on the show's intro music, which sounds like what would happen if Taylor Swift recorded a pop song about the joys of feminism under capitalism. Once the recorded intro is over, Haley jumps in with an animated promise to "deliver an ah-MAY-zing show to you guys today" featuring an interview with "young hotshot jeweler to the stars Eliza Roth." I mean, when you put it that way, it almost sounds like my life isn't on the verge of utter disaster.

In a honeyed voice, Haley zips through a segment she calls "A Broad Abroad," in which she summarizes a string of thirty-second news stories about notable women around the world, recites her personal finance tip of the week, and hits play on a prerecorded ad about teeth whitening strips. It's over sooner than I expected, and then I'm on. Haley reads notes off her phone to describe my career path, Brooklyn Jewels's launch, and the Meghan Markle success story from that *Elle* interview.

"So, Eliza, let's talk about funding. It's the biggest hurdle for so many female entrepreneurs. How did you get started?" she asks.

I don't love this question. It feels uncool to admit that getting a company off the ground is a hell of a lot harder when you don't have an inheritance to cover a chunk of your starting costs. But I have to acknowledge it, because it's an enormous privilege. It would be unfair at best, irresponsible at worst to gloss over that fact and let other aspiring entrepreneurs think Sophie and I got here solely based on our own grit. So I spit that out first, then describe the years of legwork, how I won us funding in a business plan competition, and the challenges of finding exactly the right location for our storefront. Talking about the shop makes me anxious; I still haven't gotten a response from Roy yet.

"You've gotten a ton of great press lately," Haley notes. She holds her eye contact steady as she delivers a killer next line. "Don't you think it's unfair that it all comes right on the heels of your engagement announcement?"

"Oh!" I sputter. My heart begins to pound. I hadn't anticipated this question. I swallow and launch into a rebuttal. "I sell engagement rings, you know. It's only natural that people would be curious about my personal life. My fiancé and I are flattered by the attention, and I'm excited for this next step in our lives, but ultimately, my focus is and has always been on my work."

Haley narrows her eyes. "But isn't it kind of anti-feminist bullshit that you've worked this hard for so many years, and that *this* is the moment that people finally care about you?"

I don't know what's worse—to alienate my new followers by saying yes, or to defy Haley by saying no. I take a deep breath.

"Look, it's unfortunate that we live in a world in which girls are groomed from infancy to view marriage as a prize. There's a conveyor belt that takes us directly from watching Disney princesses have their happily-ever-after kiss with their prince to watching grown women chasing engagement rings on *The Bachelor*." I can feel my voice getting stronger. "I didn't create this system. I only live in it. I sell engagement rings because I have a lifelong passion for jewelry, and my sister and business partner happens to be a talented designer. If you find something problematic about the sudden spotlight on Brooklyn Jewels because of a development in my personal life, I understand that point of view. Getting engaged isn't an achievement and shouldn't be treated as such. But if I shy away from that spotlight, it only hurts my bottom line. And I don't see anything feminist about avoiding an ethical profit."

I lean away from the mic, satisfied. The air in the room is very still. I think I nailed it. Haley's mouth twitches up into a half smile.

"Ethical," she says slowly. Her gaze flashes to my ring. "Let's talk about blood diamonds."

Now *this* is a question I'm prepared for. "We don't use them. In fact . . ."

Ten minutes later, I'm off the air. Haley slips off her headphones.

"Your speech was impressive," she says. "I don't know if I *agree*, but you defended yourself well."

"Thanks for having me."

The assistant asks me and Haley to pose for a photo together. Her follower count is huge, so of course, I say yes. When we're done,

I head to the elevator and check my phone. There's a stream of sup-portive messages from fans who tuned in and a steady spurt of new followers. One notification in particular catches my eye—an Insta-gram DM from Raj. He must have followed me.

"You killed it on air," he wrote, adding a smiley face emoji.

I can't believe he tuned in. I follow him back.

I toggle through the rest of my notifications, and that's when I see the email that makes my heart sink.

My first instinct is to call an Uber, but that's a splurge I can't af-ford these days. I hop on the subway, which is mercifully not too crowded at this lazy dip in the afternoon, and head back to Wil-liamsburg. On the train, I think through how I'll present this to Sophie. No matter how I relay the news, it won't be pleasant. But at least I can soften the blow. Wine isn't the right answer—she's not really drinking much these days, since alcohol can apparently decrease your chance of getting pregnant. (Yet another reason I'm happy to be uninterested in having children right now, or possibly ever.) But I know her weakness. I make a slight detour from the subway to the shop to pick up a whole steaming hot pie at Joe's Pizza on Bedford Avenue. It's worth it.

Her eyes light up when I carry the white box through the doors of the shop. Sophie's working on her laptop while Jess helps a couple compare stones on a black velvet display tray. I don't dare disturb the sale, so I take the pizza to the back room and work quietly until it's time to close up.

I'm not even trying to listen in, but the shop is small; I can't help but notice when I hear Jess ask in a faux-casual tone, "So, how did you hear of Brooklyn Jewels?"

The female customer's response is instantaneous and cheery. "You came up on my Instagram Explore feed!"

"Oh, love that!" Jess chirps, her voice smooth like syrup.

I hear the couple settle on a stone and a setting. Jess explains that since she doesn't have the setting in stock in the woman's size, they'll need to come back in two to four weeks to pick up the custom order. Jess takes the guy's credit card information and registers the deposit. I'm glad that Sophie must be hearing this significant sale now; it'll make the conversation we're about to have even easier.

The customers leave a little after six, and I join Jess and Sophie in the front room so we can close up together. The routine is old and well-worn; we've divided this ritual into parts ever since we were all kids together at Helen's shop. There would be upbeat music—disco, more often than not—to guide us through storing trays of jewels into the safe, wiping down counters, and taking out the trash. Here, as adults, it's no different. When we're done, Jess grabs her purse from the back room and turns to head out.

"Greg is *actually* taking me to dinner tonight," she explains, a note of excitement in her voice. Greg, her friend with benefits, rarely asks her to hang out beyond the walls of his bedroom. "Otherwise, I'd stay for pizza."

I'm glad she's not staying. The pizza is meant to soften the blow of the conversation I need to have with Sophie.

"Stay and eat with me?" I ask Sophie.

"I don't know . . . I was planning on making dinner tonight," she hedges.

"Please," I say.

I think she gets it. I let her have Helen's old leather armchair. I sit cross-legged on a gray folding chair and pull a cheesy slice from the box.

"So, I got some news," I say.

"From Roy," she supplies.

"Yeah."

She leans back in the armchair. A defeated expression crosses her face. "He said no, didn't he?"

"Yeah, he didn't go for our plan," I admit.

A half smile curls around her lips. "So you bribed me with pizza so I wouldn't get too upset."

"I tried."

She sighs heavily. "October, then. That's the deadline to decide whether or not we can keep the shop open."

What she does next burns straight into my memory: she looks slowly around the cramped, musty back room. Her eyes roam over the safes, the file cabinets containing stacks of tax documents, her design equipment on the shelf. And then she finally meets my gaze with tears brimming in her eyes. Her voice cracks when she tries to speak.

"I'm not ready to give all this up," she says.

"Not yet," I say. "It's not happening yet."

She crumples a slice of pizza in half and takes a sad bite. "You can't say that for sure."

"I'm not going to let us go under," I insist. "We're going to make this work."

I open my laptop and pull up QuickBooks, the accounting software that shows our expenses, our sales numbers, and what's left in our company bank account. I swivel the laptop to face Sophie and come around the table to lean on the arm of her chair. I tweak the data in the document to reflect projections—how much money we'll need to pull in by the end of October in order to re-sign the lease at the higher rate. I optimistically increase our sales numbers, too, explaining that we've been on the upswing for weeks and can logically expect to maintain a certain level of growth. If the math is right—and I think it is—this proves that we'll be able to squeak by just fine, as long as our sales continue to grow exponentially.

"That's a big if," Sophie points out.

I take a deep breath. "I promise I won't let you down. I want to make this work—it has to work. For both of us, and Jess, and Mom and Dad, too."

She finishes her slice of pizza, brushes the crumbs from her hands, and closes the laptop. Her eyes aren't red-rimmed with tears anymore.

"I want to trust you," she says.

"I don't want to lose this place any more than you do," I remind her gently.

She hugs me tightly. "I know, I know," she says.

On my phone, I key up a disco playlist on Spotify. The pulsing opening notes make her grin and groove in her seat. She knows exactly what I'm doing. I heap another slice of pizza onto her paper plate, swirling the dripping strings of cheese around onto the tip. And for the first time in a long time, we relax together—not talking about work, or money, or my fake engagement, or her long road to conception. Instead, we're just two sisters on a mellow Tuesday night in, trading gossip about people from back home and pulling up photos of fluffier and fluffier cats on Instagram until it's dark outside and our bellies are full.

· Chapter 10 ·

I always thought I'd want a guy to make a grand, romantic gesture. It turns out that's only because I've never had one. In reality, grand, romantic gestures catch you unpleasantly off guard. I learn this the hard way at 5:30 p.m. on Wednesday afternoon, when I'm hunched over my laptop in the front of the shop and the bell over the door *dings*. Blake sails through the door holding a bouquet of unwieldy proportions, stuffed with tulips and orchids and miles of greenery—and I'm wearing nearly thirty thousand dollars' worth of diamonds on my left ring finger.

I rip off the ring, practically dislocating a joint or two in the process, and shove it in a drawer, where he can't see it. He's beaming and apparently doesn't notice how frantic I am. Maybe I deserve to have Blake figure me out; maybe I shouldn't be doing this. Having him here in my space only emphasizes my guilt.

"Hi," he says in his low, steady voice. He leans a hip against the edge of the counter and peers into the case. "Nice shop you've got here."

"H-hi. Thank you."

He's still beaming, like he should get so many brownie points for, what, using Google to find out where I work and bringing me some flowers? I wish he would disappear, because if he's Googled my company, that means he very well could have discovered my scheme online. I feel terrible for hiding the truth from him. But wait, no—if he stumbled across anything incriminating, he wouldn't be wooing me with a gorgeous bouquet the size of the Empire State Building. That realization spurs me to breathe again.

"Those are beautiful," I say, taking the flowers from him.

"They reminded me of you," he says.

Jess simply stares. "Hi," she says, wide-eyed. Her dinner date with Greg last night was a bust; low on romance, high on him watching football over her shoulder.

Blake introduces himself.

Sophie, who had been sketching a new collection in the back room, emerges at the sound of his voice. Her eyes glitter in a way that tells me she knows exactly who this is.

"You must be Sophie?" Blake asks, extending his hand to her. "Eliza has told me so much about you. I'm Blake."

"Hi," she breathes, still starry-eyed.

Great, even my married lesbian sister thinks my fake boyfriend is hot.

"I should go put these in water," I say, somehow feeling like I'm interrupting. "Uh, I'm gonna run upstairs for a sec to grab a vase from my kitchen. I'll be right back."

I slip past Blake, take the stairs to my apartment two at a time, and proceed to sift through the cabinet beneath the sink, past a clanging, jangling mass of pots and pans I haven't used since potentially the last presidential administration, in order to unearth the one vase I own. I unwrap the flowers as fast as I can, fill the vase with water, and squeeze the bouquet inside. It's a tight fit. When I make it back downstairs, Blake, Sophie, and Jess are in a rapt discussion of the shop's wares, which makes my skin crawl with nerves. They don't necessarily know every single detail of what I've told Blake; they could trip up my ruse at any minute.

But mercifully, Blake appears to be just fine. He admires some of the pieces in the glass case, asks Sophie about where she sources some of her materials, and sends me a sunny smile when he sees me holding the overflowing vase.

"I wanted to drop by to see if I could take you out tonight," he says simply, as if men who could pass for male models swing by for surprise date nights all the time.

"I'll close up," Jess blurts out before I can answer.

Blake shrugs like it's a done deal.

I do a mental check of my life. True, at least my engagement ring is off, but I definitely did not shower this morning and not a soul on this planet would describe my underwear as "cute." I have, like, a solid amount of armpit stubble. It's not the most ideal moment for a date. But I can't turn him down.

"Uh, yeah, I guess I'm free?" I say. And then, more persuasively, "Yes, I'd love to go out with you tonight."

Walking with Blake feels like floating. He slips his hand into mine and our fingers interlock seamlessly. He rubs his thumb along the inside of my palm as we wind through hip Williamsburg, into stately DUMBO, and toward the majestic entrance toward the Brooklyn Bridge. Somehow, walking across one of the most romantic stretches of steel in the world, toward the glittering Manhattan skyline—of course, it's glittering, Blake probably arranged for the sun to set at the exact right time, because he *would*—feels natural with him.

That doesn't mean I'm comfortable. Oh, lordy, *no*. I'm well aware that our conversation is a minefield; it's entirely too possible that he's seen my boastful Instagram Stories taken inside his apartment (maybe a friend tipped him off?) or that he's stumbled across my engagement announcement. Maybe he's even turned off by how aggressively I arrived at his doorstep the other night. (Unlikely, but still.) I feel bad for lying to him. I feel like I'm teetering on a high wire, one step from doom: I have to lead Blake away from conversations about my personal and professional lives while simultaneously entrancing him into falling for me. The thought of it leaves me breathless.

"I figured it was my turn to surprise you," he says, breaking my reverie as he steers us around a group of tourists. I have to speed-walk in order to keep up with his long legs.

(It's too easy to spot tourists. The sensible sneakers, maps, and cameras are one dead giveaway. But the real trick is to watch their eyes. New Yorkers don't bother swiveling their gaze to take in the whole view anymore. Tourists walk around with gawking eyes like soup spoons, ready to slurp everything up.)

"Your turn?" I ask.

"You know, you showed up at my place last week. It's my turn."

"Oh, so we're taking turns now," I say, lifting my chin to look at him. It's important that I understand his intentions so I can play this right.

His cheeks turn the slightest shade of pink. "I'd like that, wouldn't you?" he asks.

"Of course." I lean my head onto the edge of his shoulder. It's time to take a risk. I swallow and stare out at the sharp spikes of the Manhattan skyline to give me courage; I need to remember that I moved to New York to pursue my dreams for a reason, and that if

I don't try every goddamn trick in the book to secure my place in this city, it was pointless to come here at all. "You know, Blake, I like you."

He grins. "Really," he says. It's a statement, not a question.

"Like, *like*-like you," I clarify.

"You *like*-like me," he says. "I'm flattered."

If he were a different person, it'd sound like he was mocking me. Isn't this how third-graders talk about their crushes? But there's a sweet note of pride in his voice that's impossible to ignore. As much as I see him as a prize, he seems to see the same in me. It's hard to wrap my head around—not just because Blake is such an obvious catch (look up "eligible bachelor" in the dictionary and you'll literally see Blake's face), but because for so long, dating in New York has felt like a series of men kicking me when I'm already down. Singledom in this city feels like an unfortunate game of bingo, and I've checked too many boxes for the game to be fun any longer: I've been stood up; I've suffered through dinners in total silence after it became clear that we shared radically incompatible political views; I've enjoyed four weeks of sweet, steady dates with a guy who seems like a gentleman—up until I get an angry Facebook message from his current girlfriend; I've had hookups that seem dangerously close to what some might call sexual assault.

I don't think that what I have with Blake is perfect. I'm not blind to our slightly stilted conversation, which is probably worsened by the fact that I can't be honest with him about the basic facts of my life. When I'm with him, I get the odd sensation of feeling like I'm acting in a movie about how adults date. I mean, he always wears belts that match his shoes. He has an artfully designed bar cart, flawless white sheets without any weird stains, and extra terry-cloth bathrobes just lying around, as if a prop stylist swept through his apartment before I arrived. Right now, here on the Brooklyn Bridge, we sound like we're fumbling to recall lines from a script: *You* like-*like me*.

Blake is not the love of my life right now—it's far too soon for that—but maybe he could be someday. I can see it. Our budding relationship feels like finally touching down on solid land after years of struggling against rocky waves. He's simple. He's a solution. And he's easy to like for a thousand different reasons: his old-school charm, his self-assured confidence, his innate ability to make you feel special. I want him to like me, too.

"Tell me about your watch," I say, slipping my thumb over the heavy gold band.

He lets go of my hand and stretches his wrist out in front of him. The gold glints sharply in the dwindling rays of sunshine.

"It was my dad's," he says.

He grips my hand again tightly and squeezes it. He sounds like he wants to say something more, but he doesn't.

"It's gorgeous. Vintage?" I ask.

"Twenty, maybe twenty-five years old." He hesitates. "My dad passed away when I was fourteen. He collected watches. I inherited this from him."

"That's where the idea for Bond and Time came from?"

He nods. I squeeze his hand.

"I wanted to create something he'd be proud of, yeah."

"That's beautiful. I'm sure he's very proud."

I know this isn't about me, but my throat constricts anyway. I want to say the right thing—this time, not just because Blake is a pawn, but because I feel for him. It would be devastating to lose my dad.

"It was a tough age to have him pass, you know?" he continues.

"There's so much I wish I could've talked to him about—things I would've talked to him about, if I had been older."

"Tell me about him?" I ask. "I mean, if you want? If that's okay?"

Luckily, Blake opens up. He describes his dad so vividly, I can see him: his skin tanned and creased from summers laying out on the beach down the Cape; his dorky habit of monogramming all his cable-knit sweaters; the way he pronounced his favorite hometown delicacy as "clam chowdah," never "chowder." Blake says his dad was never sick; he was fine up until the afternoon of his heart attack. I can't help but think of my own dad. He calls it "chowdah," too—in a Maine accent, not a Boston one, but similar enough.

Blake tilts his head to peer out at the skyline, which is closer than ever. I can't see his face. When he turns back toward me, his eyes lock with mine.

"Thanks for listening," he says. "Really."

He changes the subject smoothly, and by the time our feet hit concrete in Manhattan, we've covered everything from how supremely superior New England clam chowder is to Manhattan clam chowder, to the way Helen inspired my business, somewhat similar to the way Blake's dad inspired his.

And then, surrounded by zooming yellow taxis and the wafting scent of halal carts, he pulls me into a kiss. I like the way we fit together; the sturdy pressure of his hand against the small of my back unspools the pressure in my chest. I feel like melting. The awkwardness I felt the other morning in his apartment has disappeared.

"Come back to my place?" he asks.

I'm glad he asked. I'd rather not have him in my apartment, where there's too much potential for him to stumble across something incriminating. He hails a cab and we pile in.

I like that this time around, I enter Blake's apartment building alongside him. The doorman smiles at me. It's just a tiny shred of approval—but it makes me happy.

There's something oddly intimate about watching a person go through their daily routine. I watch as Blake slips his keys out of his pocket, finds the right one, and unlocks his door. Inside, he hangs his suit jacket on a hook by the door, drops his key ring onto a smaller hook, and sits on a dark wooden bench while he removes his shoes. I know from past relationships and situationships that eventually—if all goes well—I'll learn to place my shoes and purse in a certain spot here, too. Maybe I'll even have my own key someday. For now, I awkwardly tuck my shoes and purse next to his under the bench.

"You hungry?" he asks.

"Always."

He tugs open his refrigerator door and fishes around inside. When he finds what he's looking for, he holds it behind his back and gives me a coy smile.

"I may have one more surprise for you."

I step toward him, but he wrestles away from me. I reach for his hip to keep him in place and tilt my head up to kiss him. He softens, and when the kiss ends, he shows me what he's been hiding: fistfuls of Babybel cheeses. I can't help but laugh.

"You're kidding me!"

"I mean, you basically told me that cheese was the way to your heart," he says, peeling the wrapper off one and handing it to me. "So . . . I had to get you some cheese."

I plant another kiss on him, then another and another. It turns out there is plenty more where the Babybel came from. He has an array of fancier cheeses, too—a Wisconsin cheddar, a soft brie, an impressively smelly bleu—plus a spread of jam, grapes, prosciutto, mustard, and a sliced French baguette. He opens a fresh bottle of red wine, pours two glasses, and places them extra-gingerly down on the coffee table in front of the couch.

"You won't knock this one over, will you?" I tease.

"I promise I won't, as long as you behave."

"I don't make promises I can't keep!" I pop a grape into my mouth.

Once he's finished setting out our feast, he reaches for the remote. "Netflix?"

"Sure."

"I'm in the middle of rewatching *Mad Men*. I dressed up as Don Draper for Halloween basically every year of college. Or we could watch something else," he offers.

Of course Blake's rewatching *Mad Men*. It's not exactly a surprise that Blake is drawn to the story of an ambitious guy making a name for himself in Manhattan.

"Let's do it," I say. "I always loved Joan and Peggy."

I think we're both more comfortable settling in on his couch this time around. As he queues up the show, he slings his arm confidently over my shoulders and I rest my head on his chest. I feel more at ease around Blake than I have in the past. Maybe it's because we've begun to share vulnerable pieces of ourselves, or maybe every fledgling couple takes a while to find their groove. Maybe the myth of love at first sight puts too much pressure on people; even if there's an instant spark, comfort needs to develop over time.

Halfway through the opening scene, Blake gently worms his shoulder out from under my head and gets up. "Forgot the cheese knife," he says.

"Do you want me to pause it?"

"Nah, I've it seen it before."

The kitchen is a classic New York one—not a separate, closed-off room, but a collection of appliances pushed up against the far wall of the living room. He could see me any time from the kitchen. But he's taking far too long to rummage in a drawer—wait, no, he's trying another drawer—he's trying a cabinet now. I slip out my phone, stand to hover over the coffee table, and snap a photo of the impressive spread. The noise from the TV covers my movements.

He turns around sooner than I expected and catches me pressing my hair to my shoulder so it doesn't dangle in front of my bird's-eye-view shot. I freeze, flush, and press my phone to my chest. He just laughs.

"*Go ahead*," he encourages, in a slightly teasing voice. "So, you're one of those girls who takes photos of all her food for Instagram."

"Guilty as charged," I say, trying to laugh. It's way better to cop to a lesser offense.

"I don't get it, but whatever makes you happy," he says, setting down the cheese knife he found and joining me on the couch again.

This time, I do hit Pause. I want to hear what he has to say. "So, you're, like, really not on Instagram?" I ask.

He shrugs and turns to look at the TV. "I mean, look at these guys. Don doesn't need to tell anyone about his beautiful wife or expensive apartment or great job. He just . . . exudes confidence."

"I'm confident," I say automatically.

"You're telling me that every like and comment and follow isn't another little confidence booster?" he asks, lifting an eyebrow. "And that you'd feel exactly the same about yourself without Instagram in your back pocket?"

"That's not it."

"Then what is it?"

It's miraculous that I can hold my own in front of an *Elle* reporter or a radio show host broadcasting to a million people, but when it's just me and Blake in his apartment, I don't know how to defend myself. It's like all the right words have been sucked away and I'm only left with the wrong ones. I don't usually feel this dumb.

"I use it mostly for work anyway," I explain. "It's good for customers to see that I'm a real person who eats cheese and drinks wine, too. It helps them feel like, you know, they *know* me. And that translates directly to sales, I swear."

That's true, but the full truth is more complicated than that. Back when I only had a few hundred followers, life had a different filter than it does now. I used Instagram to "like" photos my friends posted from parties and to gawk at celebrities sunbathing on yachts, just like everyone else. But now, my chest twinges when I miss a photo opp, or when I see a rival jeweler get a better one. I feel like I know thousands of people I've never met in real life, simply because of the ways in which they interact with my posts—there's the Starbucks barista in Cleveland fantasizing about her dream wedding; the Real Housewife of New York, who wears so many diamonds every day they seem as much a part of her as her actual skin does; the gay teen boy from the Philippines who writes "iconic" on every single photo.

And all of this, of course, changes how I see myself. It's hard not to feel as if you're important when a hundred thousand people say that you are. I'm not, of course. I'm not important. I'm just a girl who's figured out the trick, the formula: post shiny photos of this many carats (three or more) at this time (8 a.m. or 6 p.m. EST) with this kind of caption (cheery and loaded with hashtags), and presto. But sometimes, I forget that.

I don't want to explain all of this to Blake. It feels too dangerous—like it could help him unlock my real purpose here with him. The thought makes me feel heavy and sad; I don't want to dwell on whether or not this is fair to Blake, especially when I might actually be developing real feelings for him. So instead, I slide my phone back into my jeans and curl into him.

"Let's watch," I say, hitting play on the remote.

· Chapter 11 ·

"Are you Eliza Roth?"

A woman's voice jars me to attention. I left Blake's apartment
three minutes ago; I'm in line at the coffee shop on his corner now,
absentmindedly picking at a knot in my hair that definitely wasn't
there when he pulled me into his bedroom last night. Prying myself from his arms felt impossible this morning. I always feel the
same way about getting up from the sand on the last beach day of
summer—you know you *should* move, but the thought of it actually
hurts.

I spin around and take the woman in. She's about my age, clad in
blue high-waisted leggings and a matching sports bra, and carrying
a yoga mat. A flat, round gold pendant embossed with what's probably her first initial dangles from her neck; if I had a dollar for every
necklace I've seen like that this year, Brooklyn Jewels wouldn't be
in financial trouble. Her face looks expectant.

"Yes. Hi," I say.

If this were a year ago, my reaction would've been different. I might have tried to place her—did we cross paths in college? did we meet at that party at Carmen's friend's boyfriend's place?—but not anymore. Her demeanor reminds me of that shy girl who asked for a selfie in the shop: tightly coiled, like she has something to ask me.

Sure enough, she cracks into a smile. "I thought that was you. I'm so sorry, I saw you leaving my building and I just had to say hi."

"You live in that building?" I ask, slightly alarmed.

"I just *love* your Instagram," she says, as if she didn't hear my question. "I'm kind of a fan."

"Oh, thank you! That's so sweet."

She hitches up her yoga mat and I steal a quick glance at her hand. Her left ring finger is bare, which makes sense; most of our followers are either in research mode before they make a big purchase, or they're single girls who save our photos for their secret wedding-themed Pinterest boards.

"So you live next door, too?" she asks.

"Oh, I . . ."

"I thought you lived in Williamsburg, no?" she jumps in.

"Um, I do."

"Then your fiancé lives there?"

Her brow begins to furrow. I wish I had brainstormed a cover story ahead of time.

"I was visiting a friend," I blurt out.

"Early visit," she notes.

"Um . . ."

Her gaze falls to my hand. "Where's your ring?" she asks plainly.

We both look at my finger. I look back up at her. My mind goes blank under pressure.

I hear a voice behind me. "Next? Next!"

The barista. Thank god. I turn toward him and order the fastest, easiest drink possible, just so I can get out of there.

"Small black coffee to go, please."

When I finish paying and collect my drink, I turn back to the woman.

"So lovely to meet you, thanks for saying hi! Maybe I'll see you around."

I toss her a huge smile that makes my cheeks ache and head for the door. I hurtle toward the subway, walking so fast that my toes smack into a fissure in the sidewalk and I trip spectacularly, arms flailing. I drop my cup and coffee splatters across the sidewalk. I steady myself and take a deep breath. It's one thing for a random, faraway person on Instagram to leave a comment questioning who I'm engaged to. It's another to have to confront that question in the flesh on Blake's block. I replay the interaction in my head. It could've gone wrong in so many ways: she could've kept asking questions. If the morning had gone differently, *Blake could've been there with me.* It could've been disastrous.

I get an email just as I'm heading down the grimy stairs into the subway. A publicist named Vivian Presley-Jones says she's reaching out on behalf of Adora, a wedding gown designer, to offer a complimentary gown for my big day if I promise to tag the brand on Instagram. These kinds of emails used to shock me; now, while I still feel lucky, the surprise factor has worn off. I look up Adora's designs. They're not entirely my taste—everything is sexy, sheer, plunging, encrusted in crystals, like something Kylie Jenner would've worn to prom if she had bothered to go to prom—but it's the style I see popping up all over Instagram. People seem to like that, even if I don't. I don't let myself second-guess this decision. I can't lose my nerve anymore. I write back immediately to say thank you, yes, and ask if I can visit the atelier on Monday.

I've seen enough episodes of *Say Yes to the Dress* to know how this works: you chant "sweetheart neckline" three times into a mirror while holding a champagne flute and wearing a white silk robe, and Pnina Tornai appears to swath you in tulle. I asked Sophie and Carmen to join me at the atelier to pick out my wedding dress. (That's still so weird to say. *My* wedding dress.) I'm the first to arrive at the salon, which is decorated in soothing tones of gray and cream that make the two racks of bright white gowns stand out. Soft pop music filters through the sound system. Of course, a sales assistant named Marcy pushes a champagne flute into my hand immediately and encourages me to wait on a Mongolian lamb bench. Vivian, the publicist I had been emailing with, makes small talk with me: she coos over my engagement ring and asks to hear all about how I met my fiancé.

I hesitate. I can make up a story that doesn't involve revealing an identity, can't I?

"Believe it or not, we met at a bar," I say, exhaling heavily.

"No way, which one?" she asks.

"Dorrian's? On the Upper East Side?" I feel like I'm taking a test I've barely studied for.

"No *way*," she repeats. "I'm there all the time, no fair. So sweet."

Before Vivian can ask too many more questions, my sister arrives in the most quintessentially *Sophie* way possible, bearing a spiral-bound notebook and a fistful of colorful highlighters to take notes on our favorites. Carmen slinks in a minute later with a gray cashmere hoodie pulled up over her hair and dark, bug-eyed sunglasses that cover her from brows to cheekbones. When she gets closer, I gasp. Her face is covered in bright red blotches and peeling in an eerily reptilian way. Sophie politely declines a champagne flute while Carmen lunges desperately for hers.

"Oh my god, what happened?" Sophie demands, recoiling.

Carmen grimaces and removes her sunglasses. "I'm testing out a new retinol before I include it in my business plan. It's, uh, not going well."

"Uh, yeah. That clears up, right?" I ask.

"In about a month, yeah," she says glumly.

"Well, that should give you plenty of time to heal up for wedding photos!" Marcy says in her brash Long Island accent, clapping her hands for emphasis. Her dark ponytail swings behind her.

Sophie laughs; Carmen adjusts her hoodie to cover another half inch of her lobster-red forehead.

Vivian ushers us toward a larger seating area in the back of the room. When we sit, she passes out binders for each of us. I flip through the laminated pages; they're the full set of the designer's current collection. As expected, none of the looks are what you could call subtle. Every dress has a thigh-baring slit, a Swarovski crystal belt, a bosom-boosting corset, or all three. If my mom were here, she'd make a snarky comment about shopping for wedding night lingerie instead of an actual wedding gown. With a pang, I think back to Sophie's beautifully simple wedding dress, with its chic boatneck and clean lines. At the time, I thought her dress was kind of boring. But now, under the harsh light of Swarovski-crystal reflections, it's clear—she was stunning. A minimalist's dream. Meghan Markle had nothing on her.

"Do any of these stand out to you?" Marcy asks, peering over my binder.

I swallow and sweep my arm around the room of glittering gowns. "I mean, all of them are so gorgeous."

Marcy blinks her long, tarantula-style, clearly fake eyelashes and waits for an actual answer. In my daily life, sure, I dress to stand out. But for me, that's always translated into bright colors and trendy silhouettes—not glitz and glam and a mile of cleavage. These dresses look like the Victoria's Secret Fashion Show Fantasy Bra with skirts attached.

"But sure, I guess I can pick a few to start," I add hastily.

Before I know it, I'm wrapped in a white silk robe in a dressing room, waiting for Marcy to bring the first of three gowns. I chose two and Sophie picked out one. Carmen had just laughed, sat back smugly on the couch, and said she couldn't wait to see me dressed.

Marcy raps once against the dressing room door.

"Come in!" I call, pulling the two halves of the skimpy robe over my exposed thighs.

She enters hoisting three garment bags over her head and sets each one on the metallic dressing room rack with a satisfying *clack*. As she unzips the first bag and pulls out the miles of fabric inside, it suddenly occurs to me that she's about to see me naked. I've worn the correct undergarments, per Sophie's instructions: a nude strapless bra with a nude seamless thong. And it's not that I dislike my body. I feel comfortable in my skin on most days, even if I don't love the dimpling cellulite along my thighs or the way my stomach presses into the waistband of my jeans after a big dinner. I feel lucky in that regard, that I've escaped the debilitating body image issues that plague most of my friends. But that doesn't mean I want to necessarily strip down in front of this saleswoman who sees dozens of brides every week who are #sheddingforthewedding. I don't even have a real wedding to shed for; pasta is my largest food group.

Marcy holds out the first dress expectantly. "Ready?" she asks, arching a manicured eyebrow.

I guess I'm as ready as I'll ever be. I untie the silk knot at my waist and awkwardly place the robe on the seat behind me. My skin crawls with goose bumps. Somehow, stepping into the open bodice of a wedding dress makes this entire experience feel tangible in a way that turns my blood cold. If all goes according to plan, I'm really getting married. I'm actually committing to this. A wedding. A *husband*. I've known this, of course, for weeks. But with a pool of lace swirling around my ankles, it suddenly feels more real than ever before.

Marcy expertly shimmies the gown up my legs and torso and sets on fastening the row of buttons along my spine. This dress is a sexy, skintight mermaid silhouette made from elaborately embroidered lace. There's a sweetheart neckline, a tightly cinched waist, and see-through panels between the arcs of lace that expose flashes of skin. I drink in my reflection in the long mirror. True, this is one of the gowns that I had selected from the binder, but I suddenly hate it.

Marcy hands me a pair of white strappy sandals in my size and cheers, "Let's go!"

"Okay?" I respond, slipping the shoes on.

My legs feel wobbly as I exit the dressing room and make the long, slow walk to the center of the atelier. Marcy helps me up onto a pedestal lodged between three full-length mirrors and the couch where Sophie, Carmen, and Vivian seem to be immersed in a conversation about moisturizers containing SPF.

"*Oh!*" Carmen shouts, just as Sophie mutters, "Oh . . ."

"It's a lot," Sophie adds.

"You look super fucking hot," Carmen says.

"But like, maybe in a bad way," Sophie offers.

I put my hands on my hips and swivel in front of the three-way mirror to catch every angle. My butt looks otherworldly, but I'm pretty sure this dress would cause my grandmother to drop dead of a heart attack.

"How would your fiancé feel about such a sexy look?" Marcy asks.

Sophie and Carmen fall silent. I try to stall with a long, "*Mmmmmm*," and pretend to keep examining my reflection.

"You know, he's not, like, the hugest fan," I say, with the distinctly terrifying sensation of speaking without knowing how my sentence will end up. "Like, obviously, not opposed, um, in general. Privately. But for the big day, you know, not necessarily the top priority."

"He's excited to keep those special, sexy vibes just between the two of you," Vivian rephrases cheerfully, clasping her hands together. Her eyes sparkle.

"Yes!" I exclaim. "Exactly. Just us."

Thank god for publicists—they know how to spin a story.

Marcy's eyebrow lifts again and it oozes judgment. "You look good, but fine, on to the next one," she says, shrugging.

We head back to the dressing room, where she helps me out of the first dress and into the second. This is my other pick.

I chose this gown for the long sheer sleeves covered in lace vine appliqués; I thought they'd be practical for a fall wedding on a hotel rooftop. There's a frighteningly low neckline, the kind I've only ever worn on Halloweekend in college, barely held together with a cluster of crystals hovering somewhere between my nipples and my navel. The skirt is a swishy rush of tulle that makes me feel like a ballerina.

Marcy finishes fastening the zipper, fluffs my hair around my shoulders, and steps back to examine my reflection. "Damn, girl."

My cheeks flush. I *sort of* like the dress. I mean, I can see *why* a person would like the dress. The vibe is "sexy woodland nymph," like something Holden's fiancé Faye would wear. The skirt is just pure fun; I can imagine myself swirling around a dance floor in it. But the bodice—or lack thereof—makes me feel naked. I'm half a breath away from exposing myself, and that's not how I want to feel on my wedding day. (*My* wedding day. There are those words again. It's easy to forget, surrounded by wedding gowns, that I may not actually be able to pull off this wedding at all. At least not the kind of wedding where the groom actually shows up.)

"Let's show your crew," Marcy suggests, pulling open the door of the dressing room before I can protest.

I can tell before I reach the pedestal that something is wrong. Sophie's eyes are red and puffy. Carmen is patting her arm. Vivian is frozen on the opposite end of the couch, clearly relieved at the sight of me and Marcy. I hustle as fast as the enormous skirt lets me and make it to the couch.

"What's wrong?" I ask.

Sophie's voice sounds nasal, like she's about to cry. "No, no, it's fine. We'll talk later," she insists.

I crouch down in front of her and take her hands. "Come on. What's up?"

"Your boob is about to fall out of that dress," she sniffles.

I adjust the neckline and clasp her hands again. "Thank you. Now talk."

"Is this really the right place? I mean, you're shopping," she says.

"Sophie, it's fiiine."

She sighs heavily. "I was just telling Carmen how tough it's been, you know, with the IVF process. And how we might not be able to afford another round, especially not right now."

Carmen looks at me with wide eyes. "I'm sorry," she mouths.

"Oh, Soph," I say, shooing Carmen out of the way so I can perch on the edge of the couch to hug my sister.

I can feel her ragged attempt to regain her breath.

"Shh, shh, it's going to be okay," I tell her.

"I want money," she says, pulling back. "I want to borrow fifteen thousand dollars from the business."

"That's a lot!" I protest.

"*This* is a lot," she says, waving to my ridiculous gown and heavy diamond ring.

I ignore her jab. "Soph, that's not how our company's finances work," I explain. "I can't just give you fifteen thousand dollars from our corporate bank account, even if I wanted to. It's complicated for tax reasons."

"You could legally give me a fifteen-thousand-dollar raise, couldn't you?" she asks.

"I—I don't know if I, if we, can do that right now," I say, faltering.

"So, what, we can put the company at risk for your interests, but not for mine?" Sophie asks bitterly.

I don't dare turn to see their faces, but I can only imagine that Marcy and Vivian are doing their best to look politely disinterested. But then again, this is a wedding salon. Emotions must run high here. I'm sure they're used to people crying on this couch all the time.

I swallow and try to stay calm. "That's not what I mean," I say.

"You're getting everything you want," she says, staring with red-rimmed eyes at the tulle ball gown pooling around my feet. "I just want . . ." She trails off and sighs heavily.

I can't blame Sophie for how she feels. She's right. I feel like my stomach is full of rocks. I can't pinpoint the moment when I changed; that's not how people work. You turn molecule by molecule until suddenly, you're a different person. You're the kind of girl whose ambition drives her to risk her company, her reputation, her own family's well-being. I suddenly don't recognize myself or my choices. I don't like everything I've done recently, but I can take control of at least one piece. I can do one good thing.

"No, you're right. This is important. Let's give you that raise. And we'll just find a way to increase our revenue somehow," I say.

I know it's the only appropriate decision to make, but it hurts to say the words out loud. More financial pressure is the last thing we need right now.

Her lip quavers. "Really?"

I hug her tightly. "Yeah. I mean, don't get me wrong, I can't promise everything—I can't guarantee that if you take the money, we'll be able to make it up in sales."

She wilts again.

"But I can promise you I'll do everything in my power to make this business a success so that the risk will be worth it."

Her shoulders shake with a silent sob. "Thank you," she whispers.

"I know you want a family more than anything. I'm not going to be the person to stand in the way of that," I say.

"I don't want to stand in the way of us, though," she says, wiping away a sniffle.

I take a deep breath. I don't know what else there is to say to her.

"We'll make it work," I repeat.

She peers at me through watery eyes and smiles. Then her face falls.

"Also, not to ruin the moment, but that dress is awful," she says. "Go try on the one I picked for you."

I do. And like magic, it's exactly right. Sisters always know best.

· Chapter 12 ·

After a hectic day filled with the most work possible, I feel restless—maybe I'm still on the adrenaline high of scoring a surprisingly beautiful wedding dress for free, or maybe I'm too nervous about my deal with my sister in order to relax. I don't want to go home to crash in front of Netflix alone. Sophie has concert tickets to a tuba performance by one of Liv's old marching band friends (I told her to not get *too* wild tonight), and Carmen has an emergency appointment with her dermatologist. I could reach out to some friends that I see less often, like Sasha or Caroline from college, but I'm not in the mood for catching up on the details of one another's lives; it would just be an awkward reminder of how little I've seen them since launching Brooklyn Jewels. And the prospect of either lying to my friends' faces about my engagement or risking exposure by telling more people the truth is exhausting. It used to be that whenever I felt antsy and ready to go out, I could take a quick spin through my dating apps and find a suitable suitor for the night. But with so much staked on Blake, I don't want to risk catching feelings for anyone else.

So, that's why I find myself walking into Golden Years ten minutes later. Raj is behind the bar. He does that head jerk bros use to greet one another—eyebrows shooting up, chin jutting forward, a smile on his face. By the time I've plopped onto a bar stool, he's already poured me a Brooklyn Bel Air Sour.

"On the house," he says, sliding it over to me.

"Again? I must've made it into your inner circle."

"Eh, you're okay," he says, clearly joking. "On your own again tonight?"

"Yep. Didn't feel like going home."

I reach for my beer and Raj's eyes bug out toward my ring finger.

"That's some rock," he says, letting out a low whistle.

I glance down. I've gotten used to wearing it, to the point where my blood runs cold whenever I realize it's not on. It always takes a split second to remember I'm not *really* engaged.

"Thanks. I put it on for wedding dress shopping today. I actually got one."

"Pics or it didn't happen," he says.

I pull out my phone and find the picture Marcy had taken just a few hours ago. I take in the image and get chills again; it's unsettling to see myself as a bride. The gown that Sophie chose for me didn't look like anything special when I had seen it in the binder, but in person, it suddenly felt just right. It has long lace sleeves, a delicate V-neck, and a modest slit up one leg that gives the sweeping skirt some movement. No tacky glitter or revealing cutouts in sight. I felt like myself in the dress—not like I was wearing a costume designed to appeal to my Instagram followers.

I spin around the phone to show Raj. He raises a brow.

"Whew. Lucky dude."

"Ha! We'll see if he shows up to meet me at the end of the aisle."

He shakes his head. "You're nuts. I love it."

"Are you seeing anyone?" I ask.

"Nah," he says. "I didn't have time at my last job. I mean, my parents are begging for me to settle down, but I haven't found the right person yet. So, in the meantime . . ." He mimes thumbing through a dating app.

"I feel you."

He drums his fingers rapidly across the wooden bar. "I, uh, was in a relationship a few years ago. I really thought we were happy together—and then she ended it." He stops drumming and gives the bar a final smack.

I cringe. I get it. I've been there.

"Give me your phone," I insist. "I'm going to find you someone. My friend Carmen works at Tinder and has given me all the inside tricks."

He laughs. "Sure, do your best. Barely employed brown guy who's five-foot-nine on a good day?"

"Okay, so we've had very different dating experiences. But let me try," I plead.

He slides his phone across the bar and goes to attend to a group of customers. Once he's gone, I toggle to view his profile. His bio reads, "Tech nerd, former startup guy, figuring out what's next. Funnier in person," and his photos are mostly group shots with his similarly hoodie-clad friends. In the last image, he's leaning against a pillar in a sharp suit; it's clearly a professional shot and looks like it was probably taken by a photographer at a friend's wedding. I'm not going to lie, even with his sheepish smile, he looks good.

I dive into his list of available potential matches and start swiping. I have no clue what his type is, so I express interest in pretty much everybody. Aside from using dating apps for myself, I've only ever swiped for Carmen, Jess, Sasha, and Caroline. It never occurred to me what a different game this would be for a guy. I'm almost conditioned to expect a cheery, "It's a match!" notification after every right swipe. Here, they rarely come. When one does—a match who looks strangely like me, even beyond the way that most twenty-something Williamsburg white girls look more or less the same—I find myself at a loss for words. I don't know how to flirt with women.

Raj is back. "Find the love of my life yet?"

"It's a work in progress."

"Don't I know it," he says, checking out what I've done. He takes in the single, solitary match, and slides the phone into his back pocket. "Hey, so, I actually get off in a few minutes. I'm on the early shift tonight."

I'm caught off guard by how empty the prospect of a night alone makes me feel. I like the easy comfort that Raj exudes.

"Do you wanna actually, like, hang out?" I blurt out.

Mercifully, the words don't even have time to hang in the air before he responds, "Yeah, sure! What did you have in mind?"

Oh. I didn't.

"Uh, you're probably sick of hanging out here, right?" I ask.

"Yeah, this is basically the equivalent of my old cubicle." He looks around and grimaces. "Not that I had an actual cubicle. It was all open floor plan—supposed to increase efficiency or some bullshit. Super startup-y."

"Wanna come see my shop?" I ask. "I have a bottle of whiskey there and we can pick up a pizza."

He laughs. "Those are the magic words."

Ten minutes later, we're on our way. I insist on paying for the pizza to thank him for all those free drinks. He protests, but ultimately hangs back when I hand my credit card to the cashier.

"Next pizza's on me," he promises.

I unlock the shop and bring Raj inside. When Sophie and I first rented the storefront, I used to savor this moment—showing friends the new space. It had felt so unimaginably adult, like the separate puzzle pieces of my life were finally clicking into place: I had a dream that was turning into a reality; I was self-employed, like I had always hoped I would be; I had a real brick-and-mortar store with gorgeous crown molding and light pouring in through the wide front window. True, I was also exhausted, cash poor, and constantly overbooked, but I had been so proud to show my friends what my sister and I had created for ourselves. I wonder how this all seems through Raj's eyes, especially now that he quit his job in order to find something fresh and meaningful.

He wolf-whistles when he sees the shop. "This is legit," he says, running his hand over the glass counter. "Where's the jewelry?"

"Everything's locked up," I explain.

"Aw, I'd love to see," he says.

I bring him to the back and unlock the safes. We strike up a plan: he can eat the pizza as long as he doesn't touch the jewels, and as long as he saves me at least two slices for later. Over the past two years, I've learned that most guys have no interest in what I do unless they're trying to select a piece for their girlfriend or wife. Raj, on the other hand, asks detailed questions about our business model and the intricacies of the fine jewelry industry. I like explaining the difference between an emerald cut and a princess cut, and why a low-quality large diamond can wind up costing less than a high-quality small one. I always enjoy talking about jewelry—that's one of the reasons I got into the business in the first place. He points out the pieces he likes, careful to keep his grubby, greasy hands far away from the actual wares, and honestly shrugs at the ones he doesn't. A lot of customers automatically gravitate toward the largest, flashiest stones. Raj seems to prefer unusual designs and underused stones, like peridot and tourmaline. I like his taste.

When his knee brushes mine underneath the desk, I hold my breath as I move it away. It must have been an accident. He doesn't seem to notice.

His phone vibrates noisily against the table.

"Can you open that for me?" he asks, hands full of pizza.

He recites his password between bites, and I tap open his notification.

"Oh! It's from that girl! That Tinder girl."

"Ha. Did you write to her or did she send the first message?"

"She did. She wrote, 'Hey, how's your day going?' and used a smiley face emoji."

"Eh, I'll write her back later. This is more interesting."

He peers back over a row of earrings.

Later, after wolfing down his third slice, he asks, "Is there a bathroom around here?"

"Actually, no, but there's one upstairs? You can use the one in my apartment."

"Cool, thanks."

I take care to lock everything away in the safe again. He grabs the pizza box and I take the whiskey. As we wind through the shop, into the hallway, and up the stairs, I try to remember the last time I brought a guy back to my apartment. Blake certainly hasn't seen it. Before him, I had gone out with a string of guys from apps, but none of them had made it past date two or three—either I had gone back to their place (always my preference) or we had avoided the bedroom entirely. I racked my brain. Could the last guy really have been Drummer Kevin? The musician from that gig Carmen and I had gone to in East Williamsburg? His sense of rhythm had been impeccable. (His breath was not.)

With Raj trailing behind me, I see my apartment with fresh eyes. It's a studio, so there's nowhere to hide; everything is out in the open for judgment. The chair nearest to the door is draped with a pile of assorted sweaters and unopened mail, with a cluster of shoes scattered beneath it. The bed is unmade and rumpled. I should probably have vacuumed my rug at least one level of dust ago. It's not that I love being a disgusting slob—it's just that whatever energy I can devote to cleaning, I spend in the shop. A baby could lick our floors and probably crawl out healthier than ever before.

Raj, apparently, does not seem to notice what my apartment looks like. "Dope place," he says, crossing the room to reach the open bathroom door.

And through his eyes, I see how it could be not so bad. I have a cool sheepskin rug that's plush under your toes and a row of leafy green plants lined up on my windowsill (they're fake, but at a distance, who can tell?). I finally got around to framing all my posters in matching black frames, including an original from the 1948 De Beers "A Diamond Is Forever" campaign, which cemented the modern tradition of symbolizing an engagement with a diamond ring. (Thank god.) My apartment is small and could use a good deep clean, but maybe it's not as embarrassing as I think.

I move a half-read book from one end of the couch and sink onto it. When I pull out my phone, I see a missed call and then a series of texts from Blake.

"Hey! Hope you're having a great week," the first one reads.

The next one is a long block of text. "Bond and Time bought a table at a charity gala this Saturday night. Would you happen to be free to join me as my date? The event is kind of a big deal for me and I'd love to have you there with me."

The last one is a punch to my gut. "I miss you," Blake wrote.

Raj emerges from my bathroom. His face lights up eagerly.

"Hey! Your soap? It smells *ridiculously* good." He holds his palms to his face and inhales deeply.

I freeze. It's not wrong to have Raj here. He's a friend, isn't he? There's nothing illicit between us; I'm even helping him find other women to date. Technically speaking, I'm not even really sure that Blake and I are exclusive. We're not an official couple, and we've never had a talk about whether or not to keep seeing other people. But with Blake's texts burning in my hand, I suddenly feel guilty. With so much at stake, I should be spending my time and energy on Blake—not on any other guy, regardless of my intentions.

I gulp a swallow and try to droop slightly against the couch. "Um, I'm actually not feeling super well," I say.

He drops his hands. "Oh, really?"

"Yeah, it, like, just came over me."

"I could go get you some Tylenol? Benadryl? Sudafed? Advil?"

"Oh, no, I'm good. I think I have all that here."

He grins. "You want some chicken soup? I know the *best* place for chicken soup. It's not far from here, I swear."

I'm torn. I feel even worse for lying to Raj.

"Seriously, I'm good. But I think it might be best if you head out."

For a split second, his face drops.

"Yeah, totally. You should get some rest," he says. He pushes up the sleeves of his hoodie and runs his hands through his hair.

He heads for the door and I meet him there. There's a brief pause where neither of us knows what to do. He awkwardly leans in for a hug, but it's a half-hearted one.

"Feel better soon," he says, turning away. "Maybe I'll see you around."

"Yeah!" I call down the stairs as he takes them quickly away from my door.

When Raj is gone, I sprawl belly-down on my bed and answer Blake's texts.

"Aw, I'd love to join you this weekend. That sounds amazing. Thanks for inviting me!"

He writes back a minute later. "Awesome. I'll send you the details soon."

"Perf. What are you up to, BTW?"

"Not much, actually . . . just *Mad Men*."

"Can I come over?"

Before his response even hits my phone, I know what it'll be. My heart races. I've got him.

· Chapter 13 ·

The box arrives on Saturday afternoon. It's Jess's day off, so I'm silently watching a group of customers browse when I notice movement outside the window: a bike messenger locking up his ride onto a telephone pole. He's wearing a yellow-and-orange reflective vest over a dingy long-sleeved T-shirt and has a blue canvas backpack slung over one shoulder. I'm surprised to see him enter the shop.

"I have your delivery, miss," he says, addressing me.

"I didn't order anything," I explain.

He scans the room. "This is Brooklyn Jewels?" He recites the address.

"Yes."

"Then this is for you."

He unzips his backpack, places a slick black box the size of a book on the glass counter, and hitches his backpack over his shoulder again. He's gone before I can open the mysterious box. The customers, three young women who sound French, swivel to look at me. If they seemed like they were seriously going to make a purchase, maybe I'd hold off on opening it. But they've spent the past five minutes lingering, whispering among themselves, and declining my offers for help. One is holding a McDonald's bag dotted with grease and another is furiously texting instead of actually looking at the jewels. They won't mind if I open it. There's no label or note, and my curiosity gets the better of me.

I lift the lid on the box to find a women's watch. The band is delicate stainless steel and looks like a river of shiny silver pebbles. The face is black, elegantly oblong, and framed at the top and bottom with matching arcs of round-cut diamonds. Tiffany & Co.'s logo is etched beneath the Roman numeral for twelve. The last time I wore a watch was when my eighth-grade science teacher insisted we all have them in order to be on time for our field trip to the aquarium. It had a plastic band that made my wrist sweat. But this is different—this is like a work of art.

There's a note inside the box, too. A man's spiky handwriting on a white card reads: *"Wear this tonight?—B."*

And so, of course, I do. A few hours later, Sophie comes in to take over my shift, and I scurry upstairs to shower, curl my hair into beachy waves, and slip into my dress—the same figure-hugging, emerald green gown I wore to my sister's wedding. At the time, I had winced at the cost, even with Bloomingdale's semiannual sale prices, but she'd begged me to buy it, insisting that I'd have plenty of opportunities to wear it again; tonight is the first time I've taken it out of my closet in three years.

Blake had texted me earlier today, offering to pick me up, but it truly would make no sense for him to take a cab down the Upper East Side, across the Queensboro Bridge, through Long Island City, Greenpoint, and Williamsburg in order to pick me up . . . only to turn the car right around and head back to the Upper East Side. I didn't blame him at all for not coming to get me. So instead, I call an Uber to take me to Gustavino's, the charity gala venue. I'm glad I am arriving on my own. I'm more nervous than I had expected to be.

I've spent three of the past five nights at Blake's apartment: Tuesday, after our walk along the Brooklyn Bridge; Wednesday, after Raj left; and Thursday, when he sent a heart-racing text in the middle of the afternoon: "Is there any chance I could see you one more night? My bed will feel empty without you in it." I went over after happy hour with Carmen.

We were slowly growing more comfortable with each other: he opens the door in white T-shirts now, rather than blazers and button-downs; I dared to lie next to him in bed with three full days of leg hair stubble. There were still some occasional lulls in our conversation, the kind that made my chest tight with anticipation. But we always managed to steer past them by jumping into conversation about work or the city.

And then, finally, Thursday night, we were lying awake in his bed, with nothing but a few lights from the apartment across the street to illuminate each other's faces. He was toying with my fingers.

"When I introduce you to people on Saturday, what should I . . . what should I call you?" he asked hesitantly.

"What do you want to call me?" I shot back. I aimed for sassy, not desperate—I'm not sure which side I landed on.

"I think 'girlfriend' has a pretty nice ring to it. What do you think?"

And I kissed him. I said yes. Were the circumstances different, I might have asked if we could continue getting to know each other better. I don't take the labels "boyfriend" or "girlfriend" lightly, especially not in a world where you can be sleeping with a person three times a week and they'll still only call you a "friend." If there was no external pressure whatsoever on our relationship, I would want to wait until my feelings for him were stronger before agreeing to an exclusive, official relationship. But if that's what Blake wants, so be it. I don't have time to waste. I'm grateful his feelings are progressing at a steady clip—that makes my life easier.

So tonight will count as our public debut. I'll meet his colleagues and the industry professionals he knows. There may be photographers. For the first time, we'll look like a real couple. The charity gala isn't just a fancy date night. If it goes well, it's one more significant step toward my plan working out. If it goes poorly—I don't want to think about it.

The Uber rolls to a stop outside a sprawling building tucked underneath the 59th Street Bridge. The façade is decorated with soaring granite arches. Soft amber light glows through the windows. I sweep the full length of my gown carefully out of the car and take a deep breath before starting down the stately brick path that will lead me inside.

"Walking in," I text Blake.

"I'll come meet you," he writes back.

He pushes open the glass double doors before I can reach the building. The tux is the first thing I see, and it's like he was born to wear it. The second thing I see is his smile—crinkly-eyed and genuine.

"You look so beautiful," he calls down the path.

I can't help but blush. His compliment gives me butterflies. My heel hits a slightly raised piece of brick and I trip, catching myself before I do anything *too* embarrassing.

"Uh, hello!" I say, gesturing to his tux. "You don't look too bad, yourself."

Eye contact feels too intense during my last few steps to close the gap between us, and I let my gaze drift over his shoulder into the throng of people inside. When I finally reach him, he plants his hands on my hips and draws me in close for a kiss. I try to strike the right balance between leaning into the kiss and not letting my lipstick smudge. As we part, he runs his fingers appreciatively over the watch on my wrist.

"You wore it," he says, clearly proud.

"Of course, I did. Thank you so much. I was so surprised!"

"I thought it'd be fun to surprise you at work."

"You like doing that, don't you?"

"Gotta keep a girl on her toes," he says, taking my hand and leading me into the venue.

If only he knew. I'm on my toes so often around him, I might as well be wearing pointe shoes.

Gustavino's is equally stunning on the inside. The ceiling is an undulating sea of tiled arches held up by stately pillars. Impressive white floral centerpieces top each table. The crowd is full of elegant tuxes and shimmery, silky, saturated gowns. Blake confidently leads me toward a cluster of people near the bar.

"Mind if I introduce you to a few people?" he asks.

"Sure," I say, hoping he can't feel how clammy my hands have become.

It's been years since a guy has introduced me to anyone—so long ago, in fact, that the most memorable example that springs to mind is meeting Holden's friends at a PBR-soaked basement apartment party back in college. A far cry from Blake's charity gala.

He slides easily into a circle of people; they shift to make room for us both. Each face seems expectant, like they knew I'd be coming.

"Everyone, this is my girlfriend, Eliza," he says, slipping my new title in so smoothly. "Eliza, this is my CFO, Dan, his wife, Arielle, Peter, who heads up biz dev, and his partner, Jeff."

Dan. Arielle. Peter. Jeff. I try to keep the names from swimming; I can't tell yet if Blake considers these people simply coworkers or actual friends. I shake hands with the men and expect to shake Arielle's, too, but she pulls me into a hug and kisses me on the cheek. She has a blond braided updo that shows off glittering earrings dangling nearly to her shoulder; they're kitschy costume jewelry but the nicer kind that can run well into three-digit price tags. I exhale—if nothing else, we can bond over jewelry. I'm wearing Brooklyn Jewels emerald studs to match my dress tonight. I wish more of my customers would be interested in stones other than diamonds; the variety makes them more fun to sell.

"So, we finally meet her," Dan says, offering Blake a playful grin.

"I promised you she was real," he jokes.

Am I? I feel guilty again for not being completely honest with him. I knock my knuckles against the side of my head with a solid *thunk*.

"Ha. Real. I swear," I say, trying to laugh.

"I'm going to grab us drinks—what do you want?" Blake asks, squeezing my arm.

He's already trailing off to the bar.

"Uh, whatever you're having is fine," I say, too flustered to make a decision.

And then I'm alone with his crew. I'm not normally a shy person— the opposite, in fact. But I so desperately want to play this right, I feel seized by nerves. Arielle and I stare at each other for a moment of silence before we both rush to say, "I love your earrings." The identical comments make us laugh; the tension between us softens.

"Where are they from?" she asks.

"Actually, they're my own. I run a jewelry company with my sister," I explain.

"Oh, what's it called?"

"Brooklyn Jewels."

Arielle's eyes narrow. I finger the back of my earring, suddenly terrified that she might recognize me.

"Is that . . . ?"

She pulls out her phone and begins to scroll through Instagram. My blood runs cold. I try to peer over the edge of her screen. Ten brutal seconds later, she looks up at me and shakes her head.

"No, I thought for a sec that you might have designed my friend's ring. But I guess that was some other company—*so* sorry for confusing you with someone else."

"No problem," I say, pressing my lips together into a tight smile.

Luckily, the rest of the group dives in to ask me softball questions about which bar Blake and I met at and which neighborhood I live in. I volley back questions of the same kind. Waiters flit by offering plates of hors d'oeuvres: bruschetta, croquettes, beef satay, each more colorfully garnished than the last. Before too long, Blake is back, carrying two flutes of champagne.

I sip mine and try to relax. Blake's hand lingers on the small of my back, keeping me close to him. He and his friends joke around easily—and the more I watch, the more I can tell that these are people he truly considers to be friends, not just coworkers. It seems as if he's the ringleader of the group, which would make sense, given his position as founder and CEO. Everyone in the group pivots slightly toward him, and the gala sounds like his idea.

"He never passes up an opportunity for a good tuxedo moment," Arielle tells me quietly. "He practically upstaged Dan at our wedding."

We both turn and look at the guys. Dan is also wearing a tux. Let's be honest, there is not much of a competition between who wears it better.

Chatting with Arielle kicks off a funny realization. If Blake is my boyfriend, and these are his friends, that means they could very well become *my* friends, too. This is what my life could look like: dressing for black-tie galas, bonding with Arielle over jewelry, feasting on tiny bites of passed appetizers. As foreign as that feels, it also feels right. I came to New York to have a life like this one. Blake could be the final puzzle piece that clicks everything into place.

A voice floats through the room, ushering us toward our seats. I turn to see a man on stage with a microphone. A banner above his head reads, "American Heart Association." It clicks—of course Blake wanted to be here tonight. He must support this cause in honor of his dad. Blake leads me and his friends to a table halfway between the bar and the stage, covered in a white tablecloth with more silverware than a Crate & Barrel. I hesitate, not sure exactly where to sit, but Blake instructs me to take the spot to his right. His friends fan out to his left. A blond woman I don't know approaches and asks if I mind if she and her fiancé nab the open seats next to me.

I look quizzically back at Blake.

"Oh, no, go ahead! Of course, please join us," he says.

The woman sweeps the skirt of her black embroidered gown to the side and sits down elegantly next to me, as if this is just another Saturday night for her. Her tuxedoed fiancé, a lanky guy glued to his phone, joins us.

"We actually just bought half the table," Blake admits quietly.

"So? That's amazing. Really amazing," I offer.

I hadn't even noticed there was ambient music, but it fades to silence as everyone settles in. Chatter dies down.

The host, a stout fifty-something man who looks like he intentionally matched his red bow tie to the association's banner, clears his throat. He introduces himself as a member of the board and congratulates us all for choosing to support such a worthy cause. There's a round of applause from the audience; I clap, then place a supportive hand on Blake's knee.

He gazes at me with a grateful look. "Thank you so much for being here with me," he says, leaning in so his lips brush my ear.

The host explains that he's been on the association's board for more than two decades, after his brother passed away from a heart attack. His voice doesn't waver when he tells the story of his sibling's death. It's clear that he's given this same speech too many times to count. The room's self-congratulatory aura dims to a somber one.

"And that's why it's so important to keep the American Heart Association going," the host concludes. "Thankfully, along with the money raised here tonight, I'm sure it will continue for years to come. I'd like to introduce our first guest. . . ."

The host brings up three guests to share their stories. Each has been affected by heart disease, either personally or because of a loved one, and they offer emotional speeches about how the association has saved lives. As they speak, waiters discreetly circle each table to take our orders.

When the speeches are over, the host returns to encourage us to eat and mingle. The blonde next to me shifts in her seat, shoots me an awkward glance, and turns back to her fiancé. When she sees him glued to his phone again, she sighs and takes a long sip of champagne.

"I'm Stephanie," she says suddenly, turning to me and thrusting out her hand.

Her grip is firmer than I expected. "Eliza. So nice to meet you."

"Eliza!" she exclaims. "I had a hunch that was you."

I falter, opening and closing my mouth like a fish hooked on a dangerous line.

"I'm sure you're sick of hearing this all the time, but I thought I recognized you from Instagram," she says. "I followed you back when Teddy and I were still just dating. Loved your pieces. I wound up falling in love with this other designer—no offense—but seriously, your stuff is so gorgeous." She absentmindedly runs a finger over her engagement ring, a flashy cushion-cut rock set in platinum, surrounded by a halo of tiny diamonds. I'd guess it's two and a half, maybe three carats.

"Well, thank you *so* much for considering us," I say, dropping my voice's volume to avoid catching Blake's attention. I can hear him talking to his friends, but I don't dare risk letting this woman ask any further questions. Instead, I go on the offensive and ask questions of my own to keep her distracted. "So, when did you get engaged?"

She happily chatters about her Christmas Eve proposal, the headaches of planning a destination wedding in Napa Valley, and her plans to honeymoon in Florence and the rest of Tuscany. The whole time, I freeze my face into a huge grin and punctuate her every sentence with an enthusiastic nod.

"But wait, wait, enough about me," Stephanie says. Her eyes go wide and she drops her voice even lower. "Is this . . . *him*?"

She gestures in the least subtle way possible to Blake. I want the marble floors to swallow me up.

I feel too nauseated to speak. I can't think straight—one wrong word from this woman, spoken just loudly enough for Blake to hear, and everything could crumble. I settle on a response that's as non-committal as possible: a smile and a raised eyebrow, which I hope makes me look mysterious and coy, rather than deranged.

"If you'll excuse me for just one moment," I tell Stephanie.

I turn to tug on the sleeve of Blake's jacket. "Can you come with me for a sec?"

He's mid-conversation with Dan, Arielle, Peter, and Jeff, but doesn't protest. Instead, he scoots out of his chair and places a hand on the small of my back as I weave through the sea of tables. As we walk, I notice how women's eyes flit up to Blake and I feel a swell of pride. I'm not ready to lose him.

I pull Blake into a secluded corner of the venue by the coat check. Whoever mans the station appears to have stepped out. Panic unspools in my chest like a flock of birds, frantically flapping their wings to get out. I don't know *what* to say to Blake—I only know that I have to say *something*, *anything* to justify pulling him away from dinner. We can't go back to that table. Not with Stephanie poking around with her nosy questions.

"Is everything okay?" he asks.

"I'm falling in love with you," I blurt out. Then I freeze, horrified by what I've just done. Blake's mouth twitches and his eyes go wide. "I mean, I know it's so soon. Too soon? And this isn't the time. Or the place. But I just wanted you to know, and—"

Blake places a finger to my lips. We lock eyes. I don't feel confident enough to breathe. I'm digging myself an even larger hole.

"I think I'm falling in love with you, too," he says, voice quavering. He shakes his head. "No, I *am* falling in love with you."

"You are?" I ask. His words feel like an uncomfortable jolt of electricity.

"Yeah," he says, tucking a stray piece of hair behind my ear.

When he kisses me, his hands slip easily over the green silk of my dress to pull me close to him. The sturdiness of his hands on my hips feels like an anchor, even as my heart pounds dangerously fast.

The past sixty seconds are giving me whiplash. I dropped the L-bomb purely because I needed something wild to distract him. I don't know why that was the first thing to come to mind. My only goal was to get him away from Stephanie—it hadn't even occurred to me until this very moment that Blake might actually be falling for me. We've only known each other for a month. I had no idea that a person could fall in love so quickly.

And yet.

Blake has acted more tenderly toward me than any man I've ever known. He's made me eggs most mornings this week, runny in the middle, just the way I like. It's clear that he genuinely listens when I speak, rather than waiting for his turn to interject his own stories, like so many other guys I've dated. He triple-checks for cars before we cross the street together, muttering "precious cargo" under his breath as we walk hand in hand. Just two days ago, I caught him staring at me with a soft smile spread across his face. When I asked what was up, he simply shrugged and said, "I *like* you."

Truthfully, I don't think what I feel for Blake is love. Yet. I can imagine it blooming someday. He's a good, solid guy, and I feel lucky to know him. I like spending evenings curled up in his apartment, and I like being here with him. But *love* is something else entirely—I remember vestiges of it from my relationship with Holden: at first, the obsessive way his name was always on the tip of my tongue, the giddy fireworks I felt every time we kissed; later on, the deeper understanding that he was someone special, despite his myriad flaws. Love isn't a choice. Strategizing every minute of my relationship with Blake is. I feel almost nauseous with guilt, but I'm too involved now to change course.

I have to play this next move carefully.

"Do you . . ." I look up at Blake with big, adoring eyes. "Do you wanna get out of here and celebrate?"

He looks over my shoulder at the seated crowd behind us and laughs. "Ha, you mean, like, now?"

I worry that I've gone a step too far—that this is the move that will sink me. Asking him to leave his favorite event of the year must be wrong. But he drops a kiss on the top of my head and agrees to go. "Sure, they're almost wrapping up anyway."

"I'll get our stuff from the table," I offer, stepping backward already so he doesn't have time to protest.

I don't think I'm overreacting; I don't want to risk an interaction between Stephanie and Blake.

I retrieve the phones we both left on the table, along with my purse. My phone lights up with a new text that must have come in while I was distracting Blake.

"Hey. It's Raj. I just wanted to apologize in case anything that happened the other night was out of line. . . . I know things ended kind of suddenly. Is everything okay?"

I can't help but imagine him hunched over the bar, biting his lip, punching out this apology text. I hate that he feels guilty at all. I slow my walk back to the door so I can respond appropriately.

"Hey! No, no, everything's really cool between us. Just wasn't feeling well all of a sudden. I can't talk now—but let's hang soon?"

I make a mental note to text him tomorrow. Raj is cool and hanging out together feels effortless; I don't want to mess up our budding friendship. I slip my phone back into my purse and approach Blake with another kiss. It's the kind of kiss that would've made me soul-crushingly jealous just two months ago. I know we look so right together. So smitten. His hand lingers on the small of my back when we finally break apart.

"I haven't ever shown you my rooftop, have I?" Blake suggests.

"You haven't."

"What do you say to you, me, a bottle of champagne, and a good view? It's a nice night."

My chest feels heavy. I don't want to hurt him. He deserves the truth about who I am and how I feel—not more lies. But I'm not brave enough to come clean right now. "I'd love that," I say.

He grins and pulls me close again. "And I love you."

· Chapter 14 ·

I'm curled up on Helen's old leather armchair in the back room of the shop, hunched over my laptop, a stack of printed and high-lighted bank statements, and a yellow legal pad scratched up with optimistic math. What's left of my coffee has gone cold. I have the same looming sense of dread I had while studying at the library in college, staring at numbers that start to swim as my mind turns to mush. But back then, if I made a miscalculation or failed to grasp a concept, the biggest consequence was a bad grade on a midterm or a final. Now the stakes are higher: I could come up short on rent. I could lose the shop. I could sink the business.

I know exactly which calculations to run by now, after having done them for so many months. All afternoon, I've pored over our sales, overhead costs, total income, taxes, rent, utilities, and salaries, double- and triple-checking to see how those figures might stretch and warp depending on what the future holds. Even if we take creative steps, like trimming our salaries and slightly boosting our prices, I don't see a safe way for us to re-sign the lease at the higher rent. There just isn't enough money.

I slump over the desk and let my forehead bang against the keys of my laptop. I can't fathom running out of money. I'd have to, what, work for someone else again? Relocate to a less charming neighborhood? Of course, I *could*. But I've never been in this position before, and I don't like it. Growing up, my family veered from comfortable (when we launched Mom and Dad's business) to very comfortable (when the business was doing well). The only financial hiccup I can ever recall is one year when we were little, when they debated if they could afford sending both me and Sophie to summer camp. By the time we were old enough to start thinking about college, money wasn't an issue. We knew we could go to the University of Maine and be fine or go to a private school out of state and also be pretty much fine. I chose to study business because I liked understanding the strategies behind running a successful company. It didn't occur to me until halfway through my first semester of school that running your own business could totally bankrupt you.

And so I let my thoughts drift off to last weekend with Blake. It's easy enough, now that I spend nearly as much time with him as I do at Brooklyn Jewels. The hours after the charity gala are a bubbling blur of hot, breathy kisses in the backseat of a cab; the cool rush of air when we stepped out onto Blake's rooftop, an urban ocean rippling out in front of us. I could see lit-up apartments, dark windows barely illuminated by the blue glow of a television, neat rows of brownstones, tidy squares of greenery that count for backyards, and the iconic lines that make up Midtown Manhattan sprawling out in front of us, sparkling brightly in the night sky. I braced myself against the ledge, drinking in the view. Blake came up from behind me to slip his hands around my waist, dotting my neck with kisses.

"I love you," he nuzzled into my ear. "And I want you."

He pressed himself closer to me, and I could feel the hard edge of his desire. I felt a sudden flash of guilt—for how grand and down-right romantic the evening was, and the hollow way my feelings didn't measure up to his—but I pushed it away. Instead, I turned around and slid my arms over his shoulders to kiss him. I felt lucky that I didn't exactly have to fake my passion for him. He was so dev-astatingly suave in his tux, and I truly did like him. I let him lead me off the roof, down the stairs, into his apartment, hoping that my feelings for him would develop over time.

Later, after Blake had drifted off against the cloudlike white pillows, I couldn't sleep.

"*I love you,*" I mouthed silently, staring at the ceiling, trying to get my mouth accustomed to forming the words. They rolled around on my tongue like rocks.

💍

I wondered if I was anything like Holden, who had strung me along for so many years. Was I worse? Holden kept me around while he figured out what he wanted in life—I don't think he meant to hurt me. I was using Blake outright.

I open up my conversation with Blake on my phone and hover my fingers over the keyboard.

"Hey . . ." I tap out.

I wait for the right words to come. They don't. I delete the draft. There's nothing to say that will assuage my guilt, strengthen my relationship with Blake, and keep Brooklyn Jewels running. It's like what people used to say about college: when it comes to good grades, sleep, and a social life, you can pick two. *Max.* You have to prioritize. You can't have it all.

The thing is, I know exactly what I need and want now. Over the past month, Brooklyn Jewels has managed to pull in 25 percent more sales than we expected. When I mapped out our sales per day, that became clear: there was a significant spike within the first three days of my engagement announcement, and then that success petered out over time, with smaller spikes after the *Elle* story, Haley Cardozo's *Head Bitch in Charge* radio show, and every time I posted something personal on Instagram. Considering that the rent hike will be 20 percent, that means a 25 percent jump in one month doesn't necessarily help, unless I can guarantee that we're able to keep our sales at that rate indefinitely. There need to be more spikes—bigger spikes.

What I need is a wedding.

With the numbers in harsh black and white in front of me, I see the big picture more clearly than ever before. A wedding is not guaranteed to save us, but it could offer us the best possible chance of success. The buzz around my engagement would turn into an even bigger buzz around the wedding. And with so much hanging in the balance—not just the shop, or my relationship with Sophie, but also our parents' stake in the company amid their own business's faltering year—I feel undeniably committed to seeing my plan through. Just to be safe, I recalculate my projections for how the wedding could buoy Brooklyn Jewels. It's tight, but it works. Just barely, but still. Pursuing Blake isn't just a harebrained scheme—it's also my most solid hope. That is, as long as he wants me. *If* he wants me in that way.

If I want to really profit off the wedding, I can't completely leave it up to chance. I can't just zip up my wedding dress, walk down the aisle, and expect to rake in sales from followers. I put on my Kris Jenner hat to mastermind what comes next. For the next hour, I dive into a Google hole, taking precise notes and bookmarking relevant pages. I learn that the clearest way to accomplish what I want isn't just to get a free wedding—I have to profit off my wedding.

I try a little bit of everything, like throwing spaghetti at the wall without fully knowing what will stick. I ask if *Brides* will purchase exclusive rights to my wedding photos for $10,000, angling myself to them as the hottest engagement ring designer in the industry; I pitch myself as a cover star for *The Knot;* I ask TLC to cast me in a variety of wedding-themed reality shows; I write to the editor of the *New York Times*'s Vows section and request coverage of my wedding; I invite a scarily popular YouTuber to the nuptials and ask her to film a wedding-themed vlog; I email Haley Cardozo to tell her how much I loved doing the podcast and to ask if she'll do a special episode on my wedding day. I briefly consider inviting her to be one of my bridesmaids, just for the sake of press, and stop myself when I realize that would be at least one step too far.

I close my laptop and stand up to stretch. When I enter the front room of the shop, Sophie looks like she's sketching out a design with a customer. Jess is straightening up a velvet tray. Outside, on Bedford Avenue, a group of women walk by, and one slows to examine our wares in the window before catching up to her friends. I take a seat behind the counter and spot a smudged fingerprint marring the glass. Reflexively, I grab the Windex and a roll of paper towels we keep lodged underfoot. I spray the chemicals and rub out the spot until the glass gleams. I feel at home here. I'm not ready to give this up.

Here is a partial list of things I did during that yearning, four-year stretch of singlehood: I read Susan Miller's horoscopes every month, breathlessly skimming them until I got to my luckiest days of the month for romance—then I'd swipe through Tinder and schedule dates for all of them. I shaved my bikini line before every date, regardless of how I felt about the guy, even though it irritated my skin, because I was too embarrassed to pay for waxing (how mortifying would it be if I forked over all that money and then nobody ever even saw it?). I read the *New York Times* wedding announcements and calculated how old each bride was when the couple met, just to see if I was falling behind. I dropped hundreds of dollars on brightly swirled bath bombs and pretty candles so I could sit in a glowing tub, skin prickling lobster red under the hot water, and feel desperately alone. I held my phone precariously over the bathtub to snap photos for Instagram, lauding those nights as "self-care," but that wasn't true. I only took baths when Sophie and sometimes Carmen and all my other college friends were doing date night or eating takeout in front of Netflix with their significant others. I used to lie submerged in the tub, wondering if there was a magic trick to finding a relationship, and if so, how everyone knew what it was but me.

And then everything changed.

I catch myself laughing out loud, actually laughing, as I walk down a tree-lined block on the Upper East Side to meet Blake. It was so easy to find him. I needed a guy. I spent *maybe* an hour and a half looking for a guy. And I picked one, it worked out, and here we are—supposedly *in love*. Has finding a boyfriend been this easy the whole time? Was I simply not trying hard enough all those years? Or was it that I was trying too hard, pouring my entire heart into it, when I only needed to use my brain?

Blake had suggested we meet at Brandy's, yet another spot in his neighborhood that's totally foreign to me. According to my Google search earlier that day, it's a piano bar a half block from Dorrian's, the nightmarishly preppy bar where Blake and I first met. There are hours of live show tunes and pop ballads every night.

"Just trust me," he had texted me earlier.

The bar is easy to spot from the street: a slightly faded red façade shouts its name, and two adjacent windows are painted with cheerful yellow letters that read GOOD TIME SALOON and SAME OLD BRANDY'S. Inside, the bar feels like the belly of an old ship: the floors and bar are made of the same dark, weathered, creaking wood; the patrons are mostly pairs of graying, older men leaning over glasses that don't look entirely clean. Half the room has small tables oriented toward a piano with a plastic tip jar on top.

Blake is seated at one of the tables, and he stands when I enter. His face lights up in a way that makes him look like a golden retriever.

"Hey!" he says, wrapping one arm around my shoulders and giving me a kiss.

"This is quite a place," I say, as I settle in next to him.

He laughs. "Do you like it?"

"I'm just . . . surprised? It doesn't seem like your scene."

"This is my favorite spot in the city, hands down," he says. He casts a pleased glance around the bar and shrugs. "It's easy to let go here. It reminds me of driving around with my dad. He used to sing a lot. *Loudly*. And not particularly well."

A waitress, a forty-something blonde with birdlike features, takes our drink orders. Blake runs his fingers over my thigh as he asks for a gin and tonic; I don't know if he even realizes what he's doing, but the gesture makes me smile. He tells me about his day—he led a post-mortem meeting on last quarter's revenue, an old business school colleague hit him up for a job, there weren't nearly enough croutons in his salad—and asks about mine. I briefly freeze. What am I supposed to tell him? That I spent the afternoon calculating how our wedding will save my business?

"Super boring," I lie, running a finger nervously around the edge of my glass. "Accounting stuff. All day long."

Soon enough, a broad-shouldered, dark-haired guy in a tight T-shirt takes a seat behind the piano and taps the microphone. The seats are mostly filled by now. The blond waitress sidles up to a mic stand and belts out "I Wanna Dance With Somebody." The energy in the room ratchets up; people around us are swaying and singing along (not well, either). Blake taps out the song's rhythm on my thigh. He seems so into it. I'm tempted to sing along, but I wouldn't be caught dead doing karaoke sober. I'm not a gifted singer. I want to match Blake's enthusiasm, but I need a little more liquid courage first.

The waitress finishes to a rousing round of applause, then moves seamlessly back through the throng of seats to take more drink orders. I drain what's left of my glass and order a second. The pianist has taken over with a rendition of Prince's "Purple Rain," followed by a highly meta version of Billy Joel's "Piano Man." By the time the waitress is back for another turn at the mic, I feel loosened up and ready to join in on her cover of Alanis Morissette's "You Oughta Know." A woman at the table across from ours thrusts her arms into the air and squeezes her eyes tight while shouting the lyrics.

"I like this place!" I yell over the music to Blake.

He kisses my cheek between songs.

A bartender jumps up to the mic to perform the most flirtatious version of *Hamilton*'s "You'll Be Back" I've ever heard, crooking his finger at a squealing audience member and singing directly at her. Blake moves his hand from my thigh to around my waist, pulling me closer to him. His body is warm and smells like leathery cologne. I lean my head on his shoulder when the music turns to slow ballads.

Tonight is easy, affectionate, and more comfortable than we've ever been before. True, I might feel that way because of the drinks and the atmosphere and the thrill of discovering a delightful hole-

in-the-wall spot. But maybe part of it is that something real is beginning to blossom between me and Blake. If this is what our life
would be like together, I can picture it. I'd like it. I could do this—
not just for the wedding, but for real. If my feelings for him become
real, the guilt that gnaws at my stomach will fade away. For the first
time since I dug myself into this hole, I feel true hope.

When the show's over, we take slow, easy steps back to his apartment, savoring the warm, starry evening. The rhythm of our footsteps echoes in my head—it sounds like, *do I love him? do I love
him? do I love him?* I wish I could fall fully for him. I like him a
lot, but I want more than that. I want to feel authentically smitten.

I remember something I read online once that described the
psychological effects of smiling. Even if you're having a bad day, the
act of smiling can genuinely lift your mood. When it comes to your
emotions, faking it till you make it apparently works for real. I can't
help but think about that as I follow Blake into his building's lobby.
I slip my hand into his and remind myself how good it feels to be
one half of a couple with him. As we ride the elevator upstairs, I appreciate how much fun it was to sing along with him tonight.

When he turns the key in his apartment door, we barely get
two steps inside; I lean against the door and pull him close to me. I
nuzzle a trail of kisses from his mouth to his ear to his collarbone.
In response, his hands roam my body, slipping up underneath my
shirt and running over my chest.

"Come with me," I say.

I straighten up and begin to saunter to his bedroom, undoing
the buttons of my shirt as I go. He follows, but not as fast as he usually does.

"Blake?" I ask.

He's stopped walking and is leaning against the wall, shaking his head appreciatively. "I was just looking, that's all. You're crazy hot—you know that, right?"

I have to laugh. I move toward him, grab his collar, and kiss him again. "You're not so bad yourself," I say, clasping his hand in mine and pulling him toward the bedroom.

Sex with Blake is always satisfying. He's good, sometimes even great: he's attentive, unselfish, and mercifully acquainted with the female anatomy. When I'm in bed with him, I can't help but slow down to admire the gently sculpted muscles along his arms and torso and the look of pure appreciation on his face. But today, there's something new. He moves more intensely than he typically does, as if he can't get enough of cupping my curves or can't bring us close enough.

"Say that you're mine," he says breathlessly.

I don't think twice. I do.

When it's over, he lies flat on his back with the duvet thrown toward our feet and ushers me close to his side. I rest my head on his chest.

"I love you," I say. "I really do."

I test how the words make me feel. They're growing on me.

· Chapter 15 ·

In my nine years of friendship with Carmen, I can count the number of times we've skipped our weekly Thursday happy hours on maybe two hands: a few vacations for each of us, a funeral out of town, the time I had the flu. That's it. The week that Hurricane Sandy devastated New York and we evacuated our dorm to sleep on cots pushed together in NYU's student center, we still found time to meet and drink Diet Cokes from the vending machine. We've gathered during blizzards and breakups, too. So when Carmen texted on Thursday afternoon, "SOS, work stuff is cray, let's do a quick coffee tonight?" I knew her situation must be dire.

I meet her at The Wing, the ultra-chic, women-only coworking space. Carmen forks over a full month's rent for annual membership, but she says the benefits—networking, events, amenities—are worth it. Carmen got her current job after loaning a laptop charger to the woman at the table next to her; she regularly goes to events with speakers like Hillary Clinton and a guru who helped her detox her chakras; the hand lotion in the bathroom is Chanel. Her pricey membership lets her bring guests, for which I am eternally grateful.

The airy space is oriented around a millennial pink couch in front of a bright, color-coded bookshelf. Famously, every title on the shelf is written by a woman. I find Carmen at her favorite table by the window, hunched over her laptop with her headphones in and surrounded by two coffee cups and a LaCroix. I have a sudden flashback to college. She looked just like this back then, too—only then, she was dressed in Forever 21 and H&M, not whatever was most recently stocked on Shopbop and The Outnet.

"Hiiiii," she says, tugging out her headphones when she sees me.

"What's going on?" I ask.

She exhales deeply. "Well, everything is happening at lightning speed. Fucking *finally*."

I know she's been pulling all-nighters, working her day job, then coming to The Wing to work on the early steps of her startup, then heading home once this place shuts down for the night to keep going. Venture capital firms are mostly run by old white dudes, so they haven't been exactly receptive to her pitch. And without a serious influx of cash, her idea had no chance whatsoever. She deserves a morsel of good news.

"The main thing is that I landed a meeting with Pinnacle Ventures . . . and it's tomorrow," she explains.

I squeal and hug her. This is a huge deal. Pinnacle is helmed by a woman and they mostly invest in cool projects targeted at millennial women—The Wing included.

"Carmen! That's amazing."

"Yeah, but I'm feeling massively underprepared. Like, this could be *it*. But only if I'm on my A-game, you know?"

"Okay, I'm going to get a coffee, and we're going to figure this out together. I'll help you prep," I offer.

"Love you. Seriously."

I order a large coffee from a braless barista, pick up a muffin for us to split, and help Carmen clear away the cups she's already drained.

"So, how can I help?"

She fills me in on the other recent developments. She selected a name after a few rounds of focus groups, Skindemand—"Like, skin *in demand*," she intoned—and finalized a list of indie skincare brands that would be interested in signing contracts to put their products in her monthly boxes.

"But now, the challenge is updating my business plan to reflect all of that, and also refining my elevator pitch, and also, praying that I don't sweat off my full-coverage foundation tomorrow, because my skin is *not* in good enough shape to pitch a skincare company," she says, rolling her eyes.

Her skin has improved since the last time I saw her, but it's not exactly clear. The red blotches are only half-faded. I wince.

"So I can't exactly help you with that, *but* let's work on your elevator pitch. Practice on me. Pretend I'm—what's her name? The investor you're meeting with?"

"Cecelia Sundquist," Carmen breathes, like it's the name of her lord and savior. "I think she might go by Cece. Should I call her Cece?"

"I don't know. Use Cecelia just to be safe. Pretend I'm her. Pitch me."

She does—quietly and awkwardly so that the people at the neighboring tables can't even hear.

"Again," I encourage. "Louder. You got this."

She runs through the pitch again, and this time she sounds a little more solid. But the wording is off. It takes me a minute to figure out what's wrong, but the third time Carmen runs through the thirty-second speech, I've got it.

"Stop, stop, stop. You keep saying 'I think.' You don't just *think* this is a good idea, it *is* objectively a good idea," I point out.

She tilts her head, unconvinced. "If it were a really good idea, wouldn't someone more qualified already have done it?"

"Come on. Don't discredit yourself. Show me your lines. Let's edit this together."

We workshop her pitch, and then I listen carefully as she runs through it over and over again. By the eighth run-through, her delivery is confident and clear. Hell, if I didn't have money problems of my own right now, I'd give her a sweet chunk of change to turn her business idea into a reality.

"You nailed it," I tell her.

She slouches forward over the table. "Ugh. Yeah? You think so?"

"Yeah. Want to do it one more time so I can film you?"

She shakes her head. "I mean, do you think this is all going to work? To the point where I could leave my job and do this full time?"

I hesitate. I want to make sure I say the right thing.

"It's just so much . . . effort," she continues. "And there's no guarantee that any of this could pan out, like it did for you." A wrinkle shoots up between her brows, like she's suddenly worried she said the wrong thing. "Not that you and Sophie didn't do a killer amount of prep work."

I can't help but think about the gloomy financial projections I was looking at earlier this week. If I could go back in time to tell my former self not to open Brooklyn Jewels, would I? *Should* I?

"Look, Carmen, there are no guarantees in this world at all. Honestly, my business might not make it through the end of the year. If you're looking for a simple, steady paycheck, this isn't the way to go. But you're so clearly passionate about this concept," I say. I get a warm flush recalling the moment I signed the lease on our storefront, when I knew I had transformed my love of jewelry into a physical space to help others form that same strong emotional connection to it. I want Carmen to have that, too. "You've done the research, your concept is cool as hell, and you're going to do an incredible job tomorrow with Pinnacle. Nobody ever said entrepreneurship was easy, but if anyone can do this, it's you."

She reaches across the table to squeeze my hand.

"All right. Then next, I'd really love your feedback on my deck."

She shows me the presentation she's put together and it's gorgeous. The branding is impeccable, done in clean black and white with pretty pops of yellow and sleek fonts. I'm proud of her. By the time we drain our cups of coffee, Carmen feels more confident about her meeting tomorrow.

"You should head out," she says, stifling a yawn. "I'm going to wrap up soon and head home anyway."

"You sure?" I ask.

"Yeah. I feel good. Besides, a girl's gotta get her beauty sleep." She gets up to hug me goodbye.

On my walk back to the subway, my brain buzzes with caffeine. Late spring is always my favorite time of year; this week marks nine years since I first moved to New York. The city seems to crackle with life again as the weather warms up: restaurants reopen their outdoor seating sections so people can sit alfresco on the sidewalks with big glasses of chilled rosé; the sidewalks are a sea of bare arms again; dusk glows warm violet against golden streetlights.

"Hey," I text Raj. "What are you up to right now?"

I haven't seen him since that awkward moment in my apartment. It's time to fix that.

"It's a slow night at the bar. Come hang?" he writes back.

"On my way!"

When I arrive twenty minutes later, Raj has my favorite beer and a plate of mozzarella sticks waiting for me on the counter. He's shed his usual hoodie for a black T-shirt. I'm surprised that his arms are muscled—I hadn't ever exactly considered what his arms might look like under all those sweatshirts, but this wouldn't be it.

"Where was happy hour this week?" he asks.

"You remembered!" I say. I barely remember telling him about our ritual. I slide onto the bar stool and chomp down gratefully on a mozzarella stick. "Thank you for this, by the way. You're amazing."

"Of course."

I tell him about Carmen's plans to launch her own business and our evening at The Wing. His eyebrows shoot up. He looks impressed.

"It's super cool that she's going out on her own, too. I wish I had the guts to do that."

"Would you ever consider it?"

He shakes his head. "Nah. Not for me. I always thought I might. . . . My parents have their own restaurant in Queens and raised me to work for myself. But honestly, I'm happiest working with and for others. I'm looking for jobs right now, though."

"Coding jobs?"

"Coding or design, yeah. I loved the early stages of designing and coding the app at my last startup, but the maintenance stuff toward the end got pretty boring after a while."

Something clicks.

"Raj, would you want to help out Carmen? She's looking for the right person to build her app."

He rubs a hand over his mouth. "I'm not gonna lie, I'm tempted."

"Yeah? I don't know how complicated it is, but . . ." I say, trailing off. I'm already typing out a text to Carmen to say I might have found an engineer for her.

"Yeah, clearly, says the girl who still uses an ancient MacBook from, like, the nineteenth century." His eyes light up when he teases me. "I've seen that thing in your store."

"Twenty thirteen was not *that* long ago!" I squeak.

Carmen is already typing back. "Deets?!?" she asks.

"Can I connect you to Carmen?" I ask Raj.

He shrugs. "Go for it. Would love to learn more. I like startups."

I connect them via text. It's too simple.

"Did you always know you wanted to run your own jewelry business?" he asks.

"The idea for the store came later, but I've been really into jewelry since I was a kid," I explain. "My parents own a boating shop, and there used to be this jewelry store next door run by this amazing woman named Helen. I used to hang out there all the time when I was younger, and she taught me to really appreciate fine jewelry."

"Like a mentor," he says.

"Yeah. In middle school, I couldn't afford anything she sold, obviously, so I used to wear Ring Pops—remember those?—and pretend they were real." The memory makes me smile.

Raj grins. "I used to love those."

"I'm not artistic, not the way Sophie is," I add. "But I loved the idea of working with jewelry and helping people find pieces that they really appreciate, the way Helen did. When she retired and closed down her shop, I was really upset. I missed it, you know? And that's when I knew I had to have a shop of my own."

From there, the conversation spirals into why we'd both die before racking up student loans in grad school and what we'd do if we won the lottery. By the time the mozzarella sticks and beer are gone, it's fully dark out—I don't know where the time has gone. Aside from a couple that looks like they're on an awkward first date, Raj and I are the only people left in the bar.

I've never really had guy friends before. Sure, there were guys I knew in college, and we'd hang out after class and on weekends, but that's not quite the same thing as what I have with Raj. Those were friendships of convenience. Back then, we led lives with a shared rhythm—classes, internships, parties, stumbling bleary-eyed and hungover into the library on weekend afternoons to cram. But now, there's no real gravity holding me and Raj together, aside from the fact that he's just genuinely cool. He's easy to be myself around. And these days, that's increasingly rare to come by.

"I'm glad things are okay between us," he says suddenly, giving me a sheepish look. "You know, after the other night."

"Oh my god, yeah. Yeah! I just wasn't feeling well. Thanks for being so chill about it."

He reaches over the bar to give me a hug. "So, we're cool," he says, laughing.

"Always, dude," I say, clapping a hand onto his shoulder.

When we break apart, he goes from starry-eyed to straight-faced in a split second. He coughs and looks away. His cheeks flush. I wouldn't blush just from hugging a friend—but I'm not confident enough to call him out on it, either. I push the thought away, crumple up my napkin, and formulate an excuse for why I really need to get going.

· Part 2 ·

September

· *Chapter 16* ·

Somehow, the calendar has slipped into September. I only realize summer is nearly gone when my phone buzzes with an alert to pay the rent. I was busier than ever at Brooklyn Jewels. A beloved reality star got engaged with one of our pieces in June, which instantly spurred a flood of orders for identical rings. Meanwhile, the shop's Instagram following ballooned, which translated into my spending more and more hours glued to my phone, replying to comments and keeping up with the steady stream of DMs. We're actually making *real money*. The influx of business makes me feel hopeful about the company's future—but every day that goes by is another day closer to the deadline to re-sign or give up the storefront's lease, and another day closer to a wedding that seems increasingly impossible to pull off without a cooperating groom.

My relationship with Blake has hit milestone after milestone: we've met all of each other's friends; he's met my family; we've traveled together for a weekend getaway. We're moving frighteningly fast. But the more boxes we tick, the more obvious it becomes to me that we have so many *more* milestones to hit before an engagement. Don't serious couples swap keys? They definitely have spent more than forty-eight consecutive hours together. I'm still anxious about peeing too loudly in his apartment.

There are moments when I consider telling him the full truth about our relationship. More often than I'd like to admit, I feel guarded around him, and I can't help but believe that's because I'm hiding a massive secret. The longer I hide it from him, the harder it is to fathom a point when I can tell him the truth. But if I never set the record straight, I fear he won't ever understand who I really am.

I almost came clean to him the night he met my parents. They drove down from Maine one Friday in August to pick me up the day before my uncle's retirement party in Connecticut. I arranged for Blake to join us at dinner. He and my parents were all running late, so I sat by myself at an empty table for fifteen minutes, nervously rereading the menu and second-guessing the entire evening. I had been with Holden for more than a year by the time we were ready to meet each other's parents. Was this new relationship strong enough, by comparison, to merit meeting after five months? I was halfway through texting Blake an excuse for why he shouldn't show up after all when he arrived. My parents walked through the door less than a minute later. I had no choice but to introduce everyone like nothing was wrong. Blake charmed both of them within minutes, of course. My mom giggled flirtatiously when he shook her hand.

"Oh, Eliza, he's *handsome*," she said—actually *out loud*—right in front of Blake.

Between work and Blake, my free time had been whittled down to practically nil. But still, I made time for happy hours with Carmen and nights with Raj. We ventured beyond the bar now—once, we ate gelato together in Domino Park; another time, he brought me to his friend's improv set at UCB.

The summer's momentum skids to a halt on a Thursday morning, the day before Blake and I are set to visit his family in Massachusetts for Labor Day weekend. Sophie heaves herself through the front door of the shop, wide-eyed and breathing hard.

"I practically ran from the subway," she announces, pausing in the doorframe to catch her breath. "Blake called me this morning."

"Blake called you?" I repeat. I have our black velvet trays spread out across the glass counter and I'm setting up the cases for the day.

"He says—and I quote—he's 'ready to propose and wants to do it right.'"

My heart races. I drop the edgy black diamond stacking ring I'm holding. "He said *what*?"

"He wanted my advice on choosing the right ring for you. He wasn't sure if you'd want a Brooklyn Jewels piece or not, and I was like, '*Obviously*, she has to have one to promote our brand.'"

"So you turned my boyfriend asking for my hand into a marketing meeting?" I say, on the verge of laughter.

She continues like I didn't say anything. "And he wanted to know if there was a specific piece you had your heart set on, or if there were certain styles he should look at. It was kind of sweet, to be honest. I mean, it's clear he really cares."

I start to feel light-headed, shaky. Is this real? I take a deep breath to try to steady myself. Luckily, there's a stool behind me that I can sink onto for support.

"So what did you say to him?!"

She revels in a long, slow grin. "I'm a genius. I knew you'd need him to propose with the ring you already debuted on Instagram. So I told him I knew just the right piece for you, and I'd bring it to him. So!" She holds her hand out expectantly.

I stare at her dumbly.

"Eliza? I need the ring."

"I'm sorry. I'm just overwhelmed. Yeah, here."

I gently tug the ring off my finger. This feels surreal. I know that inspiring Blake to propose quickly has been the plan all along—but now that it's actually about to happen, I can't quite believe it. I should be victorious right now. Instead, I'm scared. My hands shake when I hand the ring over to Sophie.

She laughs. "You know, I never thought about this until now, but this is the last piece I'd choose for you."

I roll my eyes. "It's like the McMansion of engagement rings."

"And now it'll be on your finger *forever*," she says.

A chill runs down my spine.

When I meet Blake at Penn Station the next afternoon, I can't help but glance toward his pockets. They look smooth—so if he *is* carrying my ring, it's not in such an obvious place. I wonder if it's in the monogrammed L.L.Bean duffel he has slung over his shoulder. We're boarding a 2 p.m. Amtrak to Boston, where his mom will pick us up and take us back to their house in the suburb of Needham for the weekend.

"You okay?" he asks, looking carefully at me.

"Just nervous, I guess," I say, shrugging.

I shift the orchid I'm carrying from one hip to the other. I had been so desperate to make a good impression, I purchased his mom's favorite flower to get on her good side. It didn't occur to me at the time how precarious schlepping such a delicate flower across several state lines would be. Blake gently takes it from me.

"Here, I'll hold this for now. Don't worry, she'll love you. Who *wouldn't* love you? I mean, don't you have, like, a million people on Instagram who adoringly watch your every move?" He laughs. "You're good with people. I know you are."

I'm suddenly flooded with panic. "You've seen my Instagram?"

He flaps his hand. "Nah, you know I don't use it. But isn't that true?"

I try to laugh. "Yeah. So lovable. *Everyone loves me,*" I say in an obviously fake, singsongy tone.

Guilt overwhelms me. The train station is grubby, grimy, and packed with New Yorkers straining to get out of town for the weekend. I have a desperate urge to jump on any one of these trains and get away from Blake: there's the 3:15 to Washington, D.C., and the 3:21 to Albany.

Blake clutches my hand and rubs his thumb soothingly over the inside of my palm. If only he knew why I was so nervous.

Soon enough, it's time to board the train. I consider telling him that I need to sit in the quiet car so I can get some work done ahead of the weekend, but the excuse feels wrong. I know he's looking forward to spending time together; I can tell from the sweet way he keeps bringing up stories and jokes and snaking his hand around my hips to fit it into my back pocket. Quarantining myself in silence in the quiet car would only drive a wedge between us now, even if the idea of four hours of peace to think about my true intentions honestly sounds like heaven. So I follow him to sit wherever he'd like. After the conductor comes to scan our tickets, Blake pulls a screw-top bottle of white wine and two Styrofoam Dunkin' Donuts cups out of his bag.

"This is the best way to do the Amtrak," he says, handing me one. "Trust me, I've got years of practice."

"Cheers," I say, maybe a little too forcefully.

Honestly, the wine does help calm my nerves. I try to relax and enjoy the fact that I've miraculously landed exactly where so many girls want to be: heading home to meet my charming, hot, successful boyfriend's family, likely with a ring burning a hole somewhere in his luggage.

Four hours later, we've drained the bottle and we're pulling into Boston's South Station. Blake takes my hand and weaves us through the crowd, holding the orchid aloft above our heads. He looks like he belongs here, even more so than he does in New York. He's one of a dozen guys streaming off the train like salmon in Nantucket red shorts, clutching L.L.Bean bags and Dunkin' Donuts cups. I flash back to visiting Holden's family in LA. Even if he claimed he didn't fit in there, that trip filled in all the blank details about him: I suddenly understood why he whined for tacos when he was drunk, and why he scoffed at the frigid summer ocean that kissed the Maine shoreline. I can only imagine the same will happen this weekend with Blake.

Outside the station, his mom rises from a navy sedan dressed head to toe in plum Lululemon Lycra and gives us a big wave. Blake makes quick strides to meet her and envelops her in a hug.

"Gosh, you brought me flowers!" his mom crows, ruffling his hair. "Oh, you shouldn't have."

I stand off to the side, waiting to be introduced.

"Mom, these are actually from Eliza. Mom, Eliza. Eliza, Mom," he says.

"It's so nice to meet you, Mrs. Barrett," I say, extending my hand.

"Oh, please, call me Michelle," she says, waving away her son and reaching out to hug me. Diamonds twinkle from her neck and her earlobes, but her left ring finger is bare. When she steps back, she smooths down her already smooth bob. "The orchid is so gorgeous, thank you."

Blake loads our luggage into the trunk and climbs into the front seat next to his mom. I wind up in the back. Boston's Revolutionary War–era monuments and collegiate scenery along the Charles River feel familiar to me; growing up in Maine, Boston was the nearest real city we had. (At 65,000 people, Portland was the biggest city in our state. Boston had seemed massive back then. Now, visiting from New York, it looks almost quaint.) As we drive toward the highway, Michelle eagerly peppers me with questions, beginning with what it's like to work with my sister.

"It sounds like a lovely idea, but, I mean, can you imagine Blake and Reid working together? It'd be chaos," she says. "They fought like cats and dogs as kids. You'll meet him tonight, you know."

From what Blake has told me, he and his brother weren't ever the closest growing up, but they made a particular effort to stay tight after their father died. Reid was a lacrosse star in high school, went on to play in college, and now manages a branch of a local bank near where they grew up.

"He puts on a front like he's this big, buff, intense guy," Blake had told me once. "But he's just a softie who wants his regular Friday night pizza delivered from the same place he's been ordering it from for the past twenty years."

"Working with my sister can sometimes be a challenge," I admit to Michelle. I feel as if I have to select my words carefully, like any slipup could create a bad impression. "But there's no one else I'd trust enough to launch a business with. She's amazing."

I don't want to say anything more about work. If Michelle knows what I do for a living, it's entirely possible that she could've looked me up online—and then stumbled across our Instagram.

The drive turns suburban, and soon enough, we're on a winding road surrounded on both sides by a tall thicket of pine trees. I can see just a sliver of Blake's face from this angle, but he looks transfixed by the trees, like the sight relaxes him.

"It's good to be home," he says to no one in particular.

"You know, you could *stay*," his mom says, giving him a pointed look.

"Nah. I'd miss the city," he replies. "And anyway, Eliza's a city girl, too."

Michelle's eyes meet mine in the rearview mirror. She raises one eyebrow and turns the car onto a leafy side street. Blake's words make my chest feel tight.

We pull into their driveway and Blake, like the gentleman he is, opens my door for me. His childhood home is generously proportioned, with blue siding and a cranberry red front door set against a lush backdrop of pine trees. A long, green backyard seems like the perfect spot for two energetic boys to practice lacrosse shots all those years ago. Another car is parked in the driveway.

"Reid and Lauren got here a while ago with the baby," she explains.

Inside the house, there's a flurry of hugs and introductions, but somehow, it takes Michelle mere seconds to pour me a glass of white wine. Reid is exactly how I expected him—he has Blake's sharp cheekbones and wavy brown hair, but his formerly athletic shape is going soft around the middle. His wife looks pretty but also completely exhausted; her hair is up in a ponytail, out of reach of the grasping infant on her lap. The decor is full of tasteful neutrals and sleek stainless-steel appliances, like in the kind of house you'd see on any TV show about upper-middle-class white people. Framed black-and-white family photos line the walls.

I hang back while Blake catches up with his family, awkwardly smiling at Belle, the baby. She shoves a few fingers in her toothless mouth and begins to slobber. Soon enough, Blake makes the requisite introductions. I do my best impression of a perfect girlfriend: beaming at his family, politely asking questions to show how interested I am in their lives, standing with my best posture while also straining to look casual and relaxed. This is hard. I had figured that because I'm naturally sociable I could get by just fine—but I forgot how stressful this situation could be. I hadn't realized until today how badly I wanted to impress Blake's family. Even if our relationship began just for show, it's hard to shake the desire for approval.

Michelle tends to a few pots on the stove, then ushers us into the dining room for dinner. I hover by the oblong table, feeling too paralyzed to select a chair. I don't want to accidentally pick anyone's favorite spot or sit at the head of the table. Finally, Blake sits down and pats the seat next to him. I take it gratefully.

Dinner is simple but lovely—salmon, brown rice, steamed broccoli—expertly cooked and plated in the way that only a mom can. Michelle tells a story from this week's Pilates class; Lauren talks about a new restaurant that opened up in town; Blake and Reid trade mostly good-natured barbs about the Red Sox versus the Yankees. I can't remember the last time I had a family dinner without intense discussions about our businesses. This is a refreshing change of pace.

"Now, how did you two say you met?" Reid asks.

Blake squeezes my thigh under the table and smiles at me.

"Well, I was at a local bar. Dorrian's—you remember it? I've taken you out there before."

Reid cocks his head, a flash of recognition spreading across his features. "That place with the . . . ?"

"Ha, it was right before you met Lauren. We met a few girls there, remember?" Blake says, waiting for his brother to catch on.

Reid does. He laughs. Lauren rolls her eyes.

"Yeah, yeah, *I've* heard that story before," she interjects.

"So the night I met Eliza, I had had a stressful day at work and just wanted to blow off a little steam with a drink at Dorrian's," Blake says. It occurs to me that I've never heard this story from his perspective before. I had no idea that he'd had a difficult day before meeting me that night. "And Eliza here was holding some sort of . . . casting call? Audition?"

"I needed to find a date to bring to my friend's wedding," I explain. "The search got a little out of hand, thanks to my best friend Carmen. She never quite does anything halfway."

"Sure. Audition, let's call it," Blake says, nodding. "We struck up a conversation at the bar, and I couldn't make it to the wedding because I was here for the weekend."

"But you liked him anyway!" Michelle says triumphantly, raising her glass in my direction.

"Of course!" I say, chuckling. "He's easy to like."

Blake's family smiles at me.

"Tell me some stories about Blake as a kid?" I ask. "I'd love to hear them."

They jump at the opportunity. Even though I see Blake as a pretty smooth guy, it's clear that his family sees him in a totally different light. Here, at home, he's the kid brother, the butt of every joke. Reid tells a story about how Blake would study for his fourth-grade science test with stacks and stacks of color-coded flash cards ("Always was a little nerd," he says fondly) and Lauren recalls how sweet and welcoming Blake was the first time they met four years ago. Michelle excuses herself from the table to grab a family photo album. There are maybe ten or fifteen pounds of Kodak photos slid into laminated sheets clipped into a three-ring binder.

"This is Blake from birth to age two," she says, flipping by memory to her favorite snapshots. "He refused to wear clothes until he was in preschool. Buck naked in every photo."

"Sorry I'm not as cute as I was back then," he deadpans to me.

"Eh, you're cute enough—in a different way," I joke back.

Seeing his family gently rag on him makes it easy to join in. I start to relax around them.

My phone begins to vibrate in my pocket. I know it's rude to check it, but I so rarely get phone calls—I figure I should at least see who it is. I pull out my phone to check the screen. It's Mom. I send her call to voicemail and put my phone away. But fifteen seconds later, my phone buzzes again with a text.

"Are you around to talk? Dad and I want to hear more about the shop's finances," Mom wrote.

They know we're in a precarious position. They'd bail us out if they could—but that's not an option right now.

"Will call tomorrow," I type back.

Michelle draws my attention back by tapping a manicured finger against a photo of toddler Blake in a lumpy pumpkin costume complete with an orange felt hat dripping in green vines.

"Halloween. Wasn't he the cutest? Look at those chubby cheeks."

♦

Saturday with Blake is delightfully low-key. Sunlight streams in through the window in his childhood bedroom to wake us up. He looks overgrown against the sky blue walls and neat rows of *Harry Potter* books lined up on the bookshelf. He drives us into the town's center for bagels at Cafe Fresh, his favorite spot since he was a kid. ("New York bagels don't even come close to these, I swear," he says, sinking his teeth into the doughy mass.) He shows me around his hometown: his high school; the parking lot where everyone went to make out in cars; the mossy, abandoned railroad tracks stretched across a river where he used to smoke pot during summers home from college.

We're perched there now, lying across the creaky wooden slats. My head is in his lap and he absentmindedly winds his fingers through my hair. There's a sense of calm and peace out here that's hard to find in the city. It's just us surrounded by sky-high pine trees and a lazy river below. I don't always know what to say to fill the silent lulls, but he does. He tells me more about growing up here and asks if we can visit Portland soon, so he can see my hometown through my eyes. He muses about how lucky he is to have met me, and how rare it is to find someone he can feel so comfortable around.

Eventually, it's time to head back to the house. Michelle had asked us to come home and change into nicer clothes before dinner at one of her favorite restaurants in a neighboring town. Blake stretches his arms overhead with a sweet grin on his face.

"You look so beautiful today," he says.

Then he drops down on one knee and my heart stops. His head lowers, and I can't see his expression anymore. Does he plan to propose and then celebrate with his family at the restaurant? He's fumbling with something by his foot—wait. He's tying his shoe.

He's not proposing; he's making sure he doesn't trip over his loose laces.

I take a deep, jagged breath. The air feels sharp within my lungs. He rises again.

"Ready for dinner?" he asks.

· Chapter 17 ·

I schedule wedding planning now, the same way I plan meetings and marked off time in my calendar to go to barre classes when I cared about having a toned butt. It's half past noon, so it's time to squeeze in a half hour's worth of work in the time I typically reserve for my lunch break. With the wedding just five weeks away, I have no other choice. I head into the back room to sit in Helen's old leather chair and finish following up with a travel company offering me a luxe honeymoon for free—as long as I promote the shit out of it on Instagram, of course. I picked the Mediterranean package. I like the idea of traipsing around the Greek islands, the beaches of Croatia, the coast of Italy, maybe Morocco, too. When that email is done, I research florists who can do bridal bouquets. I'm going low budget on the flowers. I don't need floral centerpieces on every table, since I don't even know how many tables I'll have. I just need a bouquet for me to hold as I walk down the aisle and a boutonniere for my groom. I think the flowers should be in assorted red tones—they'll pop the most in photos.

It's hard for me to wrap my head around how I feel about Blake. The more time I spend with him, the more I can imagine myself falling in love with him for real. I don't doubt that I have feelings for him, but I do doubt that they match the strength of his feelings for me. And it's hard to swallow the undeniable fact that if the circumstances were different, I wouldn't be fishing for such a quick engagement. But because of my predicament, I'm desperate for the proposal to happen soon.

I know Sophie gave him the ring as a gift on the house (because if he pays the full $45,000 for it, and the engagement goes south, New York state law says I could be legally required to return it to him—and that's a risk I don't want to take). At times, I even catch myself in a sheer panic because my ring finger is bare. Then, of course, I remember that I didn't lose the ring, but rather, I took it off on purpose. I really thought he would pop the question in Massachusetts, but the long weekend has come and gone.

I've only been waiting for six days, but the time is starting to gnaw at me. It's given me enough time to reconsider if all this— an engagement, a wedding, Blake—is what I really want. If I go through with it, I'm making a choice to irrevocably intertwine my personal life with my business and my livelihood. I can't take that back. Blake and I will be linked, romantically, financially, publicly, and that means opening up our relationship to scrutiny. My ruse could be exposed. But I can so easily envision the highlight reel of our lives together: first, a gorgeous wedding, then a generous spike in Brooklyn Jewels's sales that leads to a healthy bank account balance, and ultimately, the kind of soul-affirming love that can sustain the shared life of a marriage. If I truly let my imagination run, I can see us spending weekend mornings in bed with our laptops, each happily working on our businesses; I can see us sunbathing on his rooftop on summer afternoons; I can see the two of us eating stir-fry with Sophie and Liv and maybe their baby someday. But once I let people in to see all that, I can't take it back. I can't guarantee a happy ending. If we go public and then fizzle, it would be ruinous. Personally, it'd be mortifying. But professionally, it could be disastrous, too. All my new customers and followers who gush over our relationship could leave me cold.

I don't have to go through with it. I could say no to Blake's proposal. I could push away the wedding planning, cancel the splashy party at the Wythe Hotel, return the glitzy dress. Maybe that's the logical decision. The safe choice. But the prospect of shutting all that down makes me feel lost and lonely. After building up the idea in my head all spring and summer, I don't know how to pivot away from it. I would be so sad to lose Blake. And now that I'm hinging on an influx of business to keep the shop afloat, I'm too far gone. I have to go through with my plan or else.

So that's why I close my laptop at 1 p.m. and head over to the hotel's in-house restaurant, Reynard, for the cake tasting. Raj is meeting me there. He had texted over the weekend to ask about hanging out again, and I suggested he join me today. The plan isn't to pass him off as my fiancé necessarily, but I can say that my fiancé isn't able to make it, and I wanted a second opinion, so I brought a friend. It's not the most outrageous lie. I've certainly told worse.

Reynard's dining room is outfitted with the kind of industrial chic design that makes everyone in it look at least 10 percent hotter by association. The walls are rosy brick, the banquettes are made of sumptuous chocolate leather, the floor is rough wood, and the lighting fixtures are softly glowing exposed bulbs. Raj waits for me by the hostess stand, and we're seated at a round table in the back. A ponytailed waiter comes by to greet us.

"This is the happy couple?" he asks, clapping his hands together.

"Well, I'm Eliza, the bride," I say, jumping in to smooth over the potentially awkward situation. "And this is my good friend Raj, who's joining me for the tasting today since my fiancé can't make it."

Raj reaches his hand across the table to shake the waiter's hand. "Not the groom, but a groomsman," he says, hamming it up.

I choke on my sparkling water. The plan was to avoid bridesmaids and groomsmen entirely—it's too complicated to arrange with such a shaky, last-minute wedding. Maybe Sophie could serve as my matron of honor, and maybe Reid would be Blake's best man, but that's as far as I had gotten.

"He's a . . . *special, important* friend," I tell the waiter, who seems entirely unfazed by all of this. "Can't wait to have him stand by my side at the altar!"

The waiter launches into his spiel about the six varieties of cake we'll be tasting today. He gives us notecards and tiny golf pencils so we can jot down our reactions to each flavor. The moment he leaves to retrieve the first sample, I jab Raj with my elbow.

"So you're a groomsman now?" I hiss.

"You know I wouldn't miss your wedding for the world," he says, smiling like he's full of shit. "I am invited, right?"

I laugh hollowly. "Ha. Yeah. Sure. Invited to a wedding that will probably happen, if I can get my boyfriend to propose and marry me in five weeks flat."

His eyes bug out. "Jeez. What's going on with that?"

I fill him in on my weekend with Blake's family and the ring I know must be burning a hole in his pocket.

"You're kinda nuts. You know that, right?"

"I prefer the term 'ambitious.'"

A German chocolate cake arrives first, followed by a pumpkin spice pound cake and a vanilla cake with raspberry filling. We disagree on every cake.

"Good thing it's not you two getting married," the waiter jokes.

My favorite is the chocolate. I can't resist digging my fork into the molten, gooey center and returning to the plate until every morsel is gone. Overall, planning a wedding has been more stressful and less dreamy than I had anticipated, but this dessert is exactly as perfect as I had hoped it would be—a true highlight.

"So has Carmen told you what we're up to lately?" Raj asks, once the waiter retreats with our empty plates.

"Only a little! What's going on?"

He stretches to run his hands through his hair. "You're a genius for connecting us. The timing was amazing."

"Don't even worry about it."

He explains that Carmen had originally wanted someone to build out the entire Skindemand app right away. But Raj pointed out that that would take a ridiculously long time for a team to build, forget just one person—and she didn't really have the money to pay him properly for that anyway.

"So instead, I'm building her an MVP—minimum viable product—which is like the skin-and-bones version of the app that she can present to investors," he says. "It'll have everything she needs at this stage of the company, but it keeps the workload doable for a part-time engineer."

"Which is all she can afford at the moment," I fill in.

"But not for long," he says smugly.

From what Carmen has told me, her presentation to Cecelia Sundquist went flawlessly, and she seemed to be leaning toward making an investment. Nothing is set in stone, of course, and Carmen is still scoping out plenty of other VC firms in case this doesn't pan out. But she's by far her first choice, and I have a hunch this could work.

"And honestly, building the MVP means I get to dive into the design more than the coding, which is the piece I love the most," Raj continues.

He pulls out his phone to show me mock-ups of what he's creating for Carmen. Each slide borrows Carmen's sleek white, black, and yellow color scheme, but amplifies it to a level of polish that she wasn't quite able to capture on her own in the presentation. The app looks *real*.

"I love that you two are working together," I say.

"Worlds colliding, huh?" he says.

"In the best way possible."

The next servings of cake arrive: a strawberry shortcake, a lemon, and a red velvet with buttercream frosting. Raj and I try bites of them all, which gets increasingly more difficult as we feel more and more stuffed.

Later, the waiter returns for feedback. "Do you have any sense of what the groom's preference would be?" he asks.

It strikes me that I don't. The first time Blake and I went out for a nice dinner, the dessert menu arrived and he waved it away. He explained that he's not much of a sweets person. I was suddenly struck by how terrible it would be to live a life with a guy who only watches me scarf down cakes and pies and sundaes on my own.

"He's open to anything," I bluff. "He says he trusts me to pick whichever one I like the most."

"Which is . . . ?" the waiter prompts.

I look to Raj to back me up on this, but he simply shrugs.

"Whatever you want," he says.

This is the first time I've made a wedding decision with a guy by my side. True, he's just a guy friend, not my fiancé, but still. The significance of the moment strikes me in a bittersweet way. Not for the first time, I feel a pang of sadness. If my life had played out differently, I'd have a real partner to plan this with. Maybe he would groan over the difference between the cardstock weights on invitations, or maybe he would insist on an old-fashioned church wedding that's totally not my style, or maybe his mother would intervene and throw a fit if we didn't invite all twenty members of her book club, plus their husbands. But regardless of how the process went, it'd be a joint undertaking. Making these decisions entirely on my own feels wrong.

"The chocolate, I guess," I tell the waiter. "It was really good."

It only occurs to me hours later, after Raj and I have left Reynard's, that Blake specifically told me during that first dinner date that he doesn't even like chocolate.

· Chapter 18 ·

I realize that something is off on Saturday morning. Usually, on weekends when neither of us has anything pressing to do, we laze around in bed. If there's one thing I have to give Blake credit for, it's this: he is an excellent cuddler. His skin is warm, his arms wrap firmly around me in all the right places, and he nuzzles kisses onto the top of my head that make my entire body feel like it's glowing with comfort. But this Saturday, when I drift awake, he's tensely hunched over his phone. There's a gulf of space between us. On instinct, I roll toward him.

"Morning," I mumble, pressing my cheek against his thigh.

That's when I realize he's wearing chinos. I feel so naked. He absentmindedly rubs my back.

"Hi," he says.

"Up already?" I ask, confused.

"Yeah, couldn't sleep," he says.

He turns fully toward me on the bed and smiles. "Hey, there's something I'd like to do today."

"What is it?" I ask, suddenly suspicious.

He gives me a coy grin. "It's a surprise. I wanna take you some-where."

I summon every acting tip I gleaned from my brief dalliance with the Lincoln Middle School drama department, in which I played a tree in the seventh-grade winter production.

"You want to take me somewhere?" I repeat, lifting an eyebrow.

He dives in for a kiss. "Yeah. Get dressed."

I shift to sit up in bed. "Should I . . . dress for anything in par-ticular?"

I'm not a religious person, but in this moment, I actively con-sider praying he doesn't propose somewhere cheesy in public, like on the jumbotron at a sporting event or the crowded observatory on the 102nd floor of the Empire State Building.

"Just get dressed," he says, giving me that infuriatingly coy grin again. "You always look beautiful, no matter what."

I fish yesterday's jeans and T-shirt off his bedroom floor. Knowing that a proposal could happen at any time, I should've planned better for this moment. My hands are neatly manicured, yes, but that's nothing special. They always are. The T-shirt is old and beginning to form unsightly pit stains. I'd shower first, but I don't have any of the post-shower essentials I'd need here—no fresh clothes, no brush to detangle my wet hair, no real makeup aside from the tubes of lipstick and mascara I keep in the bottom of my purse. All I have is a toothbrush. Begrudgingly, I dress and check my reflection in his mirror. I've certainly had better-looking days.

Blake's kitchen table looks like something Martha Stewart her-self personally arranged: two plates are stacked high with eggs, pan-cakes, and home fries, surrounded by sunny cups of orange juice and steaming mugs of coffee. I realize that Blake has piped in soft jazz from a speaker somewhere.

"You did all of this?" I ask.

"Eat," he says simply, leaning in for a kiss.

We sit, but it's hard to eat or talk or relax when I know *something* is up. I want to pepper Blake with questions, but I know that it will be useless. I want to graciously enjoy this beautiful breakfast like a good bride-to-be should, but my mind is racing. Instead, I fork eggs into my mouth at a steady clip. Blake doesn't seem to notice; he seems preoccupied, too.

He checks his watch. I'm no connoisseur, but to my untrained eye, it looks like one of his fancier ones. "We should leave soon," he says.

I shovel the rest of the food into my mouth and excuse myself from the table. In the bathroom, I flip over my head and run my fingers through the underside of my hair to create volume. I reach for the tube of lipstick in my purse, but I hesitate. It's cherry red and the formula tends to smear on guys' faces whenever they kiss me. If Blake proposes, he'll kiss me, and then there will be photos. I don't want him to look like a clown in them. I skip the lipstick. My face looks colorless.

When I emerge from the bathroom, Blake is leaning against the doorway. He's wearing a navy suit jacket that's unseasonably heavy for mid-September.

"Ready to go?"

Poor thing looks terrified.

"Ready," I say, slipping my hand into his.

He exits his apartment, and when I turn to close the door, I think he sneaks a feel of his suit jacket pocket, just to make sure that whatever precious cargo he might be carrying is still there. I follow him into the elevator, across his lobby, and onto the street corner. He cranes his neck like he's looking for a car, but three available taxis with lit-up medallion numbers pass by without him hailing one.

"You don't want a cab?" I ask tentatively.

"I called us an Uber."

An Uber meant he could give the address without telling me where we were going.

"Ah," I say.

Blake has been pretty damn smooth these past few months—and it's all going out the window now. It's almost sweet to watch. It's a good reminder that we're all only human. I step back and let him look for the right Uber.

A black car pulls up in front of us a few minutes later. Blake opens the door and ushers me in first. He makes nervous eye contact with the driver.

"Hi," he ekes out.

As the driver heads toward Central Park, crosses over to the Upper West Side, and turns to head downtown, Blake stares out the window. At first, I try to guess where he's planning to propose: in one of the Central Park rowboats? At the disgustingly beautiful Natural History Museum? On a romantic side street in the West Village? But the car keeps sailing south, and I figure there's no point in guessing. I'll find out soon enough.

Ultimately, it slows to a stop by the waterfront, just west of One World Trade Center. I can see the Hudson River, and beyond that, the shoreline of New Jersey, and—wait. *Oh*. A white yacht is hitched to the pier in front of us. Blake takes my hand and leads me toward it.

"We're going there?" I ask, swallowing.

"Maybe," he says, offering that coy grin again.

He looks happier than he has all morning. Maybe the car ride calmed him down.

"Blake, did you know that I get—" I try to tell him.

But I'm cut off by a portly, fifty-something man in a white captain's uniform.

"Hello there!" he exclaims. "Welcome to Sailaway, New York's finest yachting experience. I'm Captain Edward Smith, I'll be taking you out on the water today."

The captain shakes our hands and we introduce ourselves, though it seems as if the captain has been more than expecting our arrival.

"Isn't this fun?" Blake asks. "I wanted to surprise you with a boat ride around the tip of Manhattan. The views are gorgeous, and I thought sailing would remind you of home."

Nobody in Portland walks around in crisp white sailor's uniforms. This is clearly just for effect. And if he really knew anything about my experiences with sailing—if he *really* knew me—he'd think twice.

We walk toward the yacht as a trio now. Captain Smith tells us about the history of this particular ship and the weather conditions today, and I start to panic as soon as he describes the water as "a little on the choppy side." I don't know if I should tug on Blake's sleeve, interrupt, and tell him how violently seasick boats make me. If it were just the two of us on a regular day, I might. But there's already so much pressure on this day, and I don't want to embarrass him in front of the captain. Before I can make up my mind, it's too late. We're already boarding.

We cross a gangway. The captain suggests we enjoy the view from the bow of the boat, while he disappears into the interior, presumably to steer. Even while we're docked, the gentle bobbing motion of the yacht makes me feel unsteady. When the boat starts to move a minute later, it feels like the waves rock us even harder. I clutch the guardrail. Blake doesn't seem to pick up on my discomfort. Instead, he comes around behind me, as if we're a nauseous Kate Winslet and a clueless Leo DiCaprio. I thought *Titanic* was the most heartbreakingly romantic movie on the planet the first time I watched it back in ninth grade. But I had grown up enough—and gotten cynical enough—by junior year to see that allegedly "falling in love" after three days is kind of a sham. Even saying "I love you" after four weeks, like Blake and I did, is clearly pushing it.

The yacht sails away from Manhattan and starts a wide turn, so the southern tip of the island comes into glorious view. From a distance, the city looks narrower than I'd expect, and jammed with buildings: glossy skyscrapers, mirrored towers, sturdy older buildings, and flashy new architecture press up against one another like rush-hour commuters on the subway. One World Trade Center soars majestically over it all. I try to ignore how queasy I feel so I can stay in the moment.

"This view is really spectacular," I tell him. I turn to kiss his cheek. "This is a perfect surprise. Thank you."

"I'm glad you like it," he says, breaking away from his *Titanic* pose and joining me along the guardrail. He shoves his hands into his pockets, hesitates, then plunges on. "You know, this view makes me think about when I first moved to New York. I came here for an adventure. To build something great. To become the person I wanted to be."

"I get that," I say. "I really do. I used to sit at home with a stack of magazines, reading about powerful, famous, glamorous people in New York, thinking about how big and magical my life could be here."

It's the perfect segue for me to drop in *why* I spent so many hours indoors reading magazines, because I was too seasick to join the rest of my family on our boat. But Blake clears his throat and keeps going.

"There's this quote from the writer E. B. White," he says. "I'm probably going to butcher it, but basically, he says there are three versions of New York. There's the city that's taken for granted by people who were born and raised here. There's the city that's just a nine-to-five destination for people who commute into work here. And then there's the city for people who come in quest of something. That's his exact phrase: *'in quest of something.'* He says *those* New Yorkers give the city passion. That's so clearly you, Eliza. I like to think that's me, too. And that's one of the reasons we work so well together. We want a life full of quests and passion and ambition."

Blake looks straight ahead as he speaks and so do I. My gaze is fixed on the rollicking waves below. They're stormy blue with frothy white caps. The yacht lurches dramatically, and so does my stomach. I'm nauseous to my core.

"We're a great team, you and I," he says. He turns to face me now. "I'd never be bored with you by my side. There's so much I admire about you—your big dreams, your drive to succeed, what a fundamentally *good* person you are. That's why it was so easy to fall in love with you. I love you like crazy."

If only he knew the real me, he wouldn't think I'm a good person at all. His big eyes loom overhead, but all I can see is how recklessly I had thrust my bejeweled hand out in front of me that boozed-up spring night, snapped a photo, and changed the course of my life forever. The yacht lurches again. I need to tell Blake how seasick I am. I can't hide this from him, no matter how sentimental and stunning this moment is supposed to be.

"Blake, I—"

I reach out to clutch his arm, hoping to steady myself. But my hand falls short because he's digging in his pocket and sinking down onto one knee.

"Eliza Roth, will you marry me?" he asks, voice glittering with hope.

My hand flies to my mouth, not in shock, but out of caution, in case I lose the battle with my stomach. He opens one of the black velvet boxes I've sold hundreds of times to reveal the three-carat, round-cut diamond ring I had carelessly chosen months ago. It glints harshly in the sunlight. The first thought that springs to mind is, *It's not too late to say no.* Maybe for the first time since I got myself into this whole mess, that truly sinks in. I could say no. I could reject his proposal. I like Blake; I might even love him someday. But I don't feel the kind of unshakable love in my core that I always expected I'd feel upon my engagement. I don't love Blake in the unquestioning way he claims to love me. If I were a different sort of person, that would settle the matter—that would be enough to make me walk away. I'd have to be scrappier, savvier, smarter, and maybe I'd lose Brooklyn Jewels for good. True love isn't certain, but I'm certain this isn't it.

Click. I hear what must be a photographer snapping away, and I'm reminded what drew me to Blake in the first place: he's picture perfect for me. He makes sense for me. I like him. Even if my feelings aren't as strong as I'd hoped, I'm pretty sure I can learn to love him. All good things take time—we just need more of it.

"Yes," I say, surprising myself with the strength of my own voice. "Yes, of course, yes."

Blake rises gratefully and picks the ring from its case. His hands shake as he slides it onto my finger. I flex my hand under its familiar weight. It looks so right and so wrong at the same time. He kisses me deeply, squeezing his hands around my hips and pulling me close to him. The boat rocks fiercely under our feet. The white-knuckled control I've managed to hang on to thus far evaporates. Nausea rolls through my stomach. I push Blake away just in time to vomit over the boat's guardrail. I retch and sputter. My throat tastes sour and feels raw.

"Eliza!" Blake yelps. I feel his hands scrape my hair back from my neck, but he's too late. He misses everything hanging by my face. I gag again at the sight of puke in my hair.

As if this isn't horrifyingly shameful enough, I hear the photographer continuing to click away. I squeeze my eyes shut as I wipe my mouth and try to catch my breath. It's not a stretch to imagine these images going viral.

"I should've told you I get seasick," I say. My voice sounds ragged.

"I had no idea," Blake says, looking slightly green himself. "I swear."

"I guess it never came up," I offer weakly.

A man in a white sailor's uniform comes rushing forward with a bottle of water.

"Ma'am, ma'am, are you feeling all right?" he asks.

I drink as much as I can handle in one sip. "I will be. Can we head back to land?"

"Of course, I'll tell the captain right away," he says.

"God, I had no idea," Blake says, shaking his head. His eyes are still wide with horror. "I just assumed, you know, growing up in a boat shop in Maine . . . this would be your thing."

"If it were, wouldn't I have said something?" I ask. There's a sharp edge to my voice.

I feel myself tense again, and this time, it's not from nausea. I don't want this to be our first fight. I don't want to ruin the moment any more than I already have. I exhale deeply. I can let this go.

"No, you know what? It's fine. It's not a big deal. I'm just so happy to be with you, and to be *engaged* to you."

"For a second there, I freaked out that you were throwing up because you regretted saying yes," Blake admits.

I'm mid-sip, so I can't respond right away. He freezes.

"You don't regret this, do you?" he asks.

My heart races. The way I play my next line will mean everything. Thankfully, my voice comes out steadier than I feel.

"Blake, I'm madly in love with you and I can't wait to be your wife. I'd kiss you right now if I didn't smell like vomit."

There's a set of stairs leading up to the roof deck in front of us.

"Let's get away from the edge of the boat," I say. "The center rocks less than the sides."

I climb up and Blake follows. There's a cocktail table draped in a white tablecloth and sprinkled with red rose petals. On top is an ice bucket chilling a bottle of Dom Pérignon and two crystal champagne flutes. The man in the sailor's uniform runs up the stairs to the roof deck.

"The captain is heading back now," he announces. "I don't know if you still . . . would you, um, like champagne?"

Blake gives me a concerned look. "I don't know if that's the best choice for you right now?"

I feel like shit, but the water has washed the foul taste from my mouth. I can't ruin today for good.

"The bubbles will settle my stomach," I say, aiming for bravado. "It's like top-shelf ginger ale. Let's pop that bottle and celebrate."

The boat attendant laughs. "You've got quite a fiancée there, sir," he says.

Blake rubs my arm appreciatively. "Don't I know it."

Once the Dom is popped and poured, I clink my glass to Blake's.

"Hey, at least the photos will be unforgettable," I joke.

"Ugh. I'm sure. Speaking of which, the photographer can get some shots of the ring. That's a thing, right? I did some research."

I laugh. "Yes, it's a thing. I'm sure I look disgusting, but I guess photos of my hand would be all right."

Blake picks up my hand and studies the ring. "Sophie told me this was your favorite piece Brooklyn Jewels has ever made," he says, shyly meeting my gaze. "It's quite a piece of jewelry."

"I know it's a little much, but thank you. You have no idea how much this means to me."

"Don't even mention it. It's a special ring for a special woman."

He ushers over the photographer, who runs me through modeling all the classic shots I know well: my left hand slipped into Blake's, splayed out against the backdrop of the Manhattan skyline, wrapped gently around my new fiancé's arm. The photographer works quickly.

"She knows what she's doing," Blake brags to him. "She does this for work."

"Hand model?" the photographer asks.

"Definitely," Blake deadpans. He shoots me a look and stifles a laugh.

For the rest of the ride, I lie across a row of seats with my head in Blake's lap. He doesn't mention the bits of vomit clinging to my hair. Our champagne flutes sit untouched on the floor by his feet. Even up here, on the roof deck, I can feel every lurch and wave. But I don't think that's the sole reason my stomach continues to roll.

· Chapter 19 ·

A few hours later, I'm nestled under the covers of my own bed with my laptop opened to the Wythe Hotel's site. Blake had brought me straight home, then went to Duane Reade to pick up saltines and ginger ale to settle my stomach. I take this time when he's gone to focus. I don't have time to feel queasy; I need to prepare for a pivotal moment in this months-long plan. If I can't convince him that a whirlwind trip down the aisle this fall at the Wythe Hotel is a good idea, then I'm stuck. That would mean potentially canceling on the Wythe—with no guarantee that I'll ever be #blessed enough to be offered a practically free #sponcon wedding ever again. I don't think I've ever had such a high-stakes conversation in my life. Above my laptop, my palms are glossy with sweat.

I hear the click of the lock. Blake is back. I had given him my keys so he could let himself in and out for this errand, and he had simply beamed.

"I guess we'll have to make each other copies now, won't we?" he said. "That is, until we're living under one roof."

Right, let me just add *that* to the to-do list: stage a wedding, save my business, find a new apartment in the most competitive housing market in the entire country. I don't have a shred of mental bandwidth to devote to moving right now. I can't even fathom where we'd live. I wouldn't want to move too far away from the shop, and I also can't imagine Blake living anywhere but his Upper East Side bachelor pad. I try to picture a compromise, but nothing materializes.

Blake hands me the saltines and ginger ale, then joins me on the bed.

"Looking at venues already?" he says, craning his neck to look at my screen.

"Yup."

"Should we, I don't know . . . call our families and tell them the news?"

I turn and blanch. Given the events of the past few months, I can't guarantee that Mom and Dad will have a sunny reaction over the phone, and I can't risk letting Blake hear whatever they have to say. I snuggle closer to him and drop a kiss on his temple.

"Why not just enjoy this day together? We can tell people tomorrow," I suggest.

"Fair enough," he concedes. "Show me the places you're looking at."

I launch into a hastily rehearsed speech about how much I've loved the Wythe Hotel ever since I moved to Williamsburg.

"I've been there for parties, and I'd just die to get married there," I say. "The rooftop has the most gorgeous view of the Manhattan skyline."

I can't breathe as I watch Blake's face for flickers of expression. It wouldn't be surprising, after all, if he preferred a stuffy ballroom uptown somewhere—or worse, a beloved family venue in Massa-chusetts.

"Hmmm," he says, tilting his head.

Blake pulls the computer onto his lap and clicks around on the site to see more photos. I try to breathe. Up until this point, I truly hadn't considered a plan B. I've pulled off the impossible again and again: finding a ridiculously eligible boyfriend at the exact moment I needed one, having him fall in love with me, and even propos-ing with the ring of my choice. I'm a goddamn fantasy machine—if something as mundane as Blake's taste in wedding venues throws me off course now, god help me.

"It's nice," Blake says finally. "I've been to the rooftop, actually, for a friend's birthday. The view is sick. But I guess it'd depend on how much it costs."

"Oh! My parents would pay for it," I fib. "They paid for Sophie's venue. Tradition, you know?"

"That's incredibly nice of them. I mean, this place is sweet. I'd be down to consider it, for sure."

"I'm going to send them an email, if that's cool?" I ask. "I'll see what dates they have open."

"Cool," he says.

I type up a quick email to the hotel staff while Blake watches over my shoulder. I can't let him see me not hit Send; I cast around for any excuse to get him away from me.

"Hey, would you mind turning on the AC?" I ask. "It's getting kind of stuffy in here."

He hops up from the bed, and I close out of the message. I can tell him the truth eventually—I'm just not ready to share it with him now.

"Sent," I say. "I'll let you know what they say."

He sits back down, slides an arm around me, and pulls me close. He buries a groan into my shoulder. "I didn't realize how much there would be to think about now! Budget, venues, caterers, groomsmen, and whatever else is probably on your secret Pinterest board?"

It works in my favor that he thinks I've been dreaming about my wedding forever, so I go along with it.

"I've got, like, half that stuff covered. Pinterest rules," I say. But his point jogs something important. "Actually, speaking of that, there's one thing we should probably get out of the way now."

"Yeah?" He shifts to get a better view of my face.

"I want a prenup."

Blake's face falls. "You're thinking ahead to divorce already?"

"No, no, no," I say. "Not at all. But I'm just trying to think practically here to protect both of our businesses. This isn't about our relationship—it's about our careers."

Blake bites his lip. I can tell by now that that's the face he makes when he's considering something deeply. The idea came to me one night a few weeks back, when the creeping sensation of guilt prevented me from falling asleep. This way, if we sign a prenup and Blake ultimately finds out the truth about why we got married so quickly, he'll be able to walk away without the fear of me keeping half his assets. It's the only fair thing for me to do.

"It's not exactly a romantic idea, is it?" he points out.

"No, but a marriage is more than just romance," I counter. I hesitate and continue. "It's about building a life together. Protecting each other."

"Let me think about it," he says. "We have time to work it out."

I take a deep breath. "Sure. Plenty of time. Let's go back to looking at the fun stuff, then."

Once the tension is broken, ideas begin to flow. It's fun to dream

up themes, toss around wedding songs, debate if it's tacky or ador-
able to smash cake in each other's faces. We talk about how the ceremony could combine his Episcopalian traditions with my vaguely
Jewish ones. He says he'd like to leave a chair empty to honor his
father. I savor how normal it all feels—just me and my new fiancé
planning a beautiful wedding together, the way millions of couples
have done before us.

It's moments like these in which I feel closest to Blake. When
chemistry crackles between us and I can lounge comfortably in his
arms, it's easy to forget how or why our relationship began. All of that
fades away, and it's clear that I could fall in love with him someday.

Blake is scrolling through wedding photos on Pinterest when it
hits me: maybe I already do love him. The sensation of love might
be buried under layers of anxiety and guilt and panic, but it's still
there. Blake makes me feel sturdy and safe. He's sweet, caring, and
thoughtful in a way I've never experienced before. I appreciate how
steadfastly transparent he is with his feelings—there are no games.

It's true that if I had met Blake under different circumstances, I
would have wanted our engagement to play out differently. I would
have liked to date for two or three years first, and I'd rather accept
a proposal on land than bobbing away at sea. But despite those differences, I can't ignore that my feelings for Blake have become very
real. I snuggle closer to him and rest my chin on his arm. Absentmindedly, he squeezes my thigh.

"What do you think of these?" he asks, clicking to enlarge a
photo of leafy green centerpieces.

"I love them. Let's do it," I say, burrowing a kiss into his bicep.

"You don't want to look around?" he asks tentatively. "Don't you
need to, like, make sure they match your bridesmaids' dresses or fit
with the vibe of the venue?"

I can't help but laugh a little bit.

"Come on, I've seen my brother and all my cousins and some friends get married. I get how this works," he says.

"They're perfect. I want you involved in making these decisions, too. I love you."

He beams. I can figure out how to get my hands on those centerpieces later.

By the time Blake and I consider getting out of bed the next morning, it's nearly noon. Truthfully, I could lounge under the covers with him forever. Our luxuriously lazy mornings in bed are one of my favorite parts of our relationship. Together, we could spoon while debating brunch delivery options for hours. But the moment he grabs my hand and admires the way my ring sparkles, I snap out of my sleepy, sex-addled, sun-drenched reverie. I don't have time to waste: if my plan is going to work, I have to set it into motion today.

"I'm glad Sophie told me to go with this one," he says, tilting my hand so the diamonds catch the light. "It's an impressive piece."

I flex my hand and try to see the ring through fresh eyes, the way he does. "Yeah, it's amazing," I say, kissing his cheek.

I reach for my phone on the nightstand and pretend to scroll through my notifications. He grabs his from the other side.

"Wow, okay, so I got an update from the hotel," I say finally.

He looks up from his screen. "Yeah?"

"They're available almost two years from now, or . . . they had a cancellation, so they have one date randomly open next month. October nineteenth," I offer.

"So, maybe we go somewhere else, then," he says, returning his attention to his phone.

I try not to panic. I double-check today's date on my phone. It's September fifteenth. The wedding is approaching so soon, I can practically count the days. If I can't get Blake on board with an October nineteenth wedding at the Wythe Hotel, there won't *be* any wedding. At least not on this accelerated timeline. For the first time, I dare to think past October, and I can imagine a scenario in which I have Blake, no wedding, plummeting sales, and eventually, no more Brooklyn Jewels. Would Blake care? If my ambition and drive and success are what attracted him to me in the first place, would he even still want me as a floundering failure? Without the hook of a wedding to spike sales, why bother getting married so soon anyway?

I clear my throat. I have his attention again.

"The date is October nineteenth. I know it's crazy soon, and it'd be such a whirlwind, but wouldn't that be fun?" I ask, amping up the enthusiasm in my voice. "Why bother waiting if we know we just want to get married?"

He puts his phone facedown on the bed and gives me an amused look.

"You really want to do that?" he asks.

I nod and give him my best hopeful look.

"I don't know, isn't that too soon?" he asks. "Don't we need more time to plan everything?"

"Hotel weddings are so easy," I say. "They're catered, everything is done for you. You just, like, bring your own dress and suit and guests."

He suddenly stops smiling. "You're not pregnant, are you? Is that what the rush is all about? Because if you *are*, that would be a major surprise, but still exciting, um, I mean, if you want it to be exciting news, and I would—"

"Blake, stop," I say, playfully hitting his arm. "I'm not pregnant.

I guess I just got a little too caught up with the excitement of getting married and thought a whirlwind wedding would be fun."

That much at least is the absolute truth.

"You really like this place?" he asks.

"I do."

"You realize it's crazy fast to get married a month from now, right?"

"Oh, fully."

He's silent for a moment. Then, just when I'm ready to shake him for a response, he gives me a smile.

"Let's do it," he says, giving me a kiss.

"Really?! Oh, thank you, thank you, thank you!"

I can't help but sink into his arms as an overwhelming wave of relief washes over me. I hope he can't feel the way my hands tremble. After all this time and effort, I can barely fathom that my plan is coming together seamlessly. It doesn't feel real. But it is: Blake Barrett and I will be married at the Wythe Hotel on Saturday, October nineteenth.

💍

There's still one more thing to do to kick this wedding into motion. Once Blake leaves my apartment later that afternoon, I dial my mom. When she answers, I ask if Dad is around. He is—he always is. I ask her to go get him and put me on speakerphone. This isn't how I imagined having this conversation. If anything, I had envisioned bringing home a fiancé they already considered a son. Our first dinner together over the summer was lovely, but sharing one pleasant meal doesn't mean they're ready to welcome him to the family.

"I wanted to let you know that Blake proposed," I explain.

"Oh my god!" Mom blurts out.

"*Eliza*," Dad says heavily.

"I know it's soon—*so* soon, trust me, I do—but I really do love him. I think this is going to work."

"You think?" Dad asks.

I hate that I tripped over my words. "I love him. The wedding is in October."

I brace myself for the reactions, and sure enough, they respond the way everyone does: "This October?" they screech.

"Why so soon?" Mom asks.

I take a deep breath and tell them the sweetest possible version of our proposal story, leaving out the fact that I threw up. I describe how beautiful the venue is, and how it's miraculously free. They don't sound thrilled, but at least they've stopped interrupting me with horrified comments.

"Wow," Mom muses. "Free. You really do have a knack for business, don't you?"

"I know it's been a hectic few months, and I know this all seems incredibly fast, but I really am so happy with Blake," I offer.

"If you're on board, we're on board," Dad says.

"Really?" I ask.

"Honey, I always thought you'd elope to Fiji, or never bother getting married at all," Mom says. "If this is what you want, we're just happy you're happy."

I think back to Sophie's wedding—how traditional it was, with the band playing old-fashioned classics and the caterer serving seared salmon. At the time, I assumed it was because Mom and Dad preferred not to stray from the norm. But now that they're so supportive of my own plans, I wonder if I had it all wrong. Maybe they just want us to be *us*, quirks and all. With my family's support, convincing Blake to jump into a wedding just thirty-four days away doesn't seem quite so preposterous anymore. I had once worried that hiding this wedding scheme from Blake created distance between us, so that he couldn't ever fully see the real me. But maybe he understands exactly who I am: spontaneous, impulsive, not content to settle for tradition. And it gives me comfort that I'm doing the right thing.

· *Chapter 20* ·

On Saturday afternoon, Sophie is bent over her kitchen counter, grimacing. Liv stands behind her with a look of pure concentration as she wields a syringe filled with a cocktail of hormones designed to prep Sophie for the next round of egg retrieval. My job is to lean over the kitchen island, grip Sophie's hands, and keep her distracted. I ask her to describe the glamping resort upstate that she's visiting next weekend for her friend's thirty-fifth birthday celebration.

"They have these A-frame wooden structures, kind of like a permanent tent or, like, an angular yurt? It's decorated all Scandi style, and there's apparently this gorgeous farm-to-table restaurant on the premises," Sophie explains.

"Sounds super chic," I say.

Sophie's eyes squeeze shut in pain as Liv inserts the syringe into her backside. She breathes deeply. The hormones should trigger her body to produce multiple eggs this month instead of just one. If she does, then she'll be scheduled for an egg retrieval procedure, at which point, the eggs will be combined with samples from their sperm donor. They chose a guy who could pass for Liv's cousin, if not her brother, half for his looks and half because his application noted that he's a jazz musician. They liked the idea of passing along creative genes.

"You're good, you're done," Liv says, rubbing her back.

"I know," Sophie says, hitching up her pants with a heavy sigh.

I had come by for brunch at the new Israeli place that opened in their neighborhood. This is just the sideshow beforehand. Over shakshuka and coffee, Liv grills me on wedding details. She's no-nonsense in that way; having gotten past the initial shock of my plan to lure Blake into holy matrimony, she's only concerned with logistics now. She wants to know exactly how many Instagram photos I need to post in order to get each vendor to comp their services and if I can get a photographer that way, too. I've always liked how straightforward and unsentimental she is. In some ways, she's easier to talk to than Sophie, who gets emotional over everything. And not just because of the hormones.

My phone lights up with incoming texts from Blake. My heart leaps when I realize what he's sending me: photos from our engagement.

"Let me see, let me see!" Sophie crows.

She grabs the phone and unlocks it from memory—she knows the passcode is the date we officially launched Brooklyn Jewels—and thumbs through the photos. I peer over her shoulder. I didn't even realize the photographer had caught the first few, when Blake and I were talking on the bow of the ship. The crashing waves must have covered the sound of the photographer's footsteps. Blake and I both look tense, our shoulders creeping toward our ears. An outsider might not be able to tell, but I certainly can—I look nervous.

Then there's a series of shots that capture Blake gallantly sinking onto one knee. His face is upturned and hopeful. My eyes widen and my posture hardens. One hand flies to my mouth while the other holds my stomach. I look miserable. But then there's a shot where I'm caught mid-word—that must be when I said yes. In the following shots, Blake kisses me passionately. And then, of course, there's a shot of me projectile vomiting over the guardrail while Blake leaps toward me in horror.

"Now, *there*'s a photo for Instagram," Liv jokes.

"I can't believe he caught that on camera," Sophie says, shaking her head in amusement.

"Ugh. I can't believe he sent those," I groan.

Sophie laughs and briefly zooms in on the disastrous photo before swiping toward the next one. The final few shots show off my ring. I can't help but notice a slight glisten of fluid smudged alongside the back of my hand. I must have wiped at my mouth. Of course, there are traces of vomit in these photos—that's just my luck. Or maybe it's karma.

"I'm going to post some of these on Facebook to share the good news," Blake texts.

Shit.

"Wait!" I write back.

We're about to move into dangerously murky waters. Once Blake announces our engagement, it's all but guaranteed that his friends and family are going to look me up online. I can pretend all I want that the old engagement announcement was Jess's, but there are too many other red flags: the slew of wedding blogs that covered my engagement; the *Elle* story referencing my fiancé; the hundred thousand Brooklyn Jewels followers who already think I'm engaged, and who won't react smoothly to a new engagement announcement.

Simply put, the more public Blake and I get, the more difficult it will be to hide the truth from him.

"I thought you'd be all over posting them, huh? Miss Instagram Photographer," he teases.

"What does he want?" Sophie asks.

"Wait for me to get there?" I text.

"Sure. When?" he replies.

My stomach sinks.

"I could come over now?"

"Cool, see you soon."

I run my hands through my hair and groan. "I'm off to Blake's to post our engagement announcement, I guess. I'll see you later, if I survive."

"Don't be so dramatic," Sophie admonishes.

"The girl got engaged to a near stranger while vomiting off the side of a yacht," Liv says, cracking up. "What else would you expect?"

"Not funny!" I exclaim, gathering my purse and heading out the door. "Not funny at all."

It takes almost an hour on the Q train to get from Park Slope to the Upper East Side, and I spend every minute running through plays in my head. Is there any wording I could suggest to Blake for him use in his announcement that would deflect suspicion? Is there any cover story plausible enough to explain away the truth? There's no caption I could use that looks appropriately excited for Blake's friends and family, while remaining business-as-usual to my own followers; no matter what I say, it'll look off to *somebody*. I Google myself, just to see what pops up in the top results. At first, I exhale: there's a link to Brooklyn Jewels's site, then my Instagram, then my LinkedIn. But sure enough, farther down the first page, there's a link to that *Elle* story. Could I reach out to the editor and have it pulled down? No, she wouldn't do that.

By the time I exit the train, I know what I have to do. There's only one option left for me—the right thing. The hardest thing. My stomach rolls like it did on the boat, but this time, I'm standing on solid ground. I walk the few blocks to his apartment from memory now; I've grown accustomed to the route and don't need to rely on my phone's directions anymore. When I reach Blake's apartment, the doorman waves me up automatically.

"He called down to tell me he's expecting you, Eliza," he says.

It's the first time his doorman has remembered my name. That's no small feat in a big, bustling building like this one. It's a New York relationship milestone.

"Thank you," I say, moving toward the elevator.

Inside, I fix my gaze on my reflection in the mirrored walls.

"You got this," I say out loud. "Everything will be fine."

The doors slide open on Blake's floor, and I jump at the sight of a woman entering the elevator.

"Oh!" I blurt out.

Great, so, I'm caught talking to myself. This bodes well.

The woman pauses in the elevator threshold. She cocks her head.

"Eliza, right?" she asks.

It clicks. "Oh, you're the girl from the coffee shop." The one who recognized me.

"Yeah." She holds the elevator door open for me to exit, then she enters.

"I was just, uh, talking to myself. I don't usually do that."

"Everything will be fine," she says with a smirk.

The doors slide shut. I feel watched and panicked. When I turn the corner, I see the door to Blake's apartment open. He's standing in the doorway, looking as handsome as ever. He takes an eager step forward to kiss me, catching the edge of the door with his foot.

"Hi," he says, smoothing back my hair. "I missed you."

He kisses me again and it feels like a salve. I shouldn't worry—I've never had to worry around him. Blake has always made me feel calm. Inside his apartment, he crosses the living room easily in a few bounding steps and crashes onto the couch.

"So, ready to do this thing or what?" His energy reminds me of a puppy.

"You know, actually, I was thinking on the way over here—is now the right time to post the photos? Shouldn't we, I don't know, savor it, just us, for a little while longer?" I sink onto the couch next to him.

His face falls slightly. "We have been savoring it," he points out. "Do you not want to post anything?"

"No, no, I do. Of course, I do. I was just, you know . . . checking."

He looks at me skeptically, then pulls out his phone and toggles through his photos.

"I was thinking this one," he says, turning around his phone to show me the shot of him down on one knee and my hand clapped over my mouth. "I love how surprised you look," he adds.

"Ha. Yeah."

He screws up his mouth. "Is everything okay?"

I freeze. I feel caught. "Yeah. No, I'm sorry for, um . . ." I trail off, unsure of what I'm apologizing for.

"It's a big step," he concedes. His fingers drift across my thigh. "I get it if you feel nervous. I don't want to push you into doing any-thing you don't want to do."

His eyes are round and bright with concern. I savor this view;

this could be the last moment he looks at me with any sympathy ever again. I'm terrified to tell him the truth, but I've let this ruse play out far too long. As awful as coming clean could be, the alternative would be even worse.

"Blake, there's something I need to tell you," I say, forcing the words out of my mouth before I lose my nerve. "About how we met."

"Yeah?" he asks.

"I . . ." I inhale deeply. I already feel light-headed. "I accidentally posted a photo on Instagram the night before I met you. A photo of myself wearing an engagement ring. And people thought I was really engaged."

"Okay . . ." he says, giving me a confused look.

"So the night I met you, my plan was to find a guy who could ultimately pose as my fiancé."

He cocks his head and furrows his brow. "Why, though?"

"There was so much more interest in Brooklyn Jewels," I explain. "I've never seen such a spike in sales before. I would've taken it down, but we really needed the money, especially since our rent is going up and we can't afford the new lease. And then . . . and then I met you. And things were going so well. I wondered if a wedding would drum up sales the way that 'engagement' did," I explain, making dramatic air quotes.

He simply stares at me in disgust.

"Everything happened so fast," I add. "A publicist offered me a wedding for free at the Wythe Hotel, and then there was a dress, and there was just never a good time to tell you about all of this because we were falling in love for real."

"So you've been using me this entire time," he says flatly.

"No! I mean, maybe it was convenient at first, but—"

He visibly flinches.

"But then it felt real! It *is* real. I know it's hard to understand, but I'm not lying when I say I love you. You can't say that what we have together isn't real."

"I can't? Because to me, it sounds like you manipulated our entire relationship for the sake of padding your own wallet," he accuses me.

"You proposed of your own accord," I say, jutting my chin out. "That was all you. And I was happy to say yes."

He looks at me with such bitterness, I could shatter.

He gets up from the couch and crosses the living room to lean against the kitchen island. He clutches it like it's keeping him upright. I can't help the hot tears welling up and threatening to spill onto my cheeks now.

"You used me to turn a profit and never bothered to clue me in. That's not love, Eliza."

"Please, Blake, listen," I plead. I'm dangerously close to the verge of hyperventilating. "I know that was wrong. I need to make this up to you. But you said it yourself when you proposed—we would have the best life together."

There's a long silence in which he stares at me with dead eyes. I'm too afraid to break eye contact.

"Eliza," he says quietly—so quietly I almost can't make it out. That's scarier than if he yelled. "Get out. We're done."

I can barely feel my feet as I rise from the couch.

"I'm going, I'm going," I say. I slip my shoes on and grab my purse.

He's still stony-faced and frozen in the kitchen.

"Go," he says simply.

So I leave and close my fiancé's door behind me, possibly for forever.

· *Chapter 21* ·

When I wake on Monday morning, my eyes feel sealed shut with schmutz. They're swollen like grapefruits from crying all weekend. Everything feels grubby and grimy: the dark smudges of makeup on my fingers and pillowcase, my greasy hair, my sweaty bedsheets. Outside, the sky is alarmingly blue, as if it's midday instead of my usual 7:30 a.m. wake-up. In a panic, I grab for my phone on the nightstand. It's nearly noon. Of course, I forgot to set my alarm last night. There are several texts and missed calls from Sophie.

"Accidentally slept in, coming soon," I type back, then throw my phone onto the other side of my bed.

I certainly don't *feel* as if I slept in. I was up until at least 3 or 4 a.m. as my mind churned through the same scene over and over again. I replayed Blake's bitter gaze, the cold horror of the moment he understood what I had done, and the pained way he refused to even sit near me. I couldn't help but anxiously wonder what would happen to Blake, what would happen to my company, and how this would all play out in the press. I know that I deserve every inch of panic and misery and self-flagellation. I hurt someone for my personal gain, and in the end, it might not even matter. Maybe it's karma. Maybe I deserve to lose everything.

I drag myself out of bed, throw on my most comfortable jeans and an oversized, thrifted men's button-down that's so shapeless I can get away without wearing a bra, and head into the bathroom. I simply run a makeup-removing wipe underneath my eyes, pull my hair back into a bun, and shuffle out of my apartment. I don't deserve to look any better than this.

Jess jumps when I enter the shop. "Oh, *hi*," she says. She can't disguise her alarm at my appearance fast enough.

"Hi," I say.

I'm surprised at how croaky and gruff I sound. Jess is helping a couple try on engagement rings, and they flinch as I lumber across the shop. A happy couple cooing over my own diamond rings is truly the last sight in the world I want to see right now.

In the back of the shop, Sophie is slurping a smoothie while using Matrix, a program that jewelers use to develop photo-realistic, computer-aided design models of new pieces. It's the last step of the design process before turning a sketch into a tangible piece of jewelry.

"Oh god, you look terrible," she says.

"Thanks," I wheeze.

Sophie is in Helen's leather chair, so I take one of the gray folding chairs across from her and sit down.

"What happened?" she asks tentatively.

"I told Blake the truth. He broke it off," I explain.

It's the first time I've said those awful words out loud. They don't sound real.

"Eliza, I'm so sorry," she says, reaching her hands across the table to grab mine. "I am so, so sorry he did that."

"Me, too," I say, sniffling.

"Are you okay?" she asks.

The expression on her face is one of pure pity. I shake my head; I'm too overwhelmed to speak. All I want to do is crumple up on my big sister's shoulder and bawl. I want to cry big, fat sobs and have her rub soothing circles on my back and stroke my hair. I lean forward and let her envelop me in a hug.

Ultimately, though, I can't relax in her arms. We have more pressing problems than my heartbreak. I try to inhale evenly to calm my jagged breath.

"Sophie, you realize what this means for us, right? For the business?" I ask.

Her face falls. "*Oh*," she says grimly. "Talk to me."

I straighten up. As upset as I am, my feelings aren't my only priority right now. I'm the one who got us into this mess—I have to be strong enough to pull us out.

"I thought we were on track to making enough money to re-sign the lease in October," I explain, willing myself to stop whimpering. "But that was when I was factoring in a wedding and banking on a huge spike in sales and press coverage and new customers."

I open my laptop on the table and show her our finances.

"See, everything looks fine here," I say, showing her the page with our current numbers. Then I click to another page. "I recalculated everything with predictions for what would happen with an increased rent and a smash success of a wedding."

"That looks pretty good," she observes.

"But then . . ." I click to the next page. "Look what happens when I calculated for a rent hike and no wedding."

Her face falls. "We run out of money," she says softly.

"We run out of money *fast*," I confirm.

She bites her lip and hesitates before asking, "You don't think . . . you don't think there's any way to get Blake back, do you?"

The thought of facing him again makes me want to disintegrate. "I'm not giving up just yet, but I think we need to prepare for a reality in which the wedding is off," I say.

She smooths her hands over her furrowed brow and is quiet for a moment.

"What if we lay off Jess?" she asks, just softly enough so that her voice won't carry into the other room.

"I would feel so guilty doing that," I whine. "And we really do need her help. You have more than enough on your plate with design and filling orders, and I can't always be available to do sales. We rely on her to make this place run—you know we do."

"What if we shut down the brick-and-mortar store and went online only?" she asks.

We've talked about the merits of a physical storefront versus a digital-only presence before, back when we were first planning to launch the company and weren't sure how big we dared to dream. Back then, we agreed: a storefront brings in foot traffic and lends a covetable air of legitimacy. It's a sign of a healthy business. And selfishly, we both felt that we grew up in a store—so damn it, we wanted one of our own.

Not all of our competitors have brick-and-mortar stores. Some rent tiny work spaces in nondescript office buildings where they see customers by appointment only. Some work with clients over Face-Time, though I'm not sure that would require enough man power to necessitate keeping Jess employed. There's a precedent for this; I've seen other jewelry businesses make it work. But it wouldn't feel as special. I'd feel like a failure.

"I know it's not ideal, but it seems like our only real shot right now," Sophie says.

"I worry about what that would do for our reputation," I reply.

"What, because being forced out of business entirely would be better?" she points out.

I can't help but think back to a few months ago, when I was brimming with limitless, optimistic energy for everything that *could* happen. Sure, I had a diamond ring and no man and no plan, but I felt full of possibility. It was exciting. I had choices. Now it seems as if I made the wrong ones. Like Sophie said, the cat's out of the bag, I've gotten emails from writers and editors at various wedding magazines and women's sites offering to cover my wedding if I agree to interviews. Hell, there's a seamstress out there somewhere making alterations to my wedding dress right this minute to tailor it exactly to my body. Whether it's well-advised or not, there *is* a wedding under way, and that could still save the business.

"I'm not ready to give up on our store just yet," I say finally. "I don't know how I'm going to fix this. But I have to try."

"Coming over for a drink," I text Raj the minute I leave the shop that night. "I seriously need one."

"What's wrong?" he writes back.

"Ugh. I'll tell you in person," I respond.

Golden Years is unusually crowded when I walk in; every bar stool is taken, and a party of customers stands and nurses drinks while hungrily eyeing seats along the bar. When Raj spots me, he waves me over to the seat farthest from the door. I weave my way through the crowd and am greeted by a tower of mozzarella sticks and an entire pitcher of beer.

"I figured you needed more than just *one* drink," he says, beaming at the spoils between us. "And I saved you a seat from the birthday party brigade."

For the first time in more than twenty-four hours, I actually smile. I settle onto the stool and immediately jam the topmost mozzarella stick into my mouth while Raj pours me the first glass of beer.

"Ugh, yuh uh ah-ul," I say, attempting to call him an angel with my mouth crammed with fried cheese.

"So what happened?" he asks.

I mumble an explanation into my plate so I don't have to see Raj's expression. "Blake and I broke up," I say quietly. I can practically feel the girl next to me straining to listen, and I don't have any interest in winding up in her viral tweet about the heartbroken mess she overheard at a bar. "He was ready to announce our engagement, and I just couldn't let him go through with it. Not before he knew the truth about why I pursued him and the wedding I'm planning. So I told him, and, well, he got upset."

"Eliza, oh no," he says, grimacing. "I'm so sorry. That really sucks."

It's what he says next that catches me off guard. "How are you holding up?" he asks.

I don't deserve any sympathy. I shrug and look down at my plate so I don't have to see Raj's expression.

"Hey, hey. Breakups are the worst. You don't have to put on a brave face," he says.

"Yeah, but I deserve to feel this awful," I point out.

"Maybe this wasn't your finest idea, but you're a good person," he says. "I know you are. Otherwise, you wouldn't have come clean to Blake at all."

I don't know if I believe him. I have a sudden craving to bite my nails or pick at my cuticles—anything to distract me from my feelings—but I know I can't.

"So that's it? The wedding is off?" he asks.

"I don't know. Probably. I just—I don't know. I wonder if I can talk to Blake."

He grimaces again. "That might be tough. After, you know, stomping all over his feelings."

His words spur me out of self-pity and into motion.

"Oh, shut up," I say, lightly tossing a mozzarella stick at his forehead.

He ducks just in time and flashes jokey finger guns my way to let me know he doesn't actually think I'm a dick. Or at least I hope that's what he means. He darts off to help a customer.

While he works, I scroll morosely through Instagram. It looks like Holden and Faye went to a wedding together this past weekend. He posted a photo of them posing in formal wear; she commented underneath, "My forever wedding date ♥." I grind my teeth so hard they could shatter into dust.

Raj is still working. I feel frantic with desperation. If anyone would know what to say to make me feel better right now, it would be Helen—she's the one I should be talking to about this. I draft an email to her:

> Hi Helen,
> How are you doing? I know it's been a while. I'm sorry I haven't called more often. I miss you.
> Brooklyn Jewels isn't doing well. Our rent is going way up this fall, and I don't know if we can necessarily afford it anymore. Well, that's not quite true—I know that we can't. I thought I had a plan to work it all out, but everything has fallen through, and—

Raj sails back toward me with a hopeful look in his eyes. "You look miserable. What would make you feel better? Drinks? Distractions?" he offers.

"Distract me, please. That would be perfect," I say, saving and closing the email before I can finish it.

There's nothing I can say to Helen without sounding like a failure anyway. I don't want her to see me like this; she'd be disappointed.

"Well, *my* day has been a little less dramatic than yours, but I got to make some awesome progress on Carmen's MVP—the minimum viable product," he reminds me. "It's not finished yet, but I think she's going to be really happy with it. I mean, I hope." He knocks on the wooden bar.

"Cool," I say, wishing I could sound as genuinely enthusiastic as he deserves.

"I considered working out this morning, but then just got honest with myself and canceled my gym membership, which I've used maybe twice in the past two months," he adds.

"Ha," I say. It sounds morose; I can't even laugh properly.

He thinks for a moment, then pulls out his phone. "I'm just gonna show you the cutest baby animals on the entire internet, okay?" he says.

Sure enough, a moment later, I'm looking at a wobbly-legged baby alpaca that appears to be more fluff than actual skin and bones. Next, he shows me a GIF of a pile of wriggling newborn golden retrievers, and then the most precious tuxedo kitten I've ever seen. It's a lot. The reptilian part of my brain is delighted by all of this; I actually squeal.

"Aha!" he says triumphantly. "A smile. I got it. Be right back."

He snags one of my mozzarella sticks, quickly scans the room to make sure nobody needs him, and then ducks into the room for employees only. I bide my time, sipping my drink, eating my snacks, and people-watching instead of scrolling through my phone. But eventually, I have to check the time. Fifteen minutes have passed. It's weird that Raj has been gone for so long. I can see customers getting antsy, too: nearby, it looks like a first date has run entirely out of steam, one stares boringly off into space while the other cranes for the check. Two people are actively pressed up against the bar, waiting to place drink orders. Where is Raj? I consider texting him. It's especially weird for him to vanish with no warning while I'm here. It's sort of become an unspoken rule between us: I'm not just here for the drinks anymore; I'm here for our friendship. Even if he's technically working, Golden Years is a chill place for us to hang out.

Just as the first date couple looks as if they might die of boring conversation, Raj emerges. He does a quick round of attending to customers: taking drink orders, offering refills, printing checks. He swings by my end of the bar.

"How's it going over here?" he asks.

"Everything okay?" I ask.

"Oh, yeah, yeah, yeah," he says, running a hand through his hair. "All good. Hey, did you hear what Trump tweeted today?"

"Oy, no, I must have missed it."

"Okay, so . . ." he says. His eyes bulge out.

As we talk about politics and minor bartender drama at Golden Years, and the ridiculous sexcapades of Raj's roommate, the fog of sadness that's followed me around since yesterday begins to clear. Raj is a fierce conversationalist—he has this way of talking passionately with his hands and listening closely that makes me feel like he really cares. From time to time, he has to dart away to take care of a bar patron, but he always returns to pick up the conversation seamlessly.

And then suddenly, Raj glances past me toward the door of the bar. It's loud in here, but I can just make out familiar voices. I turn and see Sophie, Liv, Carmen, Jess, and even Sasha and Caroline from college. I haven't seen Sasha and Caroline in months—I can't believe they're here. The group weaves their way through the crowd to surround me with hugs.

"Surprise!" they shout.

Carmen places a rhinestone tiara on my head, and Sophie is carrying a small bunch of sunflowers wrapped in paper.

"You guys! What are you doing here?!" I squeak.

They look sheepishly at Raj. "It was his idea," Jess explains.

I spin back on the bar stool to face him. "You did all this for me?"

He scratches the back of his neck and blushes. "I may or may not have snuck into the back to text Carmen, who helped organize this whole thing."

"Raj!"

"You said you wanted a distraction! I figured a surprise party would be a pretty good one."

I feel overwhelmed with love and support, not to mention a little choked up. It's been an active day for my tear ducts. I reach across the bar to give him the biggest hug I can manage from this angle.

"You're amazing," I whisper into his ear.

"It's a little short notice for an engagement party—or a breakup party or whatever this is—but I wouldn't miss it," Sasha says.

"Anyway, this sounds juicy, so . . ." Caroline says. She's never missed a good piece of gossip in her life.

I roll my eyes and laugh. Who knew I could still laugh? "Ha, it's a doozy."

I look around at the bar. "Mmm, I don't see any more seats right now, but maybe some will open up?"

"Actually, I got another bartender to cover the rest of my shift,"

Raj says. "He'll be here in a minute, and then I thought we could go up to the roof."

I'm floored by how quickly he pulled together such an incredibly thoughtful gesture.

"Dude, I love you," I blurt out.

"God, stop pretending to be in love with *everyone*," Carmen groans. "I can't keep up!"

· Chapter 22 ·

The eight of us slip through the employees-only room in the back of the bar, into the stairwell, and up six flights of winding, concrete stairs. When Raj pushes open the heavy door to the roof, we're greeted by a dusty blue dusk sky and a sultry late-summer night. The still-warm air is thick with possibilities. Raj has two pitchers of beer, a few of my friends are holding stacks of glasses, and I have Sophie's sunflowers clutched to my chest. There's a jaw-dropping view of the Brooklyn Bridge and the lower Manhattan skyline across the East River; when I get close enough to the edge of the roof, I can see my own building just across the street. There are glittering lights and other rooftop gatherings as far as the eye can see.

Raj knows Carmen, of course, but this is the first time he's meeting the others. I want to jump in to introduce everyone, but it turns out I don't need to. He's at ease with the group. He introduces himself to Sasha, who writes about dating and relationships for *Esquire*, and her best friend, Caroline, who has a sweet writing gig on *Law & Order: SVU*. Sasha lives just a few blocks from me, but we haven't seen each other that much since I launched Brooklyn Jewels, other than accidentally crossing paths while getting breakfast at Bagelsmith's a few times. I feel guilty about that. She was amazingly helpful when I was getting over Holden for the first (and second . . . and third) time.

I lay the sunflowers down along with my purse, grab one of the pitchers from Raj, and start filling glasses to pass out to the group. Carmen digs a speaker out of her bag, and soon a smooth electronic beat turns the gathering into a real party.

"Shouldn't someone make a toast?" Sophie asks.

She's not drinking tonight, but she'll always look out for me, like a big sister should.

"Yeah, a toast!" Liv echoes.

She at least has seen her fair share of breakup parties and divorce celebrations.

"Cheers to Eliza!" Carmen announces. "Cheers to my most brilliant, beautiful friend, who works harder than all of us combined every single day to make her dreams come true . . . and . . . and . . ."

I think she falters because she's trying to spin the reason for this party—my newfound single status—into something that doesn't sound terribly depressing. It's hard.

"And cheers to you being single," Raj interjects, raising his glass and looking directly at me, "because now we can commiserate while swiping through Tinder together."

"I'm down to cheer you on, but I don't exactly think I'm in any condition to date," I say, dramatically gesturing at my mad scientist hair and puffy eyes. "I look like a real catch right now, don't I?"

"Come on, you look great," Raj says.

"Maybe a little concealer around the eyes . . ." Jess offers.

"Oh, shush, you guys will both be *fine*," Sasha says, rolling her eyes.

I look around at a group of people who have all dropped whatever they were doing to be here with me, simply because I needed them.

"I have good people to get me through this," I say.

On that note, everyone clinks drinks and toasts with calls of "Cheers!" and *"L'chaim!"* People splinter off into separate conversations.

It's true that I feel more sad, scared, and—above all—guilty than I ever have before. But I'm pleasantly surprised to find that being surrounded by my friends means I don't feel alone. I try to imagine what Blake is up to right now—binge-watching *Mad Men* with a glass of scotch? Scoping out new girls at Dorrian's? It hurts to wonder. Instead, I scan the party, find Raj in the midst of conversation with Sasha and Caroline, and plunge into their circle to give him a hug. He jumps a little, caught off guard by my touch.

"You're amazing, you know that, right?" I say.

"Eliza!" he shouts, laughing. "You thanked me already down at the bar."

"I know, I know," I say, breaking away. "But, seriously, Raj. Nobody's ever done this kind of thing for me. It's just . . . you're a real friend."

He shrugs. "Yeah, I guess I'm amazing, then."

I drift through the party, mostly listening in on my friends' conversations, too overwhelmed by love and support and—honestly—exhaustion to contribute anything substantial of my own. Liv gives Carmen legal advice about registering as an LLC. Caroline is peppering Sophie and Jess with questions about diamond cut and clarity; it sounds as if she wants her boyfriend, Owen, to pop the question soon.

At one point, my friends roll out a series of embarrassing stories from college for Raj's benefit, zipping from my most victorious keg stand at a Bushwick loft party to the time I may or may not have made out with three off-duty sailors so they'd buy me and my friends a round of Jell-O shots.

"She's *so* much calmer now," Raj swears.

"Ha, *right*," Sophie says, shooting me a look of teasing sisterly love. "Because we all know Eliza is amazing at impulse control and playing it safe."

I pull out my phone, take a video of my perfect crew of friends against the backdrop of the city, and post it to Instagram Stories.

"You have the best goddamn life," one follower messages me back.

I want to believe that's true.

Two hours later, we're still on the roof, sitting cross-legged in a loose circle, draining the last of the beer. The conversation has turned into swapping stories of our worst breakups. The group crowns me the de facto winner, but there are some brutal runners-up. Raj finally tells me what really happened with his ex—apparently, she broke off a three-year relationship in the middle of his birthday dinner. Sasha recounts the time her boyfriend matched with her coworker on Tinder. Jess once dated a guy who abruptly ended their summer fling by announcing "I can't do this anymore" in the middle of a hookup.

Commiserating with my friends takes away some of the sting of my drama, but I still feel almost nauseous with guilt. My friends' breakups weren't their fault. And as hurtful as each one was, they were relatively low stakes, with fewer strings attached. My friends didn't mess up the way I did—they didn't break anyone's heart. I have a sinking suspicion that most breakups happen because the spark fades, or two people realize they aren't so compatible after all. I don't know anyone who triggered a breakup in such a calculating manner.

All night long, I've had a jolt of anxiety every time I feel my phone vibrate. Logically, I know it's probably just an Instagram notification or an email from J.Crew alerting me to the millionth sale they've had since I accidentally opted into their email list six years ago. But I can't help but fantasize that it's Blake. I miss the tiny, daily bursts of affirmation I felt every time he texted me. Half of me wonders if it's my job to reach out first and apologize; half of me thinks it's most respectful to give him the space he seems to want. But with a wedding planned for just four weeks away, and the potential fate of my business hanging in the balance, I don't know if I can afford to wait for him to come around.

I've been in a depressive fog all day, but there's a clock ticking on a wedding. I don't have the luxury of wallowing—I need to come up with a plan to move forward. There's too much at stake. I owe Sophie, Jess, and my parents a real chance at saving Brooklyn Jewels; I owe it to myself. I have bleary fragments of ideas floating through my brain, but they don't gel together into any cohesive plan. I don't mean to tune out of my friends' conversations—especially when they gathered here to pull me out of this miserable funk—but it's hard to focus.

There's a shred of a chance that I could apologize to Blake, he could cool off, and we could patch things up just in time for a wedding. I don't believe he would ever fully forgive me for hurting him, but it's not the craziest thing in the world to imagine that he would consider a marriage as a business partnership. He's said it himself:

together, we're a power couple. I can imagine us merging businesses, or cross-promoting our companies, or creating a luxury accessories empire together someday. He's ambitious. He could understand. I would just have to convince him that this strategy is the right one.

But I'd be a fool to rely on that plan. Sure, I'm a cappuccino-half-full kind of girl, but I'm not an idiot. I wouldn't blame Blake if he was permanently disgusted by me. He's a romantic at heart. He stocked his fridge full of cheese just because he knows it's my favorite; he messengered a gorgeous watch for me to wear when he whisked me away to a gala; he proposed on a yacht, for god's sake. I can't imagine he'd settle for me as a wife now. He probably thinks I'm a cold-hearted bitch. He's probably right.

Maybe calling off the wedding really is the right plan after all. I could put this entire mess behind me. It's not like I've shelled out deposits for the venue or the dress or the honeymoon—I've managed to get almost everything for free, save for a few expenses, like the pair of blue satin pumps I impulsively bought online. But telling my followers that Blake and I called off our engagement would only stir up more questions and drama, and given that I sell happily-ever-afters for a living, it would probably tank my reputation for good. (Not to mention that explaining to my nosy aunt Linda why she needs to get a refund on her airfare would be a special nightmare of its own. I would never live that one down.) If I walk away from the wedding, I don't think Brooklyn Jewels would survive. My credibility as a businesswoman would be shot. The company certainly wouldn't make it through the fall without a serious downsizing. I'd hate to lose the store. It would be awful to say goodbye to Jess. Sophie, Liv, and my parents would feel a real financial blow. And if the company ultimately fails, I'd be devastated.

I have a hazy beginning of an idea, but I don't know what to make of it. I'm definitely not emotionally prepared for it yet, and I don't know if it's even possible. If—and this is a Mount Everest–sized *if*—I could find a guy willing to pretend to be my groom, could I pass us off as a couple? Could we stage a wedding? It wouldn't have to be legally binding. It would only have to look real. I could let Blake heal in peace and give him the space he deserves; my reputation would survive intact; I could make a last-ditch attempt at saving Brooklyn Jewels; and even if the sales spike from a wedding isn't enough to justify signing the new lease, at least I'll have tried.

But I don't think I'm strong enough to do that right now. Missing Blake feels like the deafening roar of an airplane engine in my ears, like a gut punch, like bumping a deep purple bruise. Even if I could manage to pull off a fake wedding, I don't think I could make it down the aisle without tears in my eyes and a lump in my throat. I can't fathom having enough space in my head or heart to welcome a new relationship—not even a fake one.

I'm brought back to reality by Jess's hand on my shoulder.

"Hey, I have to go," she says apologetically. "I really hope you're okay. I'll see you tomorrow, yeah?"

"Oh!" I stand up and feel a rush to my head. "Yeah, yeah, of course. Thanks for coming out. It really means a lot to me."

She hugs me goodbye.

"We're actually going to head out, too," Sophie says.

She and Liv take turns saying goodbye.

"Honestly, consider this a bullet dodged," Liv says. "The divorce rates for couples who meet and marry in under a year are astronomical, believe me."

"And *there*'s the annoyingly practical comment I'm sure you've been holding in for months," I retort.

She holds up her hands. "Just telling the truth."

"Oh god, let's go before you make this worse," Sophie says, pulling her wife toward the door. Then she turns back to me, calling out, "Love you! Night."

The rest of the group starts to stand, now that the circle of people has been broken.

"You okay?" Carmen asks. She rubs my arm sympathetically. "You kinda spaced out there for a bit."

"Yeah. No? I don't know," I say, shrugging. "This has been the best night, really. It's all just sort of hitting me. You know, the pile of shit I've buried myself under."

"You'll find your way out," Sasha says encouragingly.

"And if not, you should go see my therapist," Caroline suggests. "She's amazing."

I would probably benefit from a good therapist session or fifty, but I don't know if I'll even have health insurance in a few months.

"I'll let you know," I say, sighing and pulling off my rhinestone tiara. It's giving me a headache.

"No more princess look?" Raj teases. "It really suited you."

I roll my eyes at him and drop into an ironic curtsy. "Look, I think I'm going to call it a night," I say. "Thank you all so much for being here for me."

"Of course," Carmen says.

Raj grabs the empty pitchers and we all grab the glasses. As we leave the roof behind, I take my sunflowers with me. Downstairs, the bar is still thrumming.

"How's it going?" Raj asks the other bartender.

"Dude, I gotta thank you," he says. "The tips are lit. I'm glad you called me in."

"Want me to stick around?" Raj asks.

"Nah, I got it covered," his coworker says.

"Eliza, I know this is a living nightmare right now, but it'll be okay in the long run," Carmen says, squeezing me into a tight hug. "I love you."

"Boys suck, you don't," Sasha says—I think that's her way of saying goodbye.

I watch my friends make their way toward the door, and I lose sight of them once they're outside. I hate that that gives me a pang of sadness. We aren't in college anymore; it's not like I should reasonably expect any of my friends to stay by my side all night, distracting me with gloriously tacky early 2000s music videos and homemade cookies. I should be strong enough to deal with this on my own. That's how grown women cope with heartbreak, isn't it?

"It's okay to be completely miserable," Raj says, as if he understands exactly what I'm thinking. "I mean, this is bad. Really bad."

I laugh hollowly. "Yeah. It is. Even though it was all my fault."

He rubs my shoulder sympathetically. "It was not your fault."

"Of course it was!" I exclaim.

"Relationships are a two-way street," he says. "Maybe you weren't honest because he didn't make you feel comfortable enough."

Raj's suggestion makes my thoughts shift and ooze in a way I don't know how to process.

"Let me walk you home?" he offers.

"Sure, thanks," I say.

I gather my things. He holds the bar door open for me. The walk to my apartment is barely thirty seconds, even if you count waiting for the crosswalk signal to change. But it's just long enough for me to make up my mind.

"Raj, would you, um, want to come up and hang out?" I ask, lingering by the door to my building. "I don't mean anything, you know, like that. I just thought we could talk or watch TV or whatever."

Even in the darkness, I can see him blink twice.

"Never mind, forget I said anything," I say, turning to unlock the door.

Is there anything I can do right lately?

"Wait, Eliza," he says. He reaches out to grab my wrist. "I'll come up."

"You don't have to," I say. I can feel my cheeks starting to burn.

"No, really, I don't mind," he says.

I bite my lip. "Okay," I say simply. "Thank you."

· Chapter 23 ·

I open the front door, lead Raj upstairs, and unlock the door to my apartment. I'm no longer embarrassed by the clutter. He's seen worse pieces of me. He plops down comfortably on the couch. I take two seltzers from my fridge, hand him one, and sit down on the opposite end of the couch.

"All right, you are officially graduating to step three of Breakup School," he says, grabbing my TV remote.

"Step three?" I ask.

"We already accomplished step one, which is alcohol and snacks," he says seriously. "And step two, which is forcing yourself to hang out with friends, so you can't just cry alone into your beer."

"I see, thank you for guiding me through this," I say, mimicking his no-nonsense tone.

"So step three. We have to find the ultimate distraction on Netflix. Sappy romances and cute rom-coms are strictly off-limits, which means we either need a dumb buddy cop thing or a really disturbing horror movie."

I love that Raj can make the worst day of my life into something remotely bordering on fun.

"I think I want the TV equivalent of comfort food," I say. "So . . . *The Office*?"

"Are you sure you're emotionally prepared to watch Jim salivate over Pam right now?" he asks.

"I think I can handle season one. He's hard-core friend-zoned."

"*The Office* it is," he says, queuing it up. "A personal favorite."

The ottoman is only wide enough to cover half the couch, so I slide it toward the center so we can both use it. He scoots a little closer to me and kicks up his feet. I prop up my feet, moving carefully so that our legs don't touch.

As the first episode rolls, Raj quotes Michael's lines and does impressively accurate impressions of Dwight and Stanley. When it's over, I'm relieved that he clicks the remote immediately to begin the next episode. (Only a person with freakish self-control could stop after just one, and let's be real, that's not my strong suit.)

At some point during the second episode, I realize that Raj's leg has brushed up against mine, but I actually don't feel weird about it. The adrenaline rush from the surprise party is tapering off, and I just want to relax. I slouch down so my head rests against the back of the couch. A few minutes later, I shift in my seat to get more comfortable and find my head leaning against Raj's shoulder. Neither of us flinches. I wonder if he cares—but if he did, wouldn't he move?

There's a third episode, and maybe a fourth, and then I lose track of what happens next. It must be midnight. Raj's arm slips around my shoulders. I shift on the couch to curl up with my head on his chest. The last thing I remember before drifting off to sleep is how easy it is to lie in his arms.

The next thing I know, a hand is stroking my hair. Last night floods back to me: Raj threw me a surprise party on the roof of Golden Years. He walked me home and we put on *The Office*. And that means . . . that means we're still curled up on the couch together. That hand in my hair? It's his. Not Blake's. Raj's.

I'd be lying if I said I was totally clueless that he might be into me. The signs are all there: he sends me free drinks; he usually texts me first; he goes above and beyond what a casual friend might do (hello, that surprise party). Even though that all seems glaringly obvious in the morning light, with his fingers gently smoothing down my hair, they were easy to push aside until now. I had my sights set on Blake. I had a boyfriend. Nothing could have happened between me and Raj, so I never bothered to address the chemistry between us.

But now that I've fallen asleep in his arms, I can't ignore it. The seamless way we slipped into instant banter the first time we met? You can't fake that. And I've been on enough dates in the past decade to know that the way he makes me laugh is truly rare. With Raj, there are never any awkward silences or boring lulls. We don't *make conversation*—we just talk. Often. Easily. I like his warm, brown eyes and wide smile. I've definitely had some lingering thoughts about the way his forearms look when he pushes his sleeves up.

The sound of his voice makes my heart race.

"Hey, you awake?" he asks.

"Yeah," I say, sitting up.

I can't quite face him right away. I run two fingers under each eye to wipe away the dark makeup smudges I can guarantee have appeared overnight. I'm embarrassed: not only am I probably all smudgy, but my morning breath can't be amazing, and I have a hunch my hair has mussed in the least sexy way possible. I take a deep breath and turn back toward him with a look that says, *Hello, I hope you remember I usually look more attractive than I do right now*. Because suddenly, I care.

"I turned off Netflix after the fourth episode," he says.

"Sorry I fell asleep on you," I say.

"Don't worry about it," he says.

He has a loose eyelash on his cheek, and before I realize what I'm doing, I brush it away.

"Eyelash," I explain.

He looks away and rubs his jaw. He's grinning, and I don't know what to do with that information.

Before my brain can catch up to my body, I lean into Raj, turn his chin toward mine, and kiss him. His lips are soft and his body is warm. I kiss him again, yearning for something more from him— more passion, more tenderness—but his posture stiffens. I pull back and inch away from him on the couch.

"Shit, I'm sorry," I apologize. "I don't know why I thought you wanted that—that you felt like that."

I've never felt self-conscious in front of Raj before, but suddenly, I worry I'm too much in every direction: too messy, too impulsive, too careless with his emotions. I feel the sinking sensation I've felt all spring and summer long, as if I've raced off the high dive without checking to see if there's water below.

"I—uh, you—" he starts to speak, but shakes his head and pauses to collect himself. He clears his throat. "I don't want you to feel pressured into anything just because I stayed over."

"I don't feel pressured into anything at all," I say quickly.

He swallows and looks at me nervously. "I don't want to be that guy who swoops in the minute a girl is single, you know? That's not why I'm here. I came as a friend. Really."

"A friend," I echo. "Oh."

"I mean, ugh, Eliza." He mops a hand over his face and gives me a pained expression. "Look . . ."

"I don't think it's shady of you to swoop in here, for the record," I say. "Remember, *I* invited *you* up. I wanted you to be here. I still want you to be here."

"True," he concedes. He glances down at my knee, like he's considering putting his hand there, but he refrains.

I bite my lip and twirl a loose strand of hair around my finger. It doesn't seem to matter how much practice I get talking about my feelings with guys; it never gets any easier. I know that if I say what's really on my mind out loud, I could ruin our friendship for good—and right now, I can't afford to lose anyone else. But despite what's at stake, I need to know how he really feels.

"You haven't always wanted to be just friends, right?" I ask.

He freezes. "I won't lie, I liked you," he admits. "But you weren't single. And if we weren't going to, you know, date . . . hanging out with you is awesome. I'd be an idiot to give that up."

I take a deep breath and steel myself to get real with him. "So here's the thing. When I invited you up last night, I wasn't expecting anything beyond friendship. At all. But having you sleep over . . . I don't know, it's made me see things differently."

"Differently?" He cocks his head.

God, vulnerability is terrifying.

"I want to kiss you again, if that's okay," I say.

I hope I sound confident and sexy, like a woman who knows what she wants and isn't afraid to ask for it. But Raj doesn't lean in to kiss me. Not at all. Instead, he hesitates and pushes himself backward on the couch.

"Eliza," he says softly.

"Yeah?"

"I'm here if you want me," he says. "But you have to choose me. For real. I'm not just your fallback guy for when you're sad. You can't kiss me because you feel lonely after your breakup. It's not fair for you to only hang out with me at the bar when there's nothing better for you to do."

I feel my cheeks burn in shame. I can't look at him. My first thought is to sputter, *I don't do that*, but I know that's not true. I feel like I've been caught naked and exposed. I want to tell him that he deserves better than to be my second choice, but suddenly, there's a lump forming in my throat. I was the one who overstepped a boundary—I don't get to cry in front of him. He's too much of a stand-up guy; he'd probably wind up comforting me. Again.

"I get it," I say, keeping my eyes cast downward. "I do. And I'm sorry."

"Don't apologize," he says, standing up and stretching. He ruffles his hair. "All I'm saying is that if you like me, treat me like you do."

I stand up, too. I don't know where to look, or what to do with my arms, or what to say to cut the suddenly thick tension between us. I place my hands on my hips, decide that might look too confrontational, and let them go limp by my sides.

"I didn't mean to give you mixed messages," I say. "But you're right."

"Yeah, I know," he says coolly. "No need to figure out anything right now. But if you want to talk, you know where to find me."

He heads toward the door and reaches for the knob.

"Eliza?" he says, turning back to look at me. "You have to slow down. Breathe. Take your time. There's no rush."

I try to force a smile. I wish I didn't have a deadline hanging over my head—the soft noise of the ticking clock drowns out all other sounds. I have to wonder: if there wasn't a reason to tie up my love life in a neat bow by October, would I be into Raj? For that matter, would I really be into Blake?

"Right, no rush," I say softly. "Bye."

He leaves my apartment. The front door clicks shut. I listen to the fall of his footsteps as he descends the stairs and exits the building. He's gone. I sprawl out belly-down on the couch, reveling in the warm spot Raj left behind, and press my face into a throw pillow.

So it's clear: I fucked up. I was right about one thing—Raj *has* liked me this whole time. I wasn't imagining the crackling chemistry between us; I didn't hallucinate the affectionate way he looks at me. But that doesn't mean I had the right to kiss him the moment I felt alone and confused and comfortable. Raj deserves more than a girl who's not done crying over someone else.

It's not fair for me to kiss Raj if I can't commit to being there for him, the way he's been there for me. I need to work out my own shit before dragging another person into it. I'm deeply mortified that none of this occurred to me *before* I tried to slip my tongue into his mouth.

The ugly combination of shame, humiliation, and rejection I feel in Raj's wake piles onto the lingering sadness, guilt, and panic I've carried ever since my breakup with Blake three days ago. I feel utterly and totally miserable, and it's entirely my fault for being such an impulsive idiot. I can't prolong my body's natural reaction anymore. I sob big, fat tears into the pillow and let myself cry until I'm worn out.

When I'm done, I wipe my tears and straighten up on the couch. I might be able to process that failed kiss with Raj another time, but there's one thing I have to do first. I fish my phone out from between the cracks of the couch cushions, open a new text message, and type in Blake's name.

"Hi. I know you must be angry at me right now, but if and when you're up for it, I'd love to talk. I have a business proposition for you."

· *Chapter 24* ·

I enter Starbucks five days later like I'm greeting a wounded, skit-
tish kitten: avoiding any sudden movements that might scare him
off. Blake ignored my first text, and I thought he might ignore my
second one, too, but he surprised me with a single-word answer:
"Why?" It took days to convince him. Rather than volley texts back
and forth every few minutes, like we used to, he sent just one reply
per day. I couldn't tell if he really needed that time to think about
my request, or if he simply wanted to punish me by drawing out our
conversation. Either way, I deserved the torturous wait.

He requested I meet him at the Starbucks two blocks from his
apartment, even though there are plenty of other cute coffee shops
in the neighborhood. The Starbucks here is forgettable, entirely de-
void of personality and charm. We could be anywhere in the world
right now. If this conversation turns out to be haunting and awful,
at least it won't ruin his regular coffee spot, the indie café on his
corner.

It takes me a minute to locate Blake. He's at the table farthest from the entrance, with a drink in front of him, and dressed in a light blue, collared button-down that's too formal for a Sunday morning. He's dressed for a business meeting. It hits me that *I* am the business. He stands when I approach; I spread my arms to give him a hug, but he doesn't show any signs of reciprocating. A handshake would be too weird, so he doesn't try that, either. I clasp my hands tightly in front of me.

"Hi," he says.

It's strange to hear him speak again, after more than a week of silence between us. The usual warmth in his voice has evaporated.

I eke out an awkward, "Uh . . ." before swiftly sitting down.

"You don't want coffee?" he asks, taking his seat again.

I glance at the cash register, but the line stretches halfway to the door. I don't want to make him wait for me. "Nah," I say. "I, uh . . ." I clear my throat and try to summon the strength to speak. I had been so paralyzed with nerves on the subway ride up here. "I wanted to talk to you. Thank you for giving me the chance."

He rests his chin on his interlaced fingers. He's waiting for me to say my piece.

"First, I'm sorry," I begin. "I'm deeply sorry for all the ways in which I abused your trust and hurt you."

He raises one eyebrow. I think that's my signal to continue.

"I should've been honest with you from the start. Well, maybe not at Dorrian's. But I won't lie: At first, being with you felt like a game. Like as long as I played my cards right, I could strategize this perfect future for us and bring it to life. But then, once we started falling for each other, things changed. There were times I wanted to come clean, and I wish I had, but I was too afraid that you'd react badly and that everything would be over. I was selfish, and for that, I'm sorry."

A line of stress creases his forehead. "'Once we started falling for each other'?" he repeats bitterly.

"Maybe you fell first," I admit. "But I did really care for you. You have to know that. I couldn't fake that."

"No? You faked everything else," he retorts.

I take a deep breath to keep the pangs of panic in my chest at bay.

"I was wrong, and I know it, and I'm sorry. I know that's probably not enough. But it's the truth."

"So, basically, you're saying you loved me, but not enough to be honest with me."

I feel breathless with shame. I wish I had a coffee to sip, or at least the cardboard sleeve to fiddle with. Right now, I could tear it to shreds.

"Blake . . ." I begin. But the words don't come.

"I'm guessing you came here because you want something from me," he says sharply.

"I . . ."

"Don't lie," he says. "You always have an agenda. I know you."

"Blake, I . . . I . . ."

I stumble over my words. He deserves to hear what I have to say, but I'm surprised by how difficult it is to explain what I want. I wish I knew how to tactfully suggest he marry me in a legally nonbinding wedding ceremony, but there's no rulebook for how to do that. I'm overwhelmed.

"God, Eliza, be *honest,* just for once!" he explodes.

I'm sure that caught the attention of other people here. I feel so enveloped by embarassment.

"Okay, look, I wasn't going to say anything unless you seemed potentially open to it, because my first and biggest priority here really was to apologize," I begin. "And again, *I am sorry*. Truly, I am. But if you want it, here's the truth: my company is in serious trouble. I won't be able to afford to re-sign my lease unless there's a major spike in sales, and based on everything I know, the interest in a wedding would lead to exactly that."

"You haven't called off the wedding," he guesses.

"No," I admit. "Not yet."

"And you came here because . . ." he says, prompting me.

I don't know if I can say it out loud. I give him a meaningful look, hoping that'll communicate everything I need him to know.

"Say it," he chides.

I gather my courage. "I came here to ask if you would go through with it for me. Walk down the aisle. Marry me."

My words hang in the air.

"You're unbelievable," he says, looking stunned.

"It wouldn't have to be legally binding," I add quickly. "It just has to look real. For my customers. We don't even need to get a marriage certificate."

He takes a long, contemplative sip of his coffee. Since this idea first occurred to me, I've tried to ponder how this would sound to him a thousand different times. Every time I come up with a slightly different answer. The truth is that a handful of months is hardly enough time to get to know someone. After all that Blake and I have been through, I've scraped just the surface of who he is. The layers of complicated nuance that we all have underneath can't be cracked so easily. That comes with time. And that's the one thing I don't have on my side.

Finally, he speaks. "This really is just business for you, isn't it?"

I consider what to say. I love him, but not in the way a wife should love her husband. I love him as one of many possible routes my life could take—currently, he's the best and safest one—but he's never been my one and only. I can imagine myself happy with any number of other lives, and I have a sinking feeling that happily engaged couples don't feel that way. Aren't we supposed to feel like we've found the most complementary match? The great love that we've been waiting for all our lives? The other soul that aligns perfectly with our own? I can't say in good conscience that I'm here out of love. So I go with the truth. It's not romantic, but it's honest. I owe him that.

"You and I make sense together," I explain. "Our customer base is essentially the same, only I sell women's jewelry and you sell men's. Separately, we each have our own appeal, but together, we'd be unstoppable. Two breadwinners on one team. Think of us like Beyoncé and Jay-Z, or Bill and Hillary Clinton."

He raises a skeptical eyebrow again. "Because those marriages are so strong," he says coldly.

This is why I loved him.

I sigh. "The personal stuff, we can work on. But just think about it from a business perspective. I've been getting incredible press lately—wouldn't you want to be named in that? What if we cross-promoted our brands? What if we collaborated on a line together? I mean, you have to admit we'd be a natural fit to work together."

He gives me a tight smile. "I used to think that."

". . . but not anymore," I finish for him.

Blake sighs and doesn't answer. He drums his fingers against the lid of his coffee cup and doesn't meet my eyes. I wish I could tell what he was thinking. The silence stretches on longer than makes me feel comfortable.

"October nineteenth?" he asks suddenly.

"What?"

"The date of our wedding," he says impatiently. "I mean, the date of the wedding. Your wedding."

"Oh, yeah. The ceremony starts at four p.m."

He nods carefully. I'm suddenly light-headed with anticipation for what he might say next.

"I'm not saying yes to you right now, but I'm not saying no, either," he says, still looking away. "You've made a solid case, and I need time to think it over."

He pushes his chair back and stands. This conversation is over. I skid back in my chair and stand, too. This time, he looks like he's contemplating whether or not to hug me. I hesitate before turning to walk toward the door, but the hug never comes. Instead, he lowers his eyes and walks past me across the coffee shop.

"Goodbye, Eliza," he says quietly. "I'll be in touch."

· Part 3 ·

October

· *Chapter 25* ·

It's Thursday. My wedding is nine days away. It's been a week and a half since I spoke to Blake at Starbucks, and a week and a half of anxiety. I'm fielding letters and emails from Roy, the landlord, about whether or not we'll re-sign the lease and a flurry of wedding-planning tasks that trigger actual waves of nausea, and I've been skipping out on Golden Years to avoid Raj, because I don't know how to speak to him with the respect he deserves while I'm still waiting on an answer from Blake. My romantic situation is too complicated. I'm tiptoeing around Sophie and Jess and dodging my parents' calls, because I can't talk about the shop or our company's finances without a lump forming in my throat. My Instagram posts have gotten more and more desperate, in hopes of squeezing out any sales possible. At this point, I would be posing naked with all the important bits covered by diamonds if it meant I could sell them. For the sake of keeping my bases covered, I'm still pretending online that the wedding will happen. If I need to cancel it, I'll do that—but I don't want to shut down that option before I need to.

Even though it's time for happy hour, I don't have the energy to trek to Bunna Cafe in Bushwick for Ethiopian sangria, or to Otto's Shrunken Head in the East Village for tiki drinks with tiny umbrellas. I text Carmen that I feel wiped out, and I can only handle something local.

"Let me buy you a drink at Hotel Delmano," Carmen texts.

"You don't have to do that," I write.

"You'll return the favor with the open bar at your wedding," she jokes.

"Don't jinx it," I fire back.

Hotel Delmano is a cocktail bar in Williamsburg that used to be on my regular rotation of first-date spots. The menu has an impressive variety of concoctions using ingredients like green chartreuse, cacao, yuzu, and beet juice. The colorful pink-and-blue walls are artfully faded, and the curved wooden bar is the most elegant thing in the neighborhood. Most crucially, it's less than a five-minute walk from my apartment. Carmen and I meet after work, and immediately order a round of cocktails and enough oysters to cover every available square inch of the table.

"Any news from Blake?" she asks, once the waiter has left.

I shake my head miserably. "Still nothing definitive. I texted him a few days ago just to check in again, but nothing."

"Ugh," she says.

There is nothing more she can say on the topic. *Ugh* just about sums it all up.

"Any news from Raj?" I ask.

"What, you still haven't spoken to him?" she asks, sinking down in her chair.

I shake my head again. "Not since he stayed over."

"Come on, Eliza, seriously?"

I groan. "It's complicated!"

I never understood how someone could develop feelings for two people at once—I assumed that was only in the realm of cheesy rom-coms, *The Bachelor*, and people in open relationships. But lately, I've come to the uncomfortable realization that I can want both men at the same time for different reasons. Once I let myself acknowledge that, the full extent of my crush on Raj burst into bloom. Stuffing it deep down inside of me while I wait for Blake's response has been torturous.

"I don't want to mess with Raj's feelings, you know?" I tell Carmen. "I feel stupid that I kissed him when he didn't want to kiss me back. He basically said that he likes me, but I don't treat him the way he deserves. It would be cruel for me to sulk about Blake in front of him. And right now, waiting for Blake's response is all I can think about, so . . ."

She bites her lip and gives me a sympathetic look. I know that she talks to Raj regularly because they work together now.

"He's fine when it comes to work stuff, but I don't know, he seems a little bummed lately," she says. "I don't know him as well as you do, obviously, but he doesn't totally seem like himself."

"Poor guy," I say.

"Poor guy," she echoes. Then, after a pause, "Do you *like* him?"

"Of course I do," I say automatically. "I'd go for him if I could, but I feel like I have to give Blake a chance to come back, since I asked him to. It's like I can't even begin to consider Raj as a real option until I know what's happening with Blake—not because Raj is my second choice, but because I've already made myself unavailable."

"So you'd settle for Blake, but if not, you'd rather date Raj?" she asks.

The waiter returns with our drinks and oysters, and I'm grateful for the interruption. We clink glasses, offer each other sips of our respective cocktails, and slurp down an oyster each.

"So . . ." she prompts again, when it's clear I'm putting off an answer.

I groan. In high school, when I couldn't fall asleep at night, I used to lie awake, imagining what my life would look like when I was older. I tried to envision how my face would mature into an adult one; I dreamed about the expensive jewelry I could finally afford to buy; I assumed that someday, there would be a job and a husband, just because that's what adults did. The idea for Brooklyn Jewels was far off. But I knew I wanted a career that felt like a big fucking deal—I wanted something meaningful and exciting that I could build my life around. But beyond that, the details were hazy.

Sometimes, I was an executive at a *Fortune* 500 company and married to the kind of husband who wears a suit and lives in a penthouse in New York or London. Or sometimes, I was the breadwinner, while my husband was a high school teacher or a stay-at-home dad, and we lived in a charming house with a garden out front in the suburbs. Certain dreams involved becoming a Hollywood stylist madly in love with a sexy guitarist who serenaded me on a sheepskin rug in front of a roaring fireplace when we escaped to our mountain house on weekends. It didn't matter precisely what the future held, because in each iteration of the fantasy, it always felt right. On those sleepless nights, it never occurred to me that I'd someday have trouble figuring out which choice was right for me.

The thing is, I finally grew up. The time to pick a version of the future is now. And I don't know what to do.

I've been banking on the fact that Blake coming around to a publicity-stunt wedding would be the best choice, but *is* it? Would

I be better off in the long run if I embraced my feelings for Raj? Or should I forget about my love life for a second and scrap Brooklyn Jewels because something even better is around the corner? Plenty of entrepreneurs fail the first time around. Maybe all I need is to put my head down for a year or two to come up with a sleek, sharp business plan for a new company. I wish I could fast-forward through life to see which choice will make me the happiest, but I know there's no way to do that.

I want to be the kind of woman who would live her life exactly the way she pleases, regardless of whom she's with (or if she's with anyone at all)—like Helen did. But I know enough to understand that choosing either man, or any man, would have some sort of impact on my life. If I wind up with Blake, our relationship would be centered on joint ambition. If I choose Raj, I bet life would feel more compartmentalized: work would be work, and then we'd have our world outside that together.

I consider trying to explain this all to Carmen, but I worry she won't get it. We've debated this for years: she believes that everything happens for a reason and that the universe has a plan for each of us. None of that makes sense to me. I think that bad things can happen to good people for no reason and vice versa, and that the only plan that matters in my life is the one I make for myself. I don't want to sit through yet another conversation in which she earnestly promises me that a silver lining is on its way when I know that's not necessarily true. Everyone makes their own choices, whether they know it or not.

"I want Raj," I say finally. "But I don't know if that's going to happen anymore. I made a mess. And I'd get it if he wanted to walk away from that."

Every time I consider this situation, my skin gets hot and I can feel my pulse ticking in my neck. I lift the back of my hand to my forehead; I'm warm.

She leans back in her chair, thoughtfully slurping down an oyster. "He's not going to walk away," she says.

"You don't know that," I say.

She gives the tiniest close-lipped smile that makes me wonder what she's not telling me. "Carmen?"

"He asks about you," she says. "Not all the time, but often enough that it's obvious you're on his mind."

"What does he want to know?" I ask.

She shrugs. "How you're doing. How your company's doing. If you're getting married. If you're happy. That kind of stuff."

"Oh."

So maybe he isn't repulsed by my behavior. Maybe that sloppy, impulsive attempt at a kiss didn't totally doom us. If that's the case, then what he said—that he wasn't upset with me, but he simply needed to be my first choice—must be true. Everyone deserves to feel like someone's first choice. Everyone deserves to feel chosen and cherished. And that makes me realize something else.

"Blake is wrong for me," I blurt out.

Carmen cocks her head. "What?"

"Blake is wrong for me," I repeat, feeling more and more sure of myself. "I should've figured this out earlier. But if I have to beg him to marry me this weekend, that's not okay. If he were right for me, then he'd be sprinting here now to walk down that aisle. He'd forgive me for hiding a secret from him. Or maybe I would've felt so comfortable with him from the start that I never would've had to keep that secret. I mean, I've always been honest with Raj."

Carmen simply nods. "Yeah. Honesty. That's how relationships are supposed to work. Like, if you're a normal person."

I give an exasperated sigh. "Yeah! But I didn't think I necessarily *was* a normal person! I thought—I wanted to think—that I was doing something out of the ordinary and it was going to be worth it. I thought I was sacrificing a regular relationship for something even better. I mean, god, look around. Every day, another girl we know announces that she's going to settle down for a boring life with some bland lawyer or a dude who thinks that lifting weights counts as a personality. And then she gets married, changes her name, and only posts wedding photos on Instagram for the rest of her life. I don't want to be one of those girls. Are we supposed to think that any of them are actually happy?"

By the end of my rant, I'm close to shouting. I sound desperate, like I'm trying to rationalize my long string of missteps to myself. Carmen's eyes widen in alarm. She tucks her hair behind her ears and leans forward, like she's winding up for a speech.

"Girl, we have a lot to unpack here, because you are freaking out." She gets ready to tick points off on her fingers, and I know that means she's fired up. "For starters, there's nothing wrong with getting married if that's what you want. But also, you don't have to do that. You can just live your life, run your business, and make out with hot men. That is plenty. That is more than fine. If you feel any rush to get married, that's your own doing. You can chalk it up to societal pressure all you want, but you're a single girl who planned a wedding before meeting her groom—I can't help you there."

I want to shrink into my cocktail.

"Second, don't assume marriage has to be boring," she continues. "I mean, sure, decades of monogamy might not always be the most *exciting* thing on the planet, but if you're dreading a marriage from the start, that's a red flag. The good is supposed to outweigh the bad: stable love, happiness, and support, in exchange for a promise to be faithful. You know, in all these months of hearing about Blake, I've never once heard you sound excited to marry him. It was more like . . . you decided you *were* going to marry Blake, and that was that. You both deserve more than that, Eliza."

"I don't—" I start to speak up to protest, but she holds out a finger to shush me.

"I've wanted to say this for months," she spits out. "It's okay to want to feel something. That's not weird; that's what makes you human. I can only imagine how stressed you've been these past few months, but the times you've seemed happiest are the times you're around Raj. He brings out a side in you I haven't seen since you launched Brooklyn Jewels—you're chill and goofy and relaxed. I just hope you realize how rare that is. You're so lucky to have found someone like that. It's one thing to make sacrifices for a relationship, but it's not worth it unless it's the *right* relationship. And you've found it . . . just not where you expected."

Even Carmen seems thrown off guard by the intensity of her speech. She slumps back into her seat, shakes her head a little, and downs a heavy sip of her drink. "All righty then," she mutters to herself. We sit and stare at each other, letting the gravity of her words sink in.

"I'm not ready to marry Raj," I say quietly. "At least not for, like, years."

Carmen's laugh echoes around the bar. "God, Eliza, I'm not telling you to marry him! I'm just saying to give him a chance. You'd be stupid to pass that up."

She's right. That would be idiotic. I am an idiot. The right answer has been sitting in front of me for months, and I've been too paralyzed by self-doubt and caught up in my own delusions to see it clearly. I look down at the empty oyster shells on the silver tray filled with ice chips, and the same drink I've nursed on a half dozen first dates at this very bar, and suddenly, sitting stationary in my own skin feels suffocating. I need to get out of here. I know what I have to do.

"Carmen, I think I have to head out. I need to fix this," I say. My voice sounds unsteady, but I feel the comforting sensation of a plan clicking into place. "Thank you for helping me fix this."

She chuckles. "Go. I'll stay and get the check. Just tell me how it goes."

· *Chapter 26* ·

I've speed-walked two blocks toward Golden Years before it occurs to me to text Raj and see if he's even there. I pause on the sidewalk to write to him. "Hey," I type, pressing send before I lose my nerve. I add, "Can we talk in person? Where are you?" I'm too wound up to wait for his reply.

I zoom through my neighborhood, past the bodega with one too many cats and the new smoothie shop that has the nerve to charge twelve dollars a pop. I can't believe I wasted almost two weeks worrying if Blake would come around and say yes to my proposition. I never thought I'd be the girl who waits for a guy who doesn't want her.

Golden Years's bright neon sign is like a lighthouse. It casts a warm glow on the sidewalk, and I race toward it. Just outside the bar, I check my phone. No response from Raj. I scroll down through my inbox to find Blake's name. It's way farther down than I expected it to be. Our conversation looks pathetically one-sided: it's a string of desperate pleas from me and silence from him.

"Blake, I'm sorry," I write. "I didn't mean to hurt you. I shouldn't have asked you to show up at the wedding. You shouldn't come. I don't think it's the right move for either of us."

I read over what I've written once, then twice, and then I press send. I get a chill of satisfaction. It's strange to feel free of wanting someone I once wanted so badly.

When I push through the door, I overestimate how much power I need to use and it bangs loudly against the wall. Raj, thank god, is working tonight, drying glasses behind the bar. He glances up when he sees me and flinches in a double take. There's just one available seat, smack-dab in the middle of the row of bar stools. In an ideal world, Golden Years would be empty so we could have this conversation privately, with dignity. But this is New York—always packed, especially when you wish it wasn't—and so I'm just going to have to say what's on my mind with three inches of elbow room on each side.

"What are you doing here?" he asks.

There's no edge to his voice. He sounds purely confused.

"I'm here to apologize," I say plainly. "I'm here to tell you that I like you. I'm here to say that I should've acknowledged that we could be more than just friends a long time ago. I didn't—that was wrong. But if you'll let me, I'd like to make it up to you."

He puts down the glass and the dishrag. "How?" he asks.

"I'm here if you want me," I say. "I'm choosing you. For real. You're not just my fallback guy for when I'm sad."

I can feel the people on either side of me turning away to give us more space. Raj's face is frozen solid with anxious anticipation. I barrel on.

"You're special, you know that, right? You're my favorite person to talk to. You're ridiculously thoughtful. You're genuine and funny and supportive, and I'd be so lucky if we could be a part of each other's lives."

He exhales. For a moment, I can't read his expression. The soaring sense of adrenaline I've been running on starts to wear thin. I wish there weren't this thick wooden bar blocking the space between us.

"What are you saying?" he asks slowly.

"I want to give us a shot," I say. "I want us to go out on dates to real restaurants that serve more than just mozzarella sticks. I want us to curl up on my couch to watch Netflix together. I want to kiss you for real and have you kiss me back. I understand if this is all too little, too late. But if I don't tell you now, I know I'll regret it."

Wordlessly, he walks along the length of the bar, away from me. Panic creeps into my chest. I can sense that people are eavesdropping on us and I wish they'd stop. I watch him turn the corner so he's no longer on the service side of the bar and stride toward me. I slide off my bar stool so I can stand and face him. I search his face for clues about what he's thinking, but he doesn't meet my eyes until he's directly in front of me. Then, he gently tilts my chin up with his finger so we're looking eye to eye. My heart pounds hard against my chest.

"Let's give this a shot," he says finally. His expression cracks into a grin.

He cups my cheek with one hand and kisses me deeply. I feel a rush of electricity, like my skin is sparkling with sheer joy. Across the bar, I hear a whooping shout that seems intended to cheer us on. In response, Raj's other hand slips around my waist to bring me closer as he kisses me again, and again, and again. In his arms, I feel confident, comfortable, and genuinely excited. I don't have to fake anything around him.

When we finally lean apart, he gazes at me with warm, vibrant eyes. He tucks a loose piece of hair behind my ear; it's an intimate gesture, but he does it with ease.

"I'm really glad you came back," he says softly.

"Me, too," I say.

"And you're not just here for the free drinks and snacks?" he teases.

"Not opposed, but nope, definitely just here for you," I say.

He shakes his head slightly like he can't quite believe that this is really happening.

"I hope you don't think that you're the only one who messed up," he says seriously. "I mean, yeah, the kiss caught me off guard, but I've liked you from the start. I should've told you how I felt sooner. I just . . . I assumed that girls like you didn't go for guys like me."

My cheeks flush. "What do you mean?"

"You're this badass who runs her own company and is kind of semi-famous, and, well, I'm currently covered in beer. A customer knocked over a whole pitcher earlier," he explains. "You could date anyone, and you *were* dating someone else—engaged to someone else, even—and yet you're here. You see how that's weird for me, right?"

"But I don't want to date just anyone," I say. "Raj, I want to date *you*. When I'm with you, I can be myself. Stress melts away. I genuinely have fun. Do you know how special it is to find a connection like that?"

I can actually see that thought sink in as he processes it; his self-conscious lip bite is replaced by a self-satisfied smile. He runs a hand through his hair.

There's a blob in my peripheral vision. I turn to realize a customer is awkwardly hovering a few feet away from us, clutching two empty beer bottles.

"Uh, can I get the check?" he asks, swiveling his glance from Raj to me and back again.

"Oh, yeah, sorry, dude," Raj says, grabbing the empty bottles and scrambling around the side of the bar. "Remind me of the name on your tab?"

I slide back onto the stool and spin around to lean my elbows on the bar. I feel loose and light and buzzing with good vibes. Since my breakup, I've felt like I was wading through molasses: sad, sluggish, stuck. Tonight, all of that has changed. I thrive on making shit happen.

Raj returns eventually. He has to work for another hour and asks if I'll hang out with him. I say yes, of course, and he automatically pours me a drink. He's not really supposed to drink on the job, but he pours himself one, too.

"What? We're celebrating," he says, clinking his glass toward mine.

In between him serving customers, we catch up on everything we've missed. He tells me about scaling down his shifts at Golden Years while taking on new clients. He's coding two small projects in addition to Carmen's now: a sleek calendar app and the fundraising site for a woman running for state senator next year. Thanks to the influx of cash, he's considering taking some time off for a vacation soon—he's thinking maybe Berlin, if he can get a group of friends together. I'm less psyched to fill him in on my life, considering it's nothing but stories about wedding planning and impending professional and financial doom.

"Can I ask what happened with Blake?" he says, squinting like he's not fully sure he wants to hear the answer.

"We're over," I say. "We weren't ever right for each other. It was a mistake."

"And the wedding? You called that off?" he asks.

I hesitate. "Not exactly," I admit.

I can see the question forming on his lips. "Isn't your wedding . . . soon?" he asks.

"Next Saturday," I say.

His eyebrows shoot up. "Is that, like . . ." He pauses to count. "Nine days away?"

"Yep."

After another pause, he asks, "So, what are you going to do?"

"I'm out of ideas," I say, shaking my head sadly. "I don't know."

He screws up his mouth and looks at me strangely. His eyes twinkle.

"What?" I ask.

"I have an idea," he says.

"Yeah?"

"I could pretend to marry you," he says.

I laugh. He doesn't.

"Dude, that is way too much," I insist.

"I mean, as long as the ceremony isn't legally binding and it's just for show, I could help you out," he says. "I know how important this wedding is for your company. You've worked too hard to see it disappear. Let me help you out."

I understand what Raj is saying, but I have a hard time believing he's serious.

"You're saying you'd pretend to get married?" I clarify. "Like, put on a suit, say 'I do,' that kind of thing?"

"I mean, this sounds like a fancy wedding. I'd rent a tux, but yeah," he says.

I stare at him over the bar. I swear I can feel my intestines sweating.

"Isn't that too . . ." I search for the right word. "Nice? Grand? Insane?"

He straightens up and runs his hand through his hair again. His eyes lock with mine while he considers how to respond.

"How's this," he suggests finally. "I already have plans when I get off work in an hour, but how about you come with me? We'll give this a try for real. It'll be a date. If all goes well, then we can consider what comes next."

"And here I was thinking the surprise party was the nicest thing you've ever done for me," I say.

I don't dare assume that anything good will come from our date tonight—for all I know, I could ruin this, too. And I don't take Raj's gesture lightly. The fact that he'd even offer his help to me after what's happened between us is enormous. I want to make sure he truly feels comfortable going through with the wedding, if it comes to that. But for the first time in weeks, I have a plan that could potentially save Brooklyn Jewels. That's enormously comforting. I lean across the bar to hug him, then pull back to give him another kiss. I stand up and collect my purse and jacket.

"What, where are you going?" he asks, looking confused.

"Heading home to get dressed," I say, walking backward toward the door. "I have a date tonight."

· Chapter 27 ·

I scurry across the street and up the stairs to my apartment. In my bathroom mirror, it's clear that the past few weeks have been tough on me: my hair is greasy, my skin looks lifeless, and the bags under my eyes are a sad shade of blue. I jump into the fastest shower of my life so I can shampoo myself into something resembling a human again. When it's time to towel off and start getting ready, it hits me: I have no idea what I'm getting ready *for*. Ninety percent of my time spent with Raj thus far has involved distracting him from bartending at Golden Years. I couldn't even tell you if his go-to first date spot is a cocktail lounge, a dive bar, or a coffee shop—or if he even *has* a go-to first date spot.

"You said you had plans in mind?" I text Raj, clutching a towel to my chest and shivering. "What are they?"

He texts me a link and I open it. It's an event at the House of Yes, the legendarily outrageous club in Bushwick, Brooklyn. I've been there for a few events before: the bar, performance space, and dance floor look like what would happen if Studio 54 had a baby with a circus. It appears that tonight's event is something called the Poetry Brothel: a mash-up of poetry performance; burlesque; and campy, gothic theater. It's a far cry from the American Heart Association Gala.

". . . too much?" he texts.

"It's perfect," I write back.

This is my cue to go overboard: the next half hour is a blur of sea salt spray, purple eyeliner, and the perfume Carmen gave me for my birthday last year. I pause before selecting an outfit. What screams "I'm sorry, I'm glad we made up, thanks for offering to pretend to marry me?" I consider a few outfits before selecting something that feels simple and sexy: an off-the-shoulder black dress that's understated enough that I can load up on fun costume jewelry. I put on color-blocked Lucite hoops and a rainbow channel-set band. I leave the engagement ring on my dresser; it feels off, somehow, to wave it in his face right now. I'm about to leave when the rumpled sheets and duvet on my bed catch my eye. I can't say for sure what will happen with Raj tonight, but I'd feel better not leaving this one particular element up to chance. I take a minute to carefully make my bed. Then I grab my leather jacket from the hook by the door and head back to Golden Years. Adrenaline rushes through my body again. After years of forgettably mediocre dates, tonight could be the outing that changes everything. It could be monumental. If tonight goes well, our lives won't ever be the same again. But, like, no pressure or anything.

When I reenter Golden Years, it strikes me how everything has changed in the past two hours. Raj meets my eyes when I walk in and my heart does a backflip. I lean against the bar; he leans over it to kiss me.

LOVE AT FIRST LIKE

"You're so beautiful," he says.

It's the first time he's ever complimented me like that, and my cheeks go hot. "Thank you," I mumble. "You look great always."

You look great always. Do I sound like some sort of AI robot reciting fragments of human speech? I hope that didn't sound too awkward.

"I'll be done here in one minute, cool?"

"Yeah!" I take a seat on a bar stool to wait for him.

He disappears into the back room. I send Carmen a text.

"You'll never guess what's happening right now," I say, baiting her into a response.

Her reply is instant. "???"

I see another text from her bubbling up. A minute later, it appears: "Won't lie, I def used Find My Friends to lightly spy on you, and I KNOW YOU'RE AT GOLDEN YEARS!"

I laugh and dash off a quick text to fill her in on what's gone down since I saw her earlier tonight.

She shoots back a GIF of Kris Jenner cooing, "You're doing amazing, sweetie."

Raj emerges from the back. "Ready to go?" he asks.

We walk to the subway. I try to focus on anything other than his hand dangling inches from mine.

"I didn't know you were into poetry," I blurt out.

"It's not really my thing, but my friend is performing tonight," he explains. "Plus, House of Yes is always fun."

"It took me two weeks to wash the glitter out of my hair last time I went," I say.

"See? Fun."

And then, as if he can read my mind, he slips his hand into mine. It's warm and comforting. He squeezes my hand, turns to me, and raises an eyebrow as if to say, "Is this okay?" I squeeze his back. From there, it's easier to relax. The more affectionate Raj is, the calmer I feel. The compliments and the hand-holding make me feel like this is for real. Carmen's words from happy hour echo in my head: I just have to take this one step at a time and focus on our chemistry—not necessarily our entire future together.

Ten minutes later, once we're off the train, we walk to the venue. House of Yes is hard to miss, partly because it's a massive aqua warehouse painted with the word "YES" on the side, but mostly due to the line of people dressed in irritatingly hip outfits and outrageous costumes that stretches halfway down the block. The men wear more interesting makeup than the women. The first room inside features a bar decorated with multicolored strips of wood fanning out like rays of sunshine, a cluster of disco balls, and a life-sized statue of a polar bear. We're waiting in line for drinks when Raj, apropos of nothing, kisses me.

"I just wanted to do that again," he says, shrugging.

We each order beers. Raj tries to pay, but I gently touch his hand.

"Please, let me get this round," I say. "You've been giving me free drinks forever."

He hesitates for a moment, but doesn't protest when I give my credit card to the bartender.

"Next time's on me, then," he says.

I try not to dwell on the implication of his words.

We move into the main room, an airy performance space. The red velvet curtain over the stage reminds me of a school play, but the vaguely sexual cage hanging from the ceiling does not. We wedge into the crowd, past a very tall man wearing nothing but a tiny pair of metallic briefs and matching suspenders. It's louder here. We curve toward each other, our shoulders and elbows and hips bumping as we talk.

Soon, a host glides onto the stage. She looks like an Old Hollywood starlet in a floor-length, gauzy, magenta robe trimmed with marabou over a matching corset and ruffled panties. She welcomes the crowd, which erupts in cheers. The host outlines how the event works: a few poets will read their work onstage, and then the rest will offer private poetry readings for a fee. The curtain sweeps up to reveal a dozen poets lounging on or draped around a brocade fainting couch. Everyone is dressed in riffs on the same theatrical Old Hollywood style. The host introduces them by their stage names: Penelope Strangelight, Cora Chaos, Beatrix Hotter, and so on. Each gives a coquettish wave or a tip of their top hat and stands to recite a line of original poetry.

"That's my friend," Raj says, nudging me when Penelope Strangelight stands. She's dressed in a sheer black tunic floating over black fishnet tights. A crown of black roses perches atop her blond hair. The effect is like a seductive Morticia Addams on her night off.

The last time I read poetry was the day I let my Tumblr account go, but tonight's performance is enjoyable. Once the introductions are complete, every poet files offstage except for one, who recites a poem about a little girl in the woods in a throaty, melodic voice. When she's finished, the spotlight swings up to illuminate the cage. Another poet, clad in old-fashioned-looking tweed trousers and a leather studded collar over a bare chest, recites a poem with vivid lines about the trouble he used to get into while performing in a punk band. It's an oddball event for sure, but it lights up my brain in places that haven't stirred in a long time. Tonight reminds me of my first few years in New York, back in college, when I had nearly limitless time to seek out adventure instead of holing up in my office to work.

"Do you go to things like this often?" I ask Raj.

"More often than I used to, now that my work schedule is a little less hectic," he says, considering it. "Not as often as I'd like."

"I like this," I tell him.

He squeezes my hand. "Good."

Soon, the host encourages us to disperse throughout the venue for private readings. The poets leave the stage to install themselves in various spots. Penelope Strangelight is making her way across the main floor when she does a double take by us.

"Raj!" she exclaims, breaking character and hugging him. "You made it. Awesome."

It occurs to me that I have no idea how close they are, or how much she knows about me.

Luckily, Raj introduces me. "This is Eliza, my . . . girlfriend?" It's like he's testing out the word for the first time. He turns to me in confusion. "*Are* you my girlfriend?"

Penelope laughs loudly. I just sputter in shock.

"Uh . . . maybe? I mean, I think so? Or not? Up to you?" I ramble.

"Come on, you two, I have a poem that's perfect for you," she says. I notice for the first time that she has a lightly lilting British accent.

Bewildered, we both follow her through the throng of people, past the bar, and outside to a patio that appears to be home to a flock of nude Greek statues. As we walk, I can't help but frantically mutter to Raj.

"I mean, it's not like I don't *want* to be your girlfriend," I explain in a panicked whisper. "We just hadn't talked about it in those terms yet."

"Even though we might get married next weekend?" he fires back.

I study his expression: he looks sheepish, maybe a little embarrassed, but not mad. That's good.

"I'm your girlfriend, then," I say. "Let's give this a real try."

He shakes his head like he can't believe me. "Girlfriend," he says slowly, grinning, like he's getting used to calling me that.

Penelope clears her throat and we fall into silence. She plants herself among the statues, makes thoughtful eye contact with each of us, and launches into a poem about new love:

Oh, darling, whoever you aren't,
we're naked in another yellow bed.
Winter's coming and I've learned enough
skin that it's like sky
to me. All the curtains in Brooklyn
are cream-colored linen and tied
in bows like nervous tongues

along white windowsills.
Indian summer spent
tumble-weeding through
subway systems, white
pavements, gardens to basement
bedrooms with rainwater blistered
ceilings to coil my body like a broken spring
in another mattress.
I would like to mean something
soon. To wake along
the frayed edge of morning
and unravel

the afternoon together, eat oranges in bed
and plant my toothbrush
in a porcelain socket like a flag.
Oh darling, whoever you aren't,
let me learn your mathematics—
the important numbers—birthdays,
siblings, alarm codes, lovers—how many
months the bread's been there, how
many days since you phoned your mother,
how many drinks until you're whiskey silly,
how many ecstasies you can find in me.
White sky over Brooklyn, the endlessness

of new skin. I'll whittle
these clouds into water—though I'm hoping
for ice, for the snap of weight and bright resistance,
for a white bone through skin—
for your bones, darling, for your skin.

It's a startling sensation to hear your own inner thoughts—the ones you might not have ever fully admitted to yourself—spoken out loud in gorgeous poetic imagery here in this bizarre sculpture garden at a fun house disco. When she's finished, Penelope concludes with a small curtsy. Raj fishes a five-dollar bill out of his wallet as a tip, per the event's rules.

"Enjoy your evening, babes," she says, slipping past us into the bar to find another group of listeners. "Good to see you, Raj."

"That was beautiful," I say, once we're alone.

"It really was," he agrees.

There's a lull, and I can tell we both want to say more.

"It made me feel . . ." I try to search for the right words. "It made me feel exactly the way I feel about you? Like this is new and good and I want more."

He nods. "Yeah. That's exactly it. It was eerie."

"Eerie, but kind of perfect," I muse.

We're close enough to kiss, but I'm not sure I'm brave enough to initiate that. I want to protect what we have from my own brash impulses. I don't want to mess up again, like I did that morning in my apartment. Maybe I shouldn't worry, because Raj leans in so slowly to kiss me I can feel his eyelashes brushing my skin. I like the way his kisses warm up from gentle to enthusiastic; one hand slides up my back and another caresses my cheek. When we eventually break apart, I can see him smiling.

"Do you want to get out of here?" he asks, ruffling his hair.

I've spent enough time with him to recognize it as something he does when he's just the tiniest bit nervous. I try to soothe him by kissing him again.

"Of course," I say. "Let's go. My place?"

"Yeah," he says. "I'd like that."

I call an Uber. Anticipation crackles between us in the backseat of the driver's car. I slouch down on the seat so I can rest my head on Raj's shoulder. He dangles his fingers on the curve of my knee. An indie pop song floats from the radio like we're in a music video. He kisses a soft trail from my temple to my ear; I shift in my seat, and soon, we're making out again.

On the surface, none of this is new: I've made out with plenty of people in the backseats of late-night Ubers. The difference is that this time, there's this odd sense of potential. This could be the last first time I take a guy back to my place. Part of me is afraid to move the wrong way and ruin the moment, but another part of me feels supremely confident—I can't make the wrong move, because whatever is between us is so perfectly right. He likes me. He gets me. Forget the lackluster chemistry and robotic kisses on my past dates: this is how dating should be. And the best part? It's *Raj*, who not only makes me feel so at ease around him, but also has his hand on my shoulder with his fingers slipping beneath the neckline of my dress. His touch is magnetic.

When the driver drops us off at my place, there's no question that Raj will come upstairs with me. His hands linger playfully on my waist as I fumble with the lock and key.

Once we're inside, I gesture vaguely to the refrigerator. "Do you want, um, a beer? Water? Seltzer?" I offer.

"I'm good," he says. "You don't have to, like, host me. I'm here for you."

"Wait," I say, suddenly inspired.

I'm struck by a desire to make tonight special. I slide down the dimmer on my light switch to minimize the stark effect of my bright white walls. I light the candle on my coffee table; the flickering golden light and heady scent of sandalwood create a softer atmosphere. I turn on my speaker and queue up the sultry R&B playlist I sometimes like to listen to when I'm alone. I take off my earrings and place them on my nightstand.

Raj doesn't even bother with the pretense of sitting politely on my couch. Instead, he follows my lead when I step out of my shoes and crawl onto my bed. I'm glad I took the time earlier to make it look cozy and inviting. I recline against the oversized pillows; he props himself up on his elbows and stretches out along the length of the bed. I expect another kiss like the one in the car, but the newfound sense of privacy stirs something in Raj. His mouth moves more passionately over mine; his hands explore more; his grip is firmer than it was before. My dress slips down over my shoulder, and he plants a row of kisses on the bare skin there.

I feel warm and relaxed in his arms, so I sit up and shimmy my dress over my head. I shake out my hair so it spills across my back. I revel in the hungry, appreciative look in his eyes. He responds by tugging his T-shirt over his head to reveal a smattering of dark chest hair and more of those well-proportioned arms I've thought about so many times. For the past few weeks, there's been an ever-present buzz of stress in the back of my mind, but now, it melts away. All I care about is the feeling of his lips and skin against mine.

I reach for his belt buckle and pause with my fingers on the smooth metal.

"Is this okay?" I ask.

"Go ahead," he says, nodding.

I loosen the buckle and his zipper, and he tugs off his pants, though he keeps his black boxer briefs on. In the past, with other guys, I've sometimes moved from kissing to stripping down to sex in rote fashion, like I was simply working my way through a checklist. A handful of times, I felt this unspoken pressure to keep progressing, even if I really wanted to slow down. But mostly, I just didn't have the desire to linger. Now, however, I find myself wanting to savor the process of discovering Raj's body inch by inch. There's something luxurious about lounging in bed with no rush. From the tender way his hands skim over my breasts and hips and thighs, I can tell he feels the same way. I explore the planes of his chest, the divot of his lower back, and the trail of hair below his belly button.

His fingers weave through my hair and his body wedges deliciously against mine, but I want more. I move more urgently against him; the way his hips roll against mine makes me think he wants

me, too. I feel his warm hand slip under the edge of my silky underwear and my breath catches. I fumble for his waistband, too.

"I want you so badly," he says, his voice low.

"Should I grab a condom?" I ask.

"If you want to later," he says, moving down my body toward the
end of the bed.

The sensation of his tongue against me makes me feel like I'm
glowing. The candlelight, the music—it all goes hazy. And eventually, when it's time to grab a condom, my fingers shake too badly to
rip open the packet. I laugh and hand it to him. He manages better
than I do.

Sex with Raj feels seamless, like the most obvious thing in the
world. I forget why we haven't done this a million times before. He
squeezes my ass in a way that makes me moan; his breath grows
ragged as his motions turn more fervent. When he finishes, he collapses with his forehead buried in my shoulder. I can feel his pulse
pounding against my chest. He rolls over and scoops his arm around
my body so there's plenty of room for me to curl up next to him. I
relax against his torso and appreciate how easy and comfortable it is.

After a moment, I mumble into his chest, "That was amazing."

"You're amazing," he replies, stroking my hair.

"No, I mean it," I say.

He laughs lightly, still catching his breath. "I do, too."

"It'd suck if after all this buildup, we were terrible together,"
I say.

"I don't think that would even be possible," he says.

If I were a different sort of person—a calmer sort of person—
this would be the moment I drift blissfully into slumber in my new,
hot boyfriend's arms with nary a worry. But, of course, that's not
who I am. My mind whirs with visions and questions. I can't help

but imagine Raj looking so sharp and handsome in a tux at the Wythe Hotel next Saturday. I hate that I can picture him stomping on the napkin-wrapped glass under the canopy of the chuppah— the one Jewish wedding tradition that always makes me cry. I wonder if the trajectory of our evening together has swayed him toward or against showing up for me in that ridiculously grand way. But as magical as tonight has been, I'm not sure it's enough. I'm not sure anything could be enough.

The more I think about it, the more my thoughts breeze past the wedding and toward something else entirely: a thousand more nights just like this one. I can envision us buying tickets to offbeat performances like the Poetry Brothel, trying foods neither of us can pronounce at new restaurants, and lounging in bed for hours on weekend mornings because nothing outside remotely measures up to the pleasures of spooning under the covers and talking until our voices are hoarse.

It scares me that these thoughts feel new. With Blake, I mostly reassured myself that I'd fall for him someday. If I'm having these types of thoughts about Raj on the night of our first date, that means my interest in him is truly greater than just saving Brooklyn Jewels. It means my feelings for him are real.

"Everything okay?" Raj asks. "You got kind of quiet."

"Yeah!" I blurt out. "Yeah. Do you want to stay over? Because you could. If you wanted to."

"I do, yeah," he says.

I get up gingerly so my hair doesn't catch under his arm and slide out of bed to blow out the candle and turn off the lights. Moving around gives me something to do rather than dwelling on how I feel. I slip back into bed. I should just relax, or god forbid, sleep. But I can't.

"So, here's the thing," I say a minute later, flipping onto my stomach and propping myself on my elbows so I can look directly at him. It's easier to be vulnerable in the dark. "I like you. Like, a lot."

Even in the darkness, I can see him smile. "I mean, I'd *hope* so," he retorts.

"I know this is all, um . . . nontraditional?" I continue. "Showing up at the bar after not talking for a while, and then you offering to fake-marry me, and then me seducing you."

"You can seduce me literally anytime," he says.

"Oh, I plan on it. But I just need you to know that I really care about you. This isn't just about you helping me out. I'm not expecting anything. I know that marriage, even if it's fake, is enormously meaningful. I just . . . I just hope you understand that my feelings for you are very real."

"I don't think you could fake this if you tried," he says.

I feel a rush of relief. "Good, I'm glad you feel that way."

"I know I offered to show up for you at the wedding earlier, but can I . . . sleep on it?" Raj asks tentatively. "I mean, I'm not ruling it out, but today has been a lot. I just want to think it through."

I hate that my heart sinks. I look down and pretend to study my cuticles so he can't see the disappointment on my face.

"Yeah, yeah, of course," I say. "That's smart."

"I know you don't have unlimited time, but I'll make a decision soon, I promise. Soon."

"Thanks," I say, exhaling.

I lie flat on my back next to him, but I feel too exposed. So I roll away from him, onto my side, where he can't see how crushed and hopeless I feel.

· Chapter 28 ·

According to a wedding-planning magazine I glanced at once at a bridal salon when Sophie was trying on dresses, there's a frighteningly long checklist of things to do the week before you tie the knot. If you don't have a wedding planner, which, of course, I do not—the last thing I need is to pay a stranger to ask nosy questions about who, exactly, the groom is—the tasks all fall to the bride: performing a complicated twelve-step skincare routine, calling vendors to confirm call times, and writing out a day-of itinerary to give to my photographer (an Instagram influencer's Instagram boyfriend who offered me a deal if I offered him a discount on an engagement ring). There's just one problem—it's difficult to get through these tasks with any gusto if you're not entirely sure the wedding will actually take place.

But it's not like I have anything else to do. Raj left my apartment quietly and quickly this morning. Running through my usual set of tasks at Brooklyn Jewels feels useless, given that there might not be a Brooklyn Jewels by next month. At least not in the way I'd want it to exist. I can't stand the uncertainties creeping up from every side.

I have to do something. So I put on my most no-nonsense jeans and the first top I grab from my dresser drawer and I head downstairs to get some goddamn work done.

Jess is already at the shop when I walk in the door.

"Morning," she says, glancing up from her work organizing a case of jewels.

"Morning," I reply.

The sight of Jess triggers an uncomfortable realization. There's a terrible conversation that I need to have with her, and I've put it off for as long as I possibly can.

"Do you actually have a minute to talk?" I ask.

She looks up from the velvet tray that she's loading with necklaces. "Yeah, what's up?"

I sigh and take the seat next to hers. "Look, there's no easy way to say this, but our finances are in rough shape," I say.

Her eyes go dead. "Oh," she says heavily.

"As things currently stand, I can't say for sure that we'll be open past mid-November first," I explain.

"But the holidays are the busiest sales season," she protests. "You can't close right before then."

"This isn't our choice, Jess," I say, frustrated that she'd even assume we'd shut down the shop of our own volition. "Our rent is going up, and it costs an exorbitant amount of money to lease this space every month. I wish I didn't have to tell you this, but you should at least know what's going on in case you need to start looking for another job. The wedding will hopefully help our sales, but right now I'm not one hundred percent sure it'll even happen."

She looks at me with her big saucer eyes, and I get the nauseating sensation that I've just completely crushed her.

"I'm so sorry. I wish things were different," I tell her.

She looks away. "Me, too," she says.

I could work in the back, but if my weeks in this shop might be numbered, I want to soak up the atmosphere. I grab my laptop and sit in the main showroom along with Jess so I can watch customers come in to shop and admire all our glittering jewels. I click open a new document and type out a list of everything I need to do today to confirm that the wedding can happen as seamlessly as possible a week from tomorrow. The idea of a concrete to-do list soothes me; it's something solid to cling to. I need to call the Wythe Hotel to check in with the event manager and the caterer; confirm arrival times and schedules with the photographer, officiant, and florist; and triple-check that my dress will be delivered to the hotel. Maybe I should book a bikini wax. Shit. Do I have time this week for a bikini wax?

As I debate adding that to my to-do list, Sophie enters the shop.

"Hey!" I say. I have so much to tell her. "So I have news."

She stops short and shoots me a nervous look. Historically, I tend to give her mostly bad news.

"No, no, I think you'll like this news," I clarify.

She shifts her weight onto one hip and sighs. "Lay it on me."

"I broke things off with Blake for good."

"Whoa, whoa, whoa," Sophie interjects.

I steamroll onto the good stuff. "And then I went to Golden Years to apologize to Raj and patch things up. And *then* he offered to consider helping us out next week by marrying me at the wedding."

"Wait, shut up, he did not!" Jess says, leaning over the counter, eyes gleaming. "I wish you had said that first thing today."

"Hold on, you decided one impulsive engagement wasn't enough this year, so you're spontaneously gonna marry Raj now?" Sophie asks. She folds her arms across her chest in disbelief, looking every inch the part of the judgmental big sister.

"Well, 'marrying' might not be the right word," I say, back-tracking. "He offered to maybe marry me in a legally nonbinding ceremony, just for show, just to help out Brooklyn Jewels, because he knows that this business means everything to me."

"Maybe?" Sophie echoes.

"What do you mean, maybe?" Jess asks.

"Well, he's still thinking it over," I explain.

Sophie stares at me for a moment, looks at the to-do list on my computer screen, then actually tips her head back to cackle.

"Wow, you've outdone yourself this time," she says, once she's composed herself. "You're really planning a wedding with no actual groom in sight, aren't you?"

I angle my laptop away from her. "He'll be there, okay? Just watch. He'll show up and say yes," I insist.

Sophie throws up her hands. "Fine. God forbid you ever do any-thing like a normal person. Have fun ruining your own life." She gets up and heads into the back room.

Jess looks at me blankly.

"I, um, have some work to do," I say pointedly.

She snaps her attention back to her own laptop.

I feel incredibly self-conscious as I dial the first number, the event manager. The line rings once, twice, three times. I'm on the verge of hanging up out of nerves. But then someone picks up the phone.

"Hi, this is Eliza Roth, I'm looking for Sharon, the event man-ager?" I ask, slipping into my most professional, take-no-bullshit voice. It's go-time.

By one o'clock, I've made my way through three-quarters of the list. I was careful with my language, subbing in "the groom" instead of

Raj's name. I didn't specify on any of the calls exactly who I was marrying. I break for lunch and head to Sweetgreen for a salad. I order my kale Caesar salad to go and carry it the few blocks back to the store. I'm distracted by texting Carmen updates from last night, so I don't notice anything strange through the glass window of the shop. It's not until I've reached the door that I notice our CLOSED sign. I look up from my phone in confusion and enter the shop.

Raj is standing alone in the middle of the shop. His usual duds—the old hoodies I've seen him wear a thousand times—are replaced by a pair of charcoal gray dress pants and a pale pink button-down shirt with the sleeves rolled up just so. As I enter the shop, he presses something on his phone and a familiar song that I can't quite place fills the room. The first few chords are bouncy and upbeat.

"Hi," I breathe, taking all of this in.

"Hi," he says, grinning.

"I've never seen you dressed like this," I say cautiously.

"Special occasion," he says.

That's when I realize what the song is. Bruno Mars's smooth voice belts out, "I think I wanna marry you." I get it. I get what's happening. I clap a hand to my mouth; I feel giddy and so absurdly relieved. I walk toward him.

"Eliza, I can't promise you that we're going to fall in love, or grow old together, or stay together forever, but I can promise you this: you're the most incredible woman I've ever met, and I want to give us a try," Raj says. "I really care about you, you know? And if that means helping you out, that's what I'll do."

I'm so flooded with gratitude I can only nod and eke out, "Thank you so much."

But then there's more. Raj looks around at the jewelry cases. He shoves his hands in his pockets nervously.

"I wanted to do this properly," he says. "And I imagine you have enough fancy rings of your own. But I . . . I brought you something, and I'd like to give it to you."

He takes out a small, colorful package and tears it open to reveal a red Ring Pop on a purple piece of plastic. He gazes down at it and then back up to me.

"You told me you used to love these when you were a kid, back when you first dreamed about opening your own jewelry store," he says. "I know this is silly and nothing much, but I thought this would remind you of how important that dream is, and how—together—we can make sure it stays a reality."

"Oh my god, Raj," I say, eyes wide. "You didn't. This is amazing. You're amazing."

I move toward him to kiss him, but he holds up his hand.

"Wait, let me do this," he says.

He sinks down onto one knee and holds up the Ring Pop as an offering. "Eliza, would you do me the honor of fake-marrying me?"

Unlike my last proposal, this time around I'm bursting with enthusiasm to say yes. I can't get the words out fast enough.

"Yes, of course, yes. Raj, you're incredible. Yes!"

He stands and carefully slides the Ring Pop onto my finger. It's a little snug (it's made for a child, after all), but somehow it's perfect for this moment. I throw my arms around his neck to kiss him.

I'm sure there are a million and one logical reasons why I should be afraid right now—and maybe Sophie is currently holed up in the back room making a list of all of them—but I don't feel that way. Forget that pre-wedding checklist. I just checked off the most important item of all. I'm fully aware that what Raj and I are about to do is unorthodox, to say the least, but I feel relieved to be taking this next step with a person I feel so comfortable around. I'm grateful that Raj and I are on the same page here. He knows that I don't need a promise of forever. I only need a promise that we'll take our relationship one day at a time.

Sophie and Jess emerge from the back of the shop with tentative expressions on their faces.

"You did it?" Sophie asks haltingly.

"They did it!" Jess shouts. "Look at them! Look at the lovebirds!"

Raj holds up my hand and kisses my Ring Pop. "We did it."

Bewildered, I look from Raj to Sophie. "What?"

"I may have had some help getting into the shop while you were at lunch," Raj admits. "And I needed someone to tell me your favorite flavor of Ring Pop."

"I knew strawberry was your favorite," Sophie says, sighing like this admission cost her a lot.

"But you were so—you were so negative," I point out.

She shrugs. "You're so far into this rabbit hole, I can't imagine another way out. If this is what you want, so be it. He's a nice guy."

That's as much of a ringing endorsement as I can ever expect from Sophie.

"Come sit and hang out here?" I offer Raj. "I'm just going through the pre-wedding checklist."

"Sure," he says. "Let me help."

"Well, first, you can start by inviting your friends and family," I point out.

He laughs. "You want to meet my parents?"

"It wouldn't be a wedding without them, right?" I ask.

"I'll see if they can make it," he says, pulling out his phone.

I take a seat behind the counter with a newfound appreciation for the fact that this place might not be in jeopardy any longer.

· *Chapter 29* ·

I never imagined I'd scarf down a semi-stale bagel straight out of a paper bag on the morning of my wedding, but these days I'm learning it's good to roll with the punches. So I'm marrying my boyfriend of nine days in a sham ceremony to save the fate of my company. Whatever. So I'm eating carbs on my wedding day, and I forgot my Spanx at home. Whatever. Carmen tosses me the bagel she picked up on her way over to the bridal suite at the Wythe Hotel; who am I to refuse food?

"You should eat *something*," she says. "My cousin refused to eat on her wedding day so she'd look skinny in her dress, but wound up literally fainting in the middle of her reception."

"Bagel it is, then," I say, giving her a thumbs-up.

Carmen, Sophie, Liv, and Jess are joining me in the bridal suite this morning for hair and makeup, along with the photographer. They're not technically my bridesmaids; with a hazy sense of exactly who the groom would be, we skipped that tradition. Anyway, even if I was planning more of a conventional wedding, I don't know if I'd want a bridal party beyond *maybe* Sophie as my matron of honor. Shouldn't wedding ceremonies be solely about the two people getting married, not forcing your closest friends to line up like a MySpace Top 8 in matching outfits?

The photographer flits around the room, snapping semi-candid pictures of us getting glammed up.

There's a knock on the door.

"Come in!" I shout from under the hands of a makeup artist dabbing concealer on my dark circles.

Mom enters the suite. It's the first time I've seen her since dinner with Dad and Blake over the summer. I called my parents last week to tell them about the drastic change of plans. They didn't quite understand why I'd want to pretend to marry a guy I've barely even dated, but after a long, tough conversation, they agreed to come and support the wedding.

"Think of it like that time I was in the school play," I had explained to them. "You and I both knew I didn't have much of a future as an actress, but you showed up with a camcorder anyway."

Mom squeezes in between me and the makeup artist to give me a hug. "I can't believe my baby's all grown up and getting married!" she says. "Well, sort of married."

"I know, Mom, I know," I say, hugging her back.

She settles onto the edge of the bed. "So you'll have to tell me more about this guy. Can you show me pictures?"

The makeup artist doesn't manage to hide her shocked expression.

Once my hair and makeup are done—I asked for long, loose waves to feel like myself and a bright red lip to pop in photos—I move toward the window for the best lighting and film a quick video for Instagram Stories.

"It's my wedding day!" I squeal. "I'm here with my friends and family in a bridal suite at the Wythe Hotel. We're all getting ready, thanks to our amazing hair-and-makeup team provided by Glamsquad."

I don't like how tentative I sound. I film it again. The framing looks off. I try it a third time, and it's finally good enough to post. This begins the process of promoting all the companies who are sponsoring the wedding—in other words, helping me pull this off for free. Seconds after it uploads, I get a flurry of excited messages in response. I exhale. I'm going to be okay. This has to be okay, right?

"Here, let me take your phone," Carmen says. "You don't need to be worrying about it all day. I'll post photos for you. Just tell me what to tag and hashtag."

I hesitate. But she's right. I've hustled to get a man here, planned a gorgeous free wedding in under six months, and hyped up my followers along the way. There's nothing else I can do. If the wedding is going to work as a marketing tactic for Brooklyn Jewels, it's going to work—but it's out of my control now. I give Carmen my phone and all the information she needs.

Suddenly, I hear a gagging noise. Sophie bolts out of the hair stylist's chair with a hand pressed over her mouth and sprints to the bathroom. A second later, I can hear her retching over the toilet. Liv scoots in behind her.

"Watch your hair!" the stylist calls.

"Honey?" Mom says, filing in behind Liv.

There are more noises, then a beat of exhausted silence. The toilet flushes.

"I'm fine," Sophie moans. Her voice echoes off the bathroom tile.

The hotel room is not set up for this many people to crowd around the bathroom door, but I squeeze in anyway. My sister looks tired but ultimately okay.

"You're not sick on my wedding day, are you?" I ask.

If she is, I hope it's not contagious.

Sophie and Liv exchange glances.

"Should we?" Sophie asks.

"Go ahead, I guess?" Liv says uncertainly.

Mom catches on first. She erupts in a happy sob and sinks onto her knees to hug Sophie.

"Mom!" Sophie squeaks, wiping the vomit from her mouth.

Our mother is hunched over, hyperventilating and howling, "I'm just—so—s-s-s-so h-h-h-happy for you!"

"We were going to keep it a surprise until after the wedding to avoid stealing your thunder," Liv explains. "And it's still so early, but . . ."

"I'm pregnant!" Sophie says.

Tears spring to my eyes, and I flap my hands to keep them at bay. I don't know who to hug first, so I scramble into the bathroom and try to embrace all three of them at once. Sophie is going to be the best mom. I know this with all my heart because she's practically been a mom to me. I'm so overjoyed for her and Liv, and their newly budding family. You think conceiving babies is the simplest thing in the world until you see someone you love struggle to have one. The good news is almost too much to process. I hear a click behind me; the photographer is either bold enough or crazy enough to catch this moment on camera, too.

"Oh no, don't you cry, too," Sophie says, squeezing my arm. "You'll ruin your makeup."

I take a deep, ragged breath and try to calm myself.

"I'm just so happy for you," I say, voice quavering. "You're getting everything you've ever wanted."

"You, too," she says with a smile.

Later, once I've collected myself and the makeup artist has touched up all our watery eye makeup, my mom helps me into my dress.

"It's so beautiful," she says, carefully zipping up the back of the dress. She runs her fingers over the delicate lace sleeves. "You're so beautiful."

"You like the dress?" I ask, trying to gauge her reflection in the mirror.

She gently adjusts the hook-and-eye closure at the top of the zipper. "I love it. It's perfect for you."

"And you're not . . . upset that you weren't there to pick it out with me?" I ask tentatively. I'm afraid to exhale.

She steps around the sweeping hem of my gown to look at me directly. She sighs.

"Do I wish I had been more involved in planning this? Sure, maybe. You're my daughter—of course, I would want to be there with you. But this is your day, and you've always done things your own way. That's just who you are."

I melt forward into a hug. I didn't realize how much her approval meant to me until I wasn't sure I had it anymore. I'm glad I do.

A high-pitched trilling sound cuts through the moment.

"Your phone alarm," Carmen says. She turns it off.

"Time to meet Raj for the first look photo," I say, hitching up my skirt so I can step into my blue satin pumps.

For something old, I dug a scarlet red lipstick out of the bottom of my bathroom cabinet; it's a kiss-proof formula I bought at the height of my dance-floor make-out phase in college. My something new is obviously my dress. The veil I'll wear later today was first worn by Sophie at her wedding; it'll be my something borrowed. And the heels are my something blue.

I take a last look at myself in the mirror. Between the stark white lace of my wedding dress and the movie-magic makeup that somehow erased months of stress from my skin, I look like a bride—not like a girl playing the part for the cameras, but like a real bride. For all the frantic effort that went into making this moment happen, I almost didn't really believe I'd ever see myself like this. I spent years after my breakup with Holden watching my friends pair off and find love—and I didn't. I knew that stumbling into a relationship is a mere matter of luck, but the darkest sliver of my anxious mind worried that being alone was my fault, somehow.

Maybe I was too busy, too ambitious, too messy, too vocal about too many of my opinions to let love in. Maybe there was something fundamentally unlovable about me. Maybe I was quick to cling to this façade of a wedding because deep down, I worried this would be my only possible shot at a happily-ever-after. The second that awful thought bubbles up, I know it's the truth.

I've spent six months stuffing these feelings down because I had a single goal: to save my company at whatever cost. But now, I can't ignore how I feel anymore. I choke up and clap my hand over my mouth to muffle a painful sob. My engagement ring catches the light and sparkles obnoxiously in front of my face. Tears pinprick at the corner of my eyes again as everything sinks in: I am a bride. There is nothing unlovable about me. And today, along with sweet, sexy Raj, in front of my family and my friends and a hundred thousand strangers on the internet, I'm going to celebrate that.

The makeup artist steps in with a damp makeup-removing wipe to dab away under my eyes one last time.

"I promise I'll stop crying soon," I tell her.

"Oh, I doubt that, but don't worry," she says. "It's normal to be an emotional wreck on your wedding day. It's why we use water-proof mascara."

I love that she uses the word "normal." I exhale a steady stream of breath to calm myself. I can do this. I *can* do this. I hug everyone goodbye. The photographer opens the door to the hotel's hallway for me. Together, we make our way to the elevator. I savor the feeling of walking down the stretch of corridor. The next time I make a walk like this in my wedding dress, I'll be heading down the aisle.

The photographer suggested we do our first look photos on the top floor of the hotel. We've booked the ceremony on the sprawl-ing, wraparound patio with uninterrupted, panoramic views of Williamsburg, the East River, and the entire Manhattan skyline. Later, the reception will be held at The Ides, the Art-Deco-meets-industrial-chic hotel bar decked out in shimmering white tiles and geometric windows. When we get off at the top floor, the photogra-pher keeps me cloistered in the narrow elevator bank to make sure that Raj doesn't see me before it's time. When I hear the two men greet each other, I'm relieved at the sound of Raj's voice. He's really here. This is really happening.

"Okay, Eliza? When you're ready, you're going to make your way around the corner to the left, through the door, and onto the patio, where Raj is waiting for you," the photographer calls. "Pretend like I'm not even here. Just walk up and say hello to him."

I feel tingly with anticipation, even though this isn't technically a real first look. The day I picked out my wedding dress, I showed Raj photos of myself in it on my phone. In hindsight, it's funny that

I had no idea I'd be marrying him in it. I fluff out my hair along my shoulders, smooth down my skirt, and take a deep breath.

Slowly, I make my way around the corner. The door from the bar to the patio is held open, and I can see Raj standing outside with his back to me. He's clad in a sharp black tux, and it occurs to me that I have no idea where it even came from—if it's a rental or if it was already hanging in his closet. There's still so much I have to learn about him.

From the way he straightens up, I can tell he senses I'm behind him. I reach out to tap his shoulder.

"Hi there, beautiful," he says, not moving.

"You don't know how I look," I say. "For all you know, I could be in my frumpiest pajamas, desperately in need of a shower."

"Hmmm, yeah, maybe," he says. "But you're always beautiful."

God, I can't believe this man is somehow real.

Raj reaches behind him to hold my hand. His thumb grazes my diamond ring.

"No Ring Pop today?" he jokes.

"I ate it!" I say.

He whips around, a playful look of surprise on his face. "You *ate* my engagement ring?"

Click, click, click.

I can't help it, I burst out into laughter. "It's candy! What was I supposed to do?!"

Click, click, click.

He softens and embraces me for a lingering kiss. I wouldn't be opposed to a lifetime of kissing this man.

Click, click, click.

"Wait, wait, wait," Raj says, stepping backward. "You're unbelievably stunning. Like, *wow*."

His jaw actually drops when he takes in the full sight of me as a bride. I'm impressed by how he looks, too. He has a fresh haircut and has tamed his usual week-old scruff into a five-o'clock shadow that makes the angles of his face look superhero sharp. He takes my hand and twirls me around to see my dress from the back. On any other occasion, I'd feel a little self-conscious and silly, letting myself be spun like a little girl. But today is a once (or twice, or three times, who knows)-in-a-lifetime kind of day. I'm surprised that I simply want to enjoy it, twirls and all.

Raj digs in his pocket and pulls out a thin cuff bracelet made of yellow gold. It's carved with an undulating wave pattern.

"My mom gave this to me this morning because she wore this on her wedding day," he says. "I know jewelry is a big deal to you, and I don't want to mess up your whole look, but . . . would you consider wearing it today? It'd mean a lot to her."

I hadn't planned on wearing any bracelets, since the gown has long sleeves that graze my wrists. I've never been a fan of mixing metals, and the gold doesn't work with the platinum-set pieces I chose to wear today (my real engagement ring, of course, plus a pair of round-cut diamond studs and an absurdly extravagant diamond pendant necklace to match, both on loan from Brooklyn Jewels). But none of that matters. A marriage is the combination of two lives, and that begins now. I'm touched by the gesture.

"Of course," I say, sliding the bracelet onto my right wrist.

It hits me that I'll be meeting his parents for the first time today, just as he'll be meeting mine.

"Wait, you need to tell me everything about your parents," I say, suddenly stressed. Meeting Michelle Barrett this summer was already trying enough.

"They're cool. I mean, my mom's a little overbearing, and my dad is kind of hard to get to know at first, but they'll like you," he says.

"Are they going to be upset that this isn't a traditional Indian wedding?" I ask.

After Raj proposed, we had discussed what the wedding ceremony should look like. I asked him to teach me about Hindu wedding traditions, and I think he considered it for a minute, but he ultimately told me that the ceremony didn't matter too much to him. "I mean, I know all weddings are about the bride," he had said. "But this one *especially* is. I'm not religious. I don't really care." So I called the officiant to pivot the Judeo-Christian ceremony I had planned for me and Blake into just a low-key Jewish one.

Raj hesitates, then says, "Our next wedding—our real, legal wedding—will be a big, traditional Indian blowout. The celebrations go on for days. There'll be a *Sangeet*; a *Mehndi*, where you'll get decked out in henna; and we'll get married under a *mandap*, which is kind of like a Jewish chuppah, actually. . . ."

"Oh, our next wedding!" I say, laughing. "We'll see about that. Let's get through one at a time."

I told Sharon, the event manager, months ago that I would probably walk down the aisle to an appropriately sappy Adele song, but Raj's proposal stirred up a new idea. When Sharon came to check on me before the ceremony, I gave her the new plan. And that's why, an hour later, after my guests settled into their seats along the rooftop patio and Raj and the officiant are stationed under the chuppah canopy of twisted branches and crawling vines, the opening notes of "Marry You" by Bruno Mars ring out. The lyrics describe a Vegas chapel wedding on a whim, which fits this situation surprisingly well. I like that it's a cheeky tribute to the whirlwind nature of our relationship.

I link my arms through my mom's on my left and my dad's on my right. Jewish tradition dictates that the bride is accompanied down the aisle by both parents; I like how egalitarian that feels. Together, we move as one unit. The guests rise and turn to face us. I spot Jess sitting with Helen, who looks regal in a purple jacket and too many necklaces spilling down her chest. Aunt Linda positively beams while her daughter Kate's eyes roam (and probably judge) my dress. I even recognize Raj's parents—they're in the front row and his features are an exact blend of theirs. As often as I've thought about this moment, it didn't occur to me until now how meaningful the walk down the aisle would feel. I've probably walked this exact same stretch of the patio a half dozen times before. But I've never done it surrounded by every important person in my life.

When I reach the chuppah, my parents each give me a kiss on the cheek.

"I love you, sweetie," my dad whispers.

There's real emotion in his eyes and it gives me goose bumps. My parents take their seats in the first row, and I join Raj in front of the officiant. His eyes sparkle when he gives me a smile.

The officiant kicks off the ceremony with a personal touch, telling the story of how Raj and I met while leaving out about 90 percent of the actual details. "So Eliza here was a single girl selling engagement rings for a living when she spotted a cute bartender. . . ." he begins. The audience laughs. We're off to a good start. The officiant segues into a speech about what it means to build a life together.

"No matter who you are, no matter how long you've been together, marriage is a tremendous leap of faith," he says. "It's a promise to do right by your partner when neither of you knows what the future may hold. There's no guarantee that it will be easy—in fact, the only guarantee is that it will not. That's not to say marriage isn't worthwhile. It's the most meaningful thing that many of us will ever do. And I don't know about you, but I believe that knowing marriage is a leap of faith makes it all the more beautiful. Today, we're witnessing two people making the leap together."

Next, he leads us each through a short set of prayers in Hebrew; he recites a few words at a time, and we follow. I make it through all right; I won't be moving to Tel Aviv anytime soon, but the guttural consonants and stretched-out vowels stir up old memories of studying for my bat mitzvah. Raj stumbles over a particularly hard-to-pronounce string of words, but keeps his eyes trained confidently on the officiant. We go through a similar process to exchange vows in English, and this time around, the words feel deeply meaningful.

After we each say "I do," the officiant places a glass wrapped in a white cloth napkin on the floor between me and Raj. He stomps on it triumphantly. The loud snap makes my body buzz with adrenaline.

"You may now kiss the bride!" the officiant announces.

I feel like I'm in a movie as Raj pulls me close for a kiss. People clap and cheer for us, and even though I'm tempted to really *go* for a kiss, I pull away a split second before we look indecent. Getting married is fun. Who knew?

"Not such a bad second date, huh?" Raj says quietly enough so only I can hear.

I grin ear to ear as we make our way down the aisle together.

The next hour—the cocktail hour—is a flurry of air-kissing relatives, a photo shoot of Raj and me with our families and friends, and endless flutes of champagne. At one point, I find myself holding a jumbo shrimp. Raj introduces me to his parents, whom I hug instantly. If they're taken aback by what must have been an incredibly bizarre phone call from their son last week—"Hi, I'm getting married next weekend, can you come?"—they don't make it into a big deal.

"Welcome to the family," his father says. "You'll have to come by for dinner sometime."

"Of course, I'd love that!" I say.

His mother touches the gold bracelet. "This is lovely on you. It should bring you luck; we've been married for thirty years now."

Aunt Linda pulls me aside to share her detailed thoughts on the ceremony, the cocktail hour, the venue, and my dress. I listen for ten solid minutes until I can pawn her off on the first person in my line of sight, who happens to be Liv's four-year-old niece.

That's when I see Helen, watching the party from her perch by a cocktail table. I hitch up my skirt and make my way toward her. When she grasps both of my hands, I feel that hers have aged; she looks more like a grandmother than she ever has before.

"Who knew you'd ever wind up in a big white dress?" she says, shaking her head with a smile. "I could see you eloping or shacking up with someone sexy, maybe, but this? I'm surprised."

"Helen!" I exclaim. "I'm happy. Raj is great."

"I'm sure he is," she says, nodding sagely. "I've heard from Jess that you two have had quite the whirlwind relationship."

"You must have heard . . . more . . . from Jess, haven't you?" I ask, wincing a little.

She raises an eyebrow. "A little something about not being able to pay the rent? I did," she says.

I sigh. "Did you ever face that? Was there ever a time when you weren't sure how to keep your store afloat?" I'm suddenly afraid that I could well up again; admitting potential defeat to Helen, the

woman who single-handedly inspired my entire career, is more devastating than I realized it would be.

"Of course, honey," she says, giving me a sympathetic look. "We
all wind up in impossible situations. But today is your wedding day,
and tomorrow, you can figure out what to do next. The right answer
will come—it just takes time."

"Time," I repeat stiffly. I don't have much time.

"And anyway, let me tell you, life after retirement? Not so bad!"
she crows. "If Brooklyn Jewels goes under, you can join me on my
next trip—I'm heading down to South America to see the Amazon."
She hugs me firmly and strokes my hair. "You'll figure it out, hon.
You always were so smart."

"Thanks," I mumble gratefully.

She swats at the rest of the room. "Now don't let me keep you all
to myself. I hear there's a party going on!"

Before I know it, it's time for the reception. If I were actually
paying for this wedding, I'd be pissed. I can't believe how quickly
time flies—especially when weddings can cost one hundred dollars
a minute or more. Raj and I make the rounds to each table of guests
as they eat. (I don't know about him, but I have too much energy
to actually sit still and focus on food.) Over and over, people say,
"I had no idea you were even dating anyone!" We fidget with our
responses, testing out new ones every time.

"Really? Didn't you see all those photos of us together on Facebook?" I fib to one cousin. (There are zero photos.)

"Huh, strange, I could've sworn I told you about Raj forever
ago," I say to another.

"Wow, it is just *so great* to see you!" I exclaim to a third person,
steamrolling right over whatever plans they had for this conversation. "Tell me about your new job. And your hair looks amazing, by
the way."

The only real moment of peace that Raj and I get together is during our first dance. I realize just how appropriate the term is; we've *literally* never danced together before.

We're rocking slowly side to side in the center of the dance floor. I can feel dozens of pairs of eyes trained on us, including the photographer's.

"Thank you," I tell Raj softly. "I mean it. Most people wouldn't step up like this."

"Trust me, I would not do this for most people," he says.

I let my head rest on his shoulder as we sway to the music for a moment.

"Oh, by the way, I have a free honeymoon booked," I blurt out, suddenly remembering. "We leave on Monday. I mean, if you want to come?"

His eyes go wide with shock. He laughs. "Um, I can try to arrange that." he says. "Where are we going?"

"A few places around the Mediterranean Sea, starting off in Santorini?" I ask.

I shouldn't have to ask my fake husband to confirm that he would like to attend our real honeymoon trip with less than forty-eight hours' notice, but alas, here we are. I've heard people say the key to keeping a relationship fresh is the ability to continually surprise each other. If that's true, I guess we're starting things off on the right foot.

"That sounds amazing," he says, kissing my forehead. "My manager is here. I'll ask him tonight if I can take some time off."

As the music transitions to a new song, more couples begin to fill the dance floor. Liv leads Sophie into a bobbing sort of waltz, and though their dance is off-kilter, their eyes are bright and glowing. I'm so happy for them. I see my mom pull my dad into the center of the crowd—he hates to dance—and I watch as Raj's parents join, too. Carmen, never one to miss a good time, sweeps onto the dance floor in a ruffled cocktail dress the color of a good pinot noir. At first, I see her dancing with friends, but a few songs later, she taps me on the shoulder.

"Raj, may I cut in?" she asks.

He obliges. "Sure."

I squeeze Carmen's hands. "This is good, right? You're having fun?"

"Of course! But listen . . . I debated showing you this, but I feel like you might want to see it," Carmen says, offering me my phone.

Blake texted me. It's short. His name feels like a sucker punch to the gut—I just wasn't expecting it.

"I'm sorry I couldn't be there for you today. You're a beautiful bride. I hope you're happy." That's the entire message.

Carmen stares at me with her teeth sunk into her lip, like an anxious squirrel.

"Are you okay?" she asks.

I furrow my brow at my phone screen and hand it back to her. "Yeah? Yeah. I mean, that's bizarrely nice of him. He didn't have to say anything. But it feels good to know that he doesn't totally hate me, which he has full license to do."

It feels odd to think about Blake in the midst of my wedding. At first, after our breakup, I couldn't imagine going through with today without him by my side. But now, our entire relationship feels so hazy and far away. Today feels right, exactly as it is.

Sharon, the event manager, sidles up to us.

"Sorry, ladies, don't mean to interrupt," she says. "But, Eliza, are you free for an interview now? A reporter from *The Knot* is here."

"Absolutely," I tell Sharon.

What happens next will be just as important as the wedding

ceremony, if not more: I offered an exclusive interview and social media promotion to *The Knot* in exchange for $5,000. Once their story publishes, I'm hoping it will be picked up by other wedding publications.

"Hi! I'm Jen from *The Knot*," a woman squeals, enveloping me in a hug and performing an air kiss. "I don't want to mess up your makeup," she explains.

"Hi!" I say, ramping up my voice to match her sorority-girl enthusiasm.

"I don't want to take up too much of your time because it's, like, your special day, obviously, but I'd love if you could record a quick fifteen-second video welcoming *The Knot* followers to your wedding that we can post on social," she says, handing me her phone. It's already unlocked and open to Instagram.

"Oh, amazing, let's go find the best lighting and a quieter space," I say, turning away from the dance floor.

We head out to the patio; I strategically stand a few inches away from the illuminated heated lamp to give my face a warm glow. I press record and coo into the phone, "Hello to everyone at *The Knot*! This is Eliza Roth, cofounder of Brooklyn Jewels. Thanks so much for celebrating my wedding with me!" I press a kiss into my fingertips and blow it out toward the camera, flashing my diamond ring in the process. I would imagine that every bride feels at least a little bit like a celebrity on her wedding day, but recording a video to go out to a bridal magazine's two million Instagram followers really hits that feeling home.

"Faaaab, thank you," Jen says, tucking her phone away in her purse. "I'll email the rest of my questions later, and you can answer them tomorrow, like we discussed."

We've gone through this—she's going to send over a basic set of

questions about my dress, my venue, my ceremony, and my relationship, plus an added series of questions about my ring and Brooklyn
Jewels. Her job will be to string my answers together into a flatter-
ing profile designed to inspire brides-to-be.

I turn up a megawatt smile and lean over to hug Jen goodbye.

"I can't wait to see the story," I tell her, giving her a dramatic
air kiss.

Jen disappears into the crowd. I make a beeline for Raj, who's
nursing a drink alongside Carmen.

"I just spoke to a reporter from *The Knot*, so hopefully, this
amps up sales even further," I tell him.

"I was watching you do your thing with her," he admits. "You
looked awesome. Totally in your element."

"You know, you two actually look like a real couple," Carmen
observes.

He slips an arm around me. "What do you mean?"

"Like, happy. In love. In sync. It's gross," she says.

I don't know how to respond to that. After years of being the
single girl, it's hard to wrap my head around the idea that I'm now
the girl who looks so obviously happy with her boyfriend. Er, fiancé.
Fake Husband. Whatever he is.

"Go talk to that guy over there," Raj tells Carmen, subtly tilting
his head toward my parents' friend's son at the other end of the bar.
"He's been checking you out."

She swivels to steal a glance at him, then swivels back to us.
"He's cute. Bye."

"I'm really happy we did this," Raj says.

"Me, too," I say, leaning my head on his shoulder.

The party spins on. It seems like a colossal waste of time to
sit and eat dinner, so we don't bother. Instead, Raj and I cut the

chocolate cake we chose together, and I carry a hefty slice on a plate as I make the rounds to say hi to more guests. I say yes to all three people who offer to get me a drink. I slip out of my pumps, hitch up my skirt, and scamper onto the dance floor to shimmy and bounce with Raj to "Kiss" by Prince, also known as the greatest love jam of all time. My heart feels like the fizzy overflow of a bubbling champagne bottle.

I close my eyes and work my hands over my head as I dance; I let the music move me. I can't remember the last time I fully let loose like this. Now that there's nothing left on my to-do list and nothing left to plan and scheme and strategize for, I'm finally free. I dance until it feels like my skin sweats glitter.

It's after midnight when the last of the guests trickle out. I think Sophie and Liv might still be around somewhere—and I know I saw Carmen leave with my parents' friend's son—but I'm too blissed-out to keep track of their whereabouts. I'm lying on the cool, hard surface of the dance floor with my head cradled on Raj's stomach. I can feel his breath slowly returning to its normal pace after eight straight hours of dancing and celebrating and *getting married*. Fake married. Whatever. It was a lot for me, and I've had six months to prepare. I can't imagine what a whirlwind this has felt like for him. His fingers interlace with mine in a lazy handhold.

Across the room, I can hear the sharp click of heels. It takes all my strength to lift up my head and see who it is. Sharon is approaching with an envelope in her hand.

"This was an amazing night," she calls across the room. "So amazing. Congratulations again to you two."

"Thanks," we say in unison.

She squats down to our level. "Here's the marriage certificate. I need both your signatures so I can mail it in."

That propels me to sit up promptly. I take the unsealed envelope and unfold the paper inside. I skim it once quickly, then read it again more carefully. This wedding has been one damn hurdle after the next. If only I hadn't had that last drink, I might be able to think faster.

"This goes to City Hall?" I ask Sharon.

"Yep. I had the officiant sign it earlier, so I just need your signatures to complete it," she explains.

"Oh, but you don't need to do that. I'm going to City Hall first thing on Monday morning anyway to change my name. I'll take it. You've been so unbelievably helpful already, you don't need to do one more thing," I tell her.

"Really, it's no trouble at all," she says.

"I would *love* to hand-deliver it," I insist.

She shrugs and stands. "Sure thing. It needs to be submitted within five days of the wedding to count, just so you know."

"Got it," I say. "Monday morning."

She walks away. Raj sits up. "You're changing your name?" he asks, looking confused.

"I just said that to get her off our case," I explain. "Just so we're all clear here, you know I'm not going to sign or submit this marriage certificate, right? This wedding was just for show."

"Yeah, I know," Raj says, nodding. "We're going to take this relationship one step at a time. If we wind up hating each other, we can always pretend to get a divorce, or whatever."

"Ugh, I need some time off before I plan my next fraudulent life event," I say, rolling my eyes.

At some point during the night, his bow tie and the top few buttons of his shirt have come undone. He looks sexy and relaxed, and I'm struck again by how lucky I am to have him in my life. I scoot closer to him and nuzzle into a kiss. But the spell is broken when I hear my name echoing through the room.

"Eliza! Liza, Liza, look, Liza, come here!" Sophie shouts, barging in.

She doubles over to catch her breath. "I ran here from the kitchen," she says, panting. "I was eating your cake, sorry."

"What is it?" I ask.

She straightens up and holds both of our phones aloft. "You need to see this," she says. "Sales."

I scramble toward the closest empty dinner table as quickly as a person in a delicate gown can scramble. She takes the seat next to mine. Raj jumps up and hovers behind us.

"I've been monitoring e-commerce all night," Sophie explains, scrolling through a list of recent sales on her phone. "Sales are zooming up like I've never seen before."

"How much did we sell tonight?" I ask.

"Sixty thousand dollars' worth," she says, leaning back in satisfaction.

"*Sixty?*" I ask. My jaw drops. I turn back to look at Raj. "Sixty?" I repeat.

"And there's more," Sophie says. "Carmen gave me your phone when she left. It's hot, by the way. Like, literally warm to the touch. I think it's genuinely overheating from all the traffic to your Instagram."

"Is that safe?" I ask.

"No idea, but the app keeps freezing from all the action. Our account jumped up by eight thousand followers," she says, showing me the new number on my screen.

Carmen must have posted a photo to my main feed. When I look, I see that it's a simple shot of me and Raj exchanging vows, and it makes me well up with pride. I tap on it and see the most overwhelming number of likes and comments I've ever gotten in my life.

"And there's more press to come. . . ." I say.

"I know," Sophie says. "Look, this is your call, and I understand if you want to crunch the numbers more thoroughly before you make a decision, but . . ."

The number *sixty thousand* echoes in my head. This is just the beginning. I know sales will continue to spike overnight as followers in other time zones tune in, and they should keep climbing throughout the week as more press rolls out. I have chills imagining what our profit margin could look like by next weekend.

I had always hoped this would happen, of course. This is exactly why I committed to the wedding in the first place. But the likelihood of every element falling into place the way I needed them to was so incredibly slim, I never let myself fully believe I could pull this off. But I have. We all did it together—me and Sophie and Carmen and, of course, Raj.

"You realize what this means? We can re-sign the lease," I say.

"We can?" Sophie asks. Tears spring to her eyes.

"I don't need to run the numbers," I tell her. "If these e-commerce figures are accurate . . ."

"They are," she interjects.

"Then we're golden."

She collapses forward to pull me into a tight embrace. I can feel her shudder and sob happy tears into my neck. Raj runs a soothing hand over my hair and rubs comforting circles over Sophie's back. We stay like this for a long time, soaking up the long-awaited sensation of success.

Eventually, Sophie pulls back and wipes her tearstained cheeks with the backs of her hands. "I'm so unbelievably proud of you," she says. "I know that I've been hard on you and that I've doubted you. Logically, this scheme never should've worked. I'm grateful that it did—but if you ever try to pull something like this again, I'm going to kill you."

It's Sophie's approval that breaks me. My face crumples and my eyes well up. Knowing that my sister appreciates everything I did for our family makes the past six months of stress worth it. I clutch her hand and blink back happy tears.

"Every family needs a fun aunt, right?" I ask.

· Chapter 30 ·

"Please turn your phones to airplane mode," the flight attendant intones over the speaker system on Monday afternoon, as Raj and I are set to fly to Athens and connect to a smaller flight to Santorini.

Getting here has not been easy. We stumbled into the bridal suite at the Wythe Hotel sometime after two in the morning, had triumphant wedding-night sex for approximately four minutes before collapsing in exhaustion, and spent all of Sunday making post-wedding, pre-honeymoon arrangements. I wrote a follow-up email to Jen at *The Knot* answering all of her questions and begged the travel company sponsoring my honeymoon to let me change the name on the second set of tickets from Blake Barrett to Raj Goyal. Meanwhile, Raj convinced his manager to let him take a week off, then sprinted to three different department stores before he could find a single bathing suit available for purchase in late October. It's been *that* long since his last vacation. Then, this morning, after helping Sophie and Jess pack and ship all the orders that tumbled in over the weekend, I re-signed Brooklyn Jewels's lease and gave our landlord a fat check. By the time Raj and I made it to our gate at the airport, we had just minutes to spare.

Now seated on the plane, I check my phone one last time. There's a text from Carmen that I must have missed while sprinting through the airport. I tap it open and see an aggressive number of words spelled out in capitals and more exclamation points than I've ever seen her use—and she's a pretty intense person.

"I know you're about to leave for your honeymoon (!!!) so I'll keep this brief, buuuuut . . . I GOT IT!!!!! I got it. FUNDING with CE-CELIA SUNDQUIST. I raised five million dollars in Series A and I am IN BUSINESS, BABY!!!!! Thank you to the moon and back for ALL YOUR HELP!!!! Love you love love you forever xoxoxoxo!!!!!"

I gasp and show Raj the text. "Carmen did it!" I exclaim.

But he's already reading a nearly identical text on his own phone. "She wants to bring me on full-time," he says. "She offered me a job! For a *lot* of money."

"Would you take it?" I ask.

"She's awesome. We'll have to talk when I get back from our honeymoon, but I don't see why not," he says.

I can't help but grin as I type a congratulatory text back to Carmen.

When I turn my phone onto airplane mode, thus entirely disconnecting myself from the outside world, I feel a wave of relief. It's been a long, stressful six months glued to my phone. Don't get me wrong, I'm grateful for the way social media has skyrocketed my business to a new level of success. I know how lucky I am to be able to garner a following and capitalize on their support. But I'm also looking forward to a week away when I can just be me, Eliza, not Eliza, the girl behind @brooklynjewels.

After the plane takes off and we're soaring comfortably through the clouds, a flight attendant comes down the aisle pushing a beverage cart.

"I overheard you talking earlier," she says in a conspiratorial tone. "I heard this is your honeymoon? Congratulations."

"Oh, thank you!" I say.

"Can I offer you something bubbly to drink?" she asks.

"Sure, thank you so much."

She takes two mini bottles of prosecco from the cart and hands them to us along with paper napkins.

"To our third date," I chuckle quietly to Raj once she's out of earshot.

He clinks his bottle against mine. "Cheers!" he says.

We both take celebratory swigs. The prosecco is sweet and fizzy; it's exactly the right way to kick off our first trip together.

"Do you want to take a photo of this?" he asks. "I know you love to keep your followers updated."

I consider it briefly, then shake my head. "Nah, let's live in the moment."

Acknowledgments

I'm so grateful to my agent, Allison Hunter, for encouraging this novel from the beginning. If not for her enthusiasm and support, this book would not exist! Clare Mao made this process so seamless. Janklow & Nesbit is a wonderful home for authors.

It was a pleasure to collaborate again with my editor, Kaitlin Olson. She brought this book to life with her savvy edits, eye for detail, and passion for jewelry. Many thanks to Lindsay Sagnette, Suzanne Donahue, James Iacobelli, Libby McGuire, Megan Rudloff, and Isabel DaSilva at Atria Books for making this book possible and for ensuring it falls into readers' hands!

Thanks to Sinem Erkas for designing the gorgeous cover and to Willa Bennett for brainstorming the winning title. Together, they're a perfect match.

I was inspired to write this novel after stumbling across talented jewelers with popular Instagram accounts. Thanks to Jillian and Tim Sassone of Marrow Fine for the inside scoop on what it's really like to run a jewelry business.

Special thanks to Lucia Stacey, who lent her poem "September" and her stage name, Penelope Strangelight, to this book. I'm honored to print my favorite piece of poetry.

I'm very lucky to work among such a supportive, passionate group of people. Thanks to Bryan Goldberg, Kate Ward, Lindsay Mannering, Kylie McConville, Veronica Lopez, Iman Hariri-Kia, Caitlin Eadie, and everyone at Elite Daily.

The day I published *Playing with Matches*, I received a flood of questions from readers who wanted to know if and when I'd publish a second novel. I couldn't get those readers' words out of my head, and so *Love at First Like* was born. Thanks to everyone who sent kind messages and cheered me on.

Thanks to my friends for celebrating this book from the start: Alexia LaFata, Annie Kehoe, Dana Schwartz, Devon Albert-Stone, Emma Albert-Stone, Elyssa Goodman, Emily Raleigh, Kelsey Mulvey, Morgan Boyer, Roshan Berentes, and more.

Thanks to Jerry and Eleanor Hart; Karen, Bob, and Jake Sykes; Bruce, Xander, Nathan, and Zoe Orenstein; and Jamie, Karin, Dani, and Rosie Orenstein for all their love.

I am so lucky to have the most supportive family in my corner. Thank you to Audrey, Jack, and Julia Orenstein for always encouraging me to pursue my love of writing, and for their thoughtful feedback on every draft.

I write love stories for a living. Thank you to Saul Hamadani for giving me one of my own—it was truly love at first like.

HANNAH ORENSTEIN is the author of *Playing with Matches* and *Love at First Like*, as well as the senior dating editor at Elite Daily. Previously, she was a writer and editor at Seventeen.com. She lives in Brooklyn.

BOOK
CLUB
FAVORITES
—
READER'S
GUIDE

Love at First Like

Hannah Orenstein

This reading group guide for Love at First Like *includes an introduction, discussion questions, ideas for enhancing your book club, and a Q&A with author Hannah Orenstein. The suggested questions are intended to help your reading group find new and interesting angles and topics for your discussion. We hope that these ideas will enrich your conversation and increase your enjoyment of the book.*

Introduction

In Hannah Orenstein's *Love at First Like*, a New York jewelry shop owner accidentally leads her Instagram followers to believe that she's engaged—and then decides to keep up the ruse.

Eliza Roth and her sister, Sophie, co-own a jewelry shop in Brooklyn. One night, after learning of an ex's engagement, Eliza accidentally posts a photo of herself wearing a diamond ring on *that* finger to her Instagram account, beloved by 100,000 followers. Sales skyrocket, press rolls in, and Eliza learns that her personal life is good for business. So she has a choice: continue the scheme or clear up the misunderstanding. With her landlord raising the rent and mounting financial pressure, Eliza sets off to find a fake fiancé.

Fellow entrepreneur Blake seems like the perfect match on paper. And in real life he shows promise, too. But Blake doesn't know Eliza is "engaged"; Sophie asks Eliza for an impossible sum of money; and Eliza feels drawn to someone else—Raj, the bartender down the street.

With a wedding to drum up more business on the horizon, Eliza's lies begin to spiral out of control, and she'll have to decide whether to stay engaged online or fall in love in real life.

Topics & Questions for Discussion

1. The novel begins with Eliza's ex-boyfriend Holden becoming engaged. They've been broken up for many years, but she worries that "his engagement means that I've officially lost the breakup." Why do you think this engagement gets under her skin so much?

2. When defending her choice to leave her Instagram photo up, Eliza notes in chapter 2 that there are some female entrepreneurs "whose businesses are bolstered *because* the founders have enviable lives." Do you agree with this statement? Can you think of other business owners who have grown their brands by having what seem like interesting personal lives?

3. When Carmen and Eliza look for a potential fake fiancé at Dorrian's in chapter 3, Carmen describes Eliza's ideal as "eligible bachelors who would look amazing on Instagram and are dumb enough to not question whatever scheme you're cooking up." Do you think Blake meets these criteria?

4. Eliza and Sophie are inspired to open their own business by their parents, who own a boating store in Maine. How do you think opening a small business has changed since the time when their parents did so?

5. How do you think Sophie feels about Eliza being the face of the brand, especially when Sophie worries Eliza may hurt the business in the long run?

6. Eliza's many Instagram followers are a significant presence in this novel. In chapter 10, she claims that, "It's good for customers to see that I'm a real person who eats cheese and drinks wine, too. It helps them feel like, you know, they *know* me. And that translates directly to sales." How do you think having so many strangers following her life affects her? Is Eliza using Instagram as a tool for promoting her business or as an outlet for herself?

7. When Sophie asks Eliza for a large sum of money for her IVF in chapter 11, she tells Eliza, "You're getting everything you want." Do you agree? Why or why not?

8. Eliza wrestles with her feelings for Blake for much of the book, saying in chapter 17, "It's hard for me to wrap my head around how I feel about Blake. . . . I don't doubt that I have feelings for him, but I do doubt that they match the strength of his feelings for me." Do you think her ruse hinders her ability to express her feelings for him?

9. Blake and Raj represent two opposites: the guy who looks good on paper and the guy Eliza's drawn to in real life. Think about the way her relationship with each progresses. How do they differ?

10. Why do you think Eliza keeps Blake in the dark about the fake engagement and wedding for so long?

11. In many ways, Eliza's ruse picks up steam when she's offered free or sponsored products for her wedding. Do you think her sponsored wedding is something she would have picked for herself?

12. Sophie and Eliza are very different people, and yet they share a close bond as sisters and business partners. How is their closeness tested throughout the novel?

13. When we talk about dating in the digital age, we often talk about dating apps. How do you think other forms of social media—like Instagram—influence the way we find and fall for partners?

14. At the end of the novel, Eliza turns down Raj's suggestion that she take a photo on her flight in order to "live in the moment." Months earlier, in chapter 8, she was staging covert vignettes at Blake's apartment with the hashtag #ElizaFoundHerJewel. What do you think this says about Eliza's growth throughout the story?

Enhance Your Book Club

1. Read Hannah Orenstein's first novel, *Playing with Matches*, with your group. (Did you catch Sasha's and Caroline's cameos in *Love at First Like*?) Think about the differences between these characters and stories.

2. Look up the Instagram profiles of some of the influencers mentioned here, such as @emilywweiss, @leandramcohen, and @whitney. Do you have favorite Instagram influencers you follow? Share them with your friends.

3. Do as Eliza and Carmen and plan a happy hour night out. If you're in New York, try AOC East, Le Boudoir, or Dorrian's. If not, visit your favorite local spot or the place where you would most likely find a fake fiancé.

A Conversation with Hannah Orenstein

You last novel, Playing with Matches, *was about a matchmaker in her early twenties. This is about a small jewelry shop owner nearing thirty. What was it like to write these two different protagonists?*

I started writing *Playing with Matches* when I was twenty-two. I wanted to create a protagonist who struggled with the same postgrad challenges that I did, like adapting to adulthood, navigating the ways in which old friendships evolve over time, and striving to create a fulfilling career. I loved writing about that exciting, exhausting, exhilarating time. By the time I wrote *Love at First Like* three years later, I wanted to explore the life of a protagonist who was a little bit more confident in her career and her own capabilities. People say to write what you know; I felt a little older and wiser than I did with my first book, and that helped me find Eliza's voice.

Stories about fraud or cons—like the Fyre Festival or Anna Delvey— particularly about "influencers," are popular right now. Why do you think this has become a cultural fascination of ours? Did these kinds of real-life stories help inform Eliza's?

Yes! I had been playing around with the concept of a jewelry store owner whose lies start to spiral out of control when I first learned about Anna Delvey. The cultural fascination with her story gave me confidence that I was on the right track.

Jewelry is a big part of this novel. How did you come up with the pieces Eliza and Sophie might sell in the store?

I did a lot of research on jewelers like Eliza—people who found big success on Instagram. The jewelry sold at Brooklyn Jewels is inspired by a lot of current trends I've seen lately (yellow gold, three-stone settings, pear-shaped diamonds), as well as trends that have been popular for several years now (diamond halos, diamond pavé bands, birthstone jewelry). Eliza's engagement ring is actually inspired by Meghan Markle's!

Who was your favorite character to write and why?

I loved getting inside Eliza's mind. It's easy to see Instagram influencers and assume their lives are a certain way, so to explore the messy, impulsive, imperfect aspects of her life—all while she maintains a façade of success and perfection—was a really enjoyable challenge for me.

Dating apps aside, how do you think social media affects the way we pair up and settle down?

Social media isn't important to everyone, but if you do care a lot about it, it can be frustrating when the person you're dating doesn't respect your interest. In the grand scheme of things, it's pretty harmless if you like to photograph your brunch before you dig in, or if you ask your significant other to take a picture together on date night. But anecdotally, I've experienced and heard so many stories of men who seem to have really negative opinions of women who love social media.

Because of that, it was important to me to include scenes in which Eliza discusses social media with both Blake and Raj, respectively. Blake challenges her interest in it and teases her for it, while Raj later encourages it (in that final moment on the plane).

Raj and Blake are so different from each other. What do you think they represent for Eliza?

Growth! There are a lot of books out there in which the heroine falls in love at first sight. This is not one of them. In real life, dating can be messy and complicated; the process of figuring out who you're compatible with can be tough. Ultimately, as Eliza gets to know Blake and Raj better, she gets to know herself better. Through the process of dating both men, she learns a lot about the kind of life she'd like to lead. Blake represents the life she feels she's supposed to want—he's ambitious and successful, just like she is, though their connection isn't the strongest. Raj offers her a new way to imagine her life: she can pursue her career with a supportive partner who makes her feel like the best version of herself.

Friendship and sisterhood are big parts of this novel. As people pair off in their late twenties and thirties now, how do you think we rely on these relationships?

Friendship is important at every age, but particularly in your twenties when you're single. Eliza has different relationships with Sophie and Carmen—one is her sister and one is her best friend—but functionally, they fulfill very similar roles in her life. I liked casting Eliza and Carmen with their dynamic because it's important to me to celebrate strong friendships in my writing.

Eliza and Carmen have a weekly happy hour date where the location changes each week. In Playing with Matches, *Sasha frequents Hotel Tortuga on Fourteenth Street. What's your go-to spot in New York?*

Hotel Tortuga was my go-to spot with my friends for years. The same year that *Playing with Matches* came out, though, the restaurant was bought by new owners, and I'm sad to say it's no longer quite the same. Many of the spots in *Love at First Like* are tributes to places I love dearly in New York—Golden Years and the Wythe Hotel in Williamsburg, and AOC East, Dorrian's, and Brandy's on the Upper East Side.

In the last few years, we've seen a lot of influencer weddings that are partially if not completely sponsored. Were you thinking of any in particular while you were writing? How do you think these sponsored weddings influence those that are not?

The first time I remember a wedding from an "influencer" type (I'm using that term loosely in this case) is 2014, when #nellandteddy, the Instagram hashtag for Nell Diamond and Ted Wasserman's wedding, suddenly appeared all over my feed. There's even a HarpersBazaar. com story from that week with the headline, "The Internet Is in Love with Nell Diamond's Gorgeous Wedding Photos." It was one of the first times that wedding photos from a noncelebrity really dominated social media and digital media, and that concept certainly influenced *Love at First Like*. Just as I finished the first draft of the novel, *Brides* announced that fashion blogger Chiara Ferragni would appear on the cover of their Weddings of the Year! issue. The fact that an influencer would get that honor—instead of Meghan Markle or any number of other high-profile celebrities who got married that year—speaks volumes about how influencer love stories and weddings are a source of cultural fascination right now.

What do you want readers to take away from this story?

My number one goal is always to entertain. If readers have a great time reading about Eliza's adventures, I'm happy! Beyond that, I hope this novel helps people consider what roles ambition, love, passion, and social media play in their own lives.

What's next for you? Are you working on anything new?

I'm currently writing a third novel set in the world of elite gymnastics, due out summer 2020 (in time for the Olympics!). I also work as the senior dating editor at Elite Daily, editing stories about single life, dating, and relationships, and I stay busy taste-testing every cheese plate in New York City.